BEYOND

BETRAYAL

By: L.T. Ryan

Beyond Betrayal

(Clarissa Abbot)

L.T. Ryan

Give feedback on the book to:

http://LTRyan.com

ltryan70@gmail.com

@LTRyanWrites

ISBN-13: 987-1495295034

ISBN-10: 1495295036

PUBLISHED BY:

L.T. Ryan

Copyright © 2013

Other Books Featuring Clarissa Abbot

Noble Beginnings

Noble Intentions Season One

Noble Intentions Season Two

Noble Intentions Season Three

In memory of Nick Reider.

One of the greatest men I ever knew. One of the best friends I ever had.

Dedicated to his wife, Lyne, and their five children.

Believe in miracles.

Always.

Chapter 1

General Edward Lawrence Logan International Airport. Logan International for short. Adjacent to East Boston and the Boston Harbor. Six runways, and over one hundred gates divided among four terminals. All located on twenty four hundred acres.

Nearly thirty million people pass through those gates each year. Business, pleasure, returning home, going home, and some who fly for the hell of it because they can.

Clarissa Abbot, one of those thirty million passengers, had no choice in the matter. She departed the 777, proceeded through the hot and humid jetway, and walked out into the open gate adorned with blue and white striped seats, and manned by three disinterested airline employees, because Sinclair, her boss, told her to do so.

Or suffer consequences that would induce words such as 'fatal,' 'dismemberment,' and 'never to be found again.'

Sinclair hadn't told her who would carry out the acts. She had no reason to ask. Clarissa knew. They had people in their employ who could do such things without batting an eye, and without leaving a shred of evidence behind. These were the kind of men who didn't care who it was they were terminating. They lived for their jobs. They got antsy when they went too long without cleaning a scene or ridding the world of a bad seed.

Is that what she had become?

In both her heart and her head, she didn't think so. Clarissa had done everything she'd been asked. Relationships that meant the world to her at one time were now fading memories, like a paper boat placed on the water as the tide receded. Whether those relationships drifted away or sunk into the abyss, she had no idea, and it did not matter.

Neither did her last assignment. *Forget it now, Clarissa.* Those had been Sinclair's final words to her while she worked frantically to eliminate evidence in her room in London. Clarissa destroyed all her belongings, including her cell phone and laptop, in the compound's incinerator. She left with the clothes on her back, a few thousand in cash, and a passport with a false identity. She boarded the plane and departed from Heathrow shortly after nine in the morning. Her flight flew back in time and arrived at noon Eastern.

Her gate was located at the end of the terminal. Glancing back, a wide window offered a panoramic view of a runway. A plane, she couldn't tell what style, lifted off. Dust and dirt and exhaust swirled in two sideways mini-tornadoes. She turned her attention forward. A sparse crowd walked away from her, down a hall that split the terminal in two. She joined the other travelers, attempting to blend in. Not an easy task for a woman like her. She was tall. Her dark red hair, pale skin, and looks drew the eyes and attention of most men and some women. Hatred, scorn, lust, curiosity. She saw it all.

She didn't fear them, though. Her concern laid in the fact that Sinclair had provided no further instructions for her to follow after departing the plane. Unfamiliar faces turned into potential enemies. Throughout her time in Sinclair's group, she had been exposed to few of the members. It had been in her best interest, he'd said. The fewer people that knew her, the better off she would be.

You never know, he had told her, *who might turn on you.*

Would Sinclair? Better yet, had he?

A pair of dark eyes fixed their gaze on her. Eyebrows flexed down. The man's face was cut from steel, handsome, and covered with four day's growth. His black hair was adorned with flecks of silver. He wore a dark suit and no tie. He left the top two buttons of his white pinstripe shirt unbuttoned.

She had no recollection of ever seeing or meeting the man. He stared at her like they'd been lovers the night before.

Clarissa kept her stride at an even pace. She didn't deviate to the left or the right. She couldn't. There wasn't room on either side. She stayed true on a path that led her right past the man.

He glanced over her head. She resisted the urge to look back. His focus shifted from above, to the left, to the right, then back on her. She watched as his right hand slipped into his pocket. He couldn't have traveled this far through the airport with a weapon. Even something as discreet as a ceramic knife would be spotted in the new imaging machines they had installed at the security checkpoint.

He pulled a black cylinder from his pocket. Maybe two or three inches in length. Before she could identify the object, he'd tucked it in his palm and passed it off to his other hand. His fingers wrapped around it.

The guy took a step forward. A couple walking along the outer edges of the corridor took two steps in. The man nodded, flashed a smile, and merged into the line. He was three paces in front of her. She glanced down at his shoes. They looked expensive. The soles were hard and thick. The uppers made from leather. A lot of the guys paid for custom shoes, she'd heard. They wanted comfort, the ability to kick ass, and to look good.

The man slowed his pace. He took a step and a half for every two Clarissa made. She saw the object in his left hand. They were almost side by side. He glanced over his shoulder, made eye contact, smiled. They became even with each other. She matched his pace. They stayed close to the outer edges of the walkway. His left hand permeated her peripheral vision. She reached for it with her right. They continued on as if they were a couple reunited after time spent away. Between their hands, the cylinder pressed against both their palms.

"Central Parking Garage," he said. "Level three. Backed into a spot in the middle of the last row. Now close your hand."

The man unthreaded his fingers from hers. She made a fist around the object, pulled her hand tight to her side, and slipped it into her jean's pocket beside her cell phone. She left her hand on top of the object. Her index finger traced it. Six buttons, and a hole at the top. Something metal, pointed inside the hole.

"I'll go back and get it for you, honey," the guy said, stopping and stepping out of the flow of traffic. He leaned in and kissed her cheek. The stubble around his mouth scratched at her. "I'll catch up at baggage claim."

Clarissa looked around, smiled, and continued on. In the end, no one there would care. Unless they did. And if there were someone there who took anything from the interaction other than a husband or boyfriend going back to claim his significant other's laptop or carry-on, then the rest of the act wouldn't have fooled them either.

She pulled the object out. It was a car key. Everything was built into the device, the key, alarm, remote start, and lock and unlock buttons.

She continued on, navigating through the airport. At one point she reached into her purse and pulled out a pair of knock-off designer sunglasses. She wasn't sure if they were supposed to be Gucci or Armani or Prada or some other brand. Clarissa didn't care about those things anymore.

Baggage claim was packed with hundreds of people. The result of dozens of flights arriving at one time. Midday madness. She stopped and stood on the tips of her toes and looked for the man who handed her the key. Had he meant it when he said he'd catch up at baggage claim, or had he said that to make the act believable? She wandered the snaking area full of travelers, conveyor belts and yet-to-be-claimed bags. A tall man in an airport uniform pulled a red suitcase off a belt that had stopped moving. The bag looked overstuffed. He pulled the extendable handle all the way out and wheeled it to an office.

The land of abandoned luggage, she thought.

Ten minutes later the man from the terminal still had not arrived. She took one final glance around. Two-thirds of the faces had changed over. That was fine with her. The fewer people around to remember her standing there, the better.

It was the middle of June, not even officially summer yet. But when she stepped outside, it felt like North Carolina in August. The temperature was over ninety, as was the humidity. By the time she found the parking garage, the bottom half of her shirt was in danger of sticking to her back. It grew worse in the garage. Airflow was non-existent. The structure reeked of exhaust and gas fumes.

Some idiot honked his horn in tune with a song. Or perhaps he was just a jerk. The sound echoed off the floors and walls and ceiling. The car drove past her. The young man behind the wheel looked over at her and winked. Although her first instinct had been to extend a gesture toward him, Clarissa ignored the guy. There was no point in getting involved in something that could result in her being arrested, especially while using an identity that could have been compromised without her knowledge.

She found the stairs and walked down one flight. The air felt thicker on the third level. It smelled worse. The front of her head ached, and she felt nauseous.

"Keep it together," she told herself. "A little further is all."

The last row was visible from where she stood. Rather than following the road to the left or right, then back, she cut through the middle, sidestepping between cars whose owners were incapable of parking in the middle of a spot.

She reached the last row, pulled the key from her pocket and pressed the alarm. A silver G Coupe chirped and screamed and honked and flashed in response. She mashed the lock and unlock buttons with her thumb until the car went silent.

"Not bad, Sinclair," she muttered, approaching the vehicle from the driver's side.

She pressed the ignition button on the key. The engine roared to life. She hoped the air conditioning had been left on full blast. She turned to the side in front of the car and shuffled to the door. Voices and laughter and footsteps echoed throughout the concrete structure. She glanced around while pulling the door open and sliding into the driver's seat. The leather seat and steering wheel felt cool. The vents piped ice-cold air out. She felt the ends of her hair lift and blow in the artificial breeze. The radio had been left on a local classic rock station. She didn't bother to change it. The navigation unit had a destination pre-programmed. She pressed buttons in an attempt to pan out or display a list of the directions.

She was interrupted before she could figure it out.

Chapter 2

Clarissa jumped at the sound of knuckles rapping against the passenger side window. Her head jerked to the right. She saw the handsome stubbled face from the terminal. The man smiled and pointed toward the door lock. She felt along the armrest with her left hand and located the window and lock controls. She glanced down, then pressed the unlock button.

The man stepped back. The door swung open. He stuck his left leg in, lowered himself into the seat, then dragged his right leg in and shut the door. His cologne blew past her. She hadn't noticed it in the terminal.

"Who are you?" she asked.

"You can call me Beck," he said.

"That your first name or last name?"

"Who says it's my name at all?" The right side of his mouth lifted upward. A small dimple formed under his cheek.

"Then you can call me Sally," she said.

His smile broadened. "You should know it doesn't work that way, Clarissa. If you were sent to meet me, you know you would have been provided with all the necessary information. Think about it for a moment. What would he have told you about me?"

"At a minimum, your name," she said.

"Yes," he said. "Go on."

"Possibly any combination of birth date, social, current and former addresses, recent operations to assess threat and experience level. Perhaps he'd include any living family members in case the target was uncooperative."

"And maybe even the names of those who are closer than family?"

She nodded. "Good thing I don't have any of those."

Beck grabbed his seatbelt and pulled it across his chest. It locked with a solid click.

"I only know your name, Ms. Abbot. The rest of your secrets are safe with you, and Sinclair."

She reached for the shifter. Her hand brushed his. She pulled back like a crocodile had lunged out of the water at her.

This drew a laugh from Beck. "If I were here to kill you, you wouldn't be driving this car, Ms. Abbot." He made a show out of lifting his hand and dropping it on his lap. "That better?"

Clarissa said nothing. With her left hand she lowered her sunglasses, fixing them on the bridge of her nose. She made a fist around the shifter with her other hand, slammed it into first and peeled out of the parking spot while spinning the wheel to the left. She expected the maneuver to be met with calls for her to be careful with Beck's vehicle.

He had no reaction.

She slammed the brakes at the end of the aisle. People fifteen feet away jumped and sprinted away from her.

Still, Beck said and did nothing.

Clarissa rolled her eyes. Otherwise, she showed no outward reaction to his failure to display any reaction. She turned right and remained under the speed limit until she reached the exit. Beck extended his hand in front of her. He dangled a twenty in front of her. She passed the money onto a woman reading a book inside a bulletproof enclosure. The woman never made eye contact. Clarissa collected the change, set it in between her and Beck, and followed the curved ramp. The guided navigation spat out directions. She followed them to I-90 and the Ted Williams Tunnel.

The tunnel was close to a half-mile long. A sign hung at the entrance and said, "No passing," in all caps and bold, black letters. She ignored the warning. She took advantage of every break in the double-wide line of cars, weaving left to right to left again. She glanced at Beck. His eyes were closed.

They emerged from the tunnel. Though there were no clouds, the sky looked anything but blue. Hazy smog filled the space between the horizon and the sun, which glared from overhead. The air blowing through the vents, while cold, smelled like an ashtray that hadn't been emptied in a week. The car appeared to be new. Didn't it come with some kind of filter to protect against poor air quality?

"Beck?" she said.

He lifted his chin from his chest and turned his head toward her. "Yeah?"

"Where are we going?"

"Wherever that GPS tells us to go."

She glanced at the LCD screen. A number was fixed to the upper right corner. Four hundred thirty-five miles to go. In her head, Clarissa pictured the eastern seaboard. That distance would put them close to Philadelphia or D.C. if she continued south. The tension in her muscles slipped away like a dying man's last breath. Sinclair wouldn't bring her home if he were going to kill her. He might have her arrested, but not terminated.

Why not have her fly directly to Reagan or Dulles?

She glanced to her right. Beck had his head down and eyes closed again. His chest rose and fell in a steady rhythm. Either he'd fallen asleep, or he was deeply relaxed. Either way, he didn't pose an immediate threat to her. She did wonder whether he knew the reason for them to travel together. Perhaps the man lived in the Boston area. Or maybe it was a mutual dependence thing. She knew she could drive herself crazy trying to figure it out. She worked through possible reasons and explanations, but none of them reached a conclusion she deemed plausible. And none of it mattered. The only one who truly knew was Sinclair.

And there was little chance he'd tell her until he had to. *If* he had to.

They continued southwest. The sun continued its westward trajectory. It would be hours before its light no longer benefited them. The longest day of the year was close. Only a few days away.

Three hours into a seven hour drive, Beck woke. He lifted his arms over his head and twisted at the waist. Something popped in his back or his shoulders.

"Pull over at the next exit," he said.

"There's nothing at the next one," she said.

"How do you know?"

"The sign on the side of the interstate had nothing under gas, food and lodging. It'll be a waste to pull over if you need any of those three things."

"Okay, take the following exit, then."

They passed the off-ramp to nowhere. She crossed into the right hand lane in advance of the next one. The sign indicated there were multiple gas stations there. He could get a drink or food or use the restroom, whatever it was he needed.

She studied the cars behind them. So far, there hadn't been a single one that paced her. That didn't mean anything, though. An experienced team would use five or six different vehicles, changing places as often as possible. Possibly even having the drivers switch out cars along the way. There was no guarantee of a pattern, other than the people behind the wheel. She'd been on the lookout for a certain type of person. The problem was, between Boston and New York, half the drivers on the road matched that type. Even halfway to Philadelphia, at least four out of every ten cars had someone who fit the profile in her head.

So she let it go and watched for a constant tail.

She pulled off the interstate, made a right at a blinking red light. They had a choice between three different gas stations. She turned left into the first one they encountered. This way, she wouldn't have to cross traffic to drive back to the interstate. The gas gauge read half-full. She pulled up to a pump, got out, reached for the hose. A man wearing greasy blue coveralls trotted over. He waved his arms and whistled and yelled at her to stop.

Beck had stepped out of the car. He looked at her over the roof.

"We're in New Jersey, Clarissa. You can't pump your gas here. If you touch that hose, you'll be in violation of a state Supreme Court ruling that dates back to 1951."

She'd driven through the state enough to know this, yet it escaped her mind. When was the last time she'd stopped for gas in Jersey?

The man smiled as he placed himself between her and the gas pump, like he guarded an endangered species. She lifted her hands and backed up. Looking to her left, she noticed Beck stepping into the convenience store. She decided to join him inside and grab a cup of coffee.

A bell dinged when she pulled the door open. Three people stood in line, staring straight ahead. None of them appeared to be with one another. Clarissa walked behind them, taking note of the largest of the three, a man wearing a Mets t-shirt with the sleeves cut off. He was big, but out of shape. His gut protruded over his waist. She deemed him not much of a threat, and moved on.

She found the coffee maker in the back corner. The brew in the pot looked old and smelled stale. The odor lingered in her nose even after she took a step back. She imagined the bottom quarter of the pot was thick sludge.

Beck emerged from a hallway and walked up to her.

"High octane," he said, wincing at the sight of the coffee.

"I think I'll pass," she said, looking toward the cooler. "Grab a soda instead."

He followed her to the fridge, then the register. They stood next to each other. The appearance of a couple again. It worked, she figured. He used the change from the parking garage and another twenty to pay for two drinks, a bag of sunflower seeds and the gas.

Outside, he asked, "Want me to drive?"

"I got it." She detested the idea of giving up control of the vehicle. At least behind the wheel she had the option of running. She wasn't armed. Neither was he, best she could tell. The only thing he could do was hit her. And if she pushed the gas to eighty or so miles per hour, he'd be less inclined to lay a hand on her.

They took their seats in the Infiniti. She turned the key in the ignition. The LCD screen lit up. It calculated their route time and distance. A little over three hours to go.

Chapter 3

Traffic thickened as they neared Philadelphia. She glanced at the dash clock for the seventieth time. Almost five o'clock. The sun still lingered overhead. Plenty of daylight remaining. As long as they got through the city in a reasonable amount of time, they'd arrive in D.C. before sunset.

A sign told her they had entered Cherry Hill, New Jersey. They traveled at a pace of thirty miles per hour. It felt like crawling. Cars gathered around them on the sides, front and back. Along the long line of vehicles, brake lights rhythmically lit up and faded away in front of her. She kept two car lengths of distance between the Infiniti and the vehicle in front of her. The man behind her didn't give her the same consideration. She saw his oversized face in her rear-view as if he sat in the back seat.

"Pull off at the next exit," Beck said.

Clarissa glanced at him. He did not return the look.

"Why?" she asked.

He said nothing.

"Beck, why?"

"Relax." The man let out an exaggerated exhale through his nose. "Do you like being in this traffic?"

"No."

"Well, it's only going to get worse. So let's get off here, find a place to eat, and pick up later. We're not getting to D.C. until after eight, anyway."

Clarissa watched the passenger side mirror for an opening. A gap appeared and she took it. The person behind her honked his horn and flashed his lights and flicked her off. She managed to keep herself from responding. It was enough knowing what she could do to the man in a one-on-one situation that helped her remain calm.

She pulled onto the exit ramp. She asked, "What's going to happen when we get to Washington?"

Beck shrugged. "To tell you the truth, I don't know. I'm out of it at that point. I suppose Sinclair will want to meet with you. Brief you, or debrief you, whatever."

"You're not going to accompany me to see him?"

"Why would I?"

She glanced over at him. His gaze met hers. She hiked her shoulders an inch while clutching the wheel with both hands.

"I don't know, Beck. I mean, why are you here in the first place? If I'm going to D.C., why didn't I fly in there to begin with? Why Boston?"

"You're with me because I flew in today, too."

"From where?"

"Somewhere."

"We weren't in long term parking. It only cost us five dollars to get out." She thought back to the chart near the exit. Two dollars for the first hour, one dollar each additional hour. "Your car hadn't been there for more than four hours."

"First, who says I parked it? Second, who says it is mine?"

The stoplight turned green. Clarissa pulled forward and made a left turn. They drove over I-95. A passing eighteen-wheeler caused the overpass to feel like it shook beneath them.

"Why would it matter if I flew into Reagan or Dulles?" she asked.

"I see you're trying to figure this out, Ms. Abbot. I'll help you. There's nothing nefarious going on here. You couldn't fly into either of the D.C. airports because someone might spot you there. Same for me. Logan is close enough, yet far enough away. It's not as big as some of the others, so there's less likely to be attention drawn to someone like yourself."

"That makes no sense. What do you mean, spot me there? I've flown in and out of both before."

Beck said nothing. Clarissa glanced in his direction. He turned his head away. His eyes reflected off the side window. She noticed a solid streak of white hair behind his ear. Birthmark? A single frightening moment in his life? Or just because?

"Are you like me?" she asked.

"What do you mean by that?"

"Outsourced help." She paused, added, "Expendable."

He shook his head.

"CIA, then?"

He pointed at a Ruby Tuesday's.

"NSA? Is this happening behind the Agency's back? Am I still supposed to be in London?"

"I could go for a steak," Beck said.

"Screw your steak," Clarissa said. She jammed her feet down on the brake pedal and the clutch while shifting the transmission into neutral. The rear of the car slipped. She over-corrected and barely missed the curb and sidewalk, where several people sat on a bench or stood near the curb waiting for the bus.

An old man swore at her through Beck's partially open window.

Beck turned his head toward her. He smiled. "I think you could use one, too. And I'll be driving the rest of the way to D.C."

Clarissa shifted into first and eased forward, turning into the restaurant's parking lot. All the spaces near the front door were occupied by Mercedes, Lexus, and Audis. Happy hour for the high profile. She found a spot behind the building that put them out of sight of the road. She cut the engine, pulled the key from the ignition, then handed it to Beck.

"Ready?" he asked.

"Wait." She shifted in the seat and turned at her waist. Her left arm remained outstretched, her hand draped over the leather-wrapped steering wheel. "Do you have a weapon for me?"

His smile returned. "I thought you'd never ask." He reached for the glove box with the key extended. It slid into a lock and it turned with ease. The cover lowered an inch per second. Beck reached inside. When his hand emerged, it wrapped around the handle of a pistol. He extended it.

Clarissa grabbed the barrel.

Beck didn't let go. "There's no ammunition in it yet. I'm going to retrieve mine out of the trunk. You'll go into the restroom after we are seated. When you return, I'll get up. After I've left the table, you grab my napkin. You'll find the magazine there."

She nodded. He released the weapon.

"Are you familiar with the M9?" he asked.

"Yeah, plenty."

"Okay." He pushed his door open and stepped outside. "Now, let's go deal with the natives and put something in our stomachs."

Just don't piss me off, Clarissa thought. *Or your dessert will be made of lead and covered with glycerine.*

Chapter 4

Everything went as planned. No one around them noticed the exchange. Clarissa loaded the magazine into the M9 while both items were in her purse. She felt relaxed again after having gone twenty hours unarmed. Had to be a new record.

They both ordered the rib eye. Beck had fries and a potato. She had a salad. Beck drank three beers. She drank one. Neither of them was affected by the alcohol.

The bar filled up with men wearing ties and women in pants suits. They shook hands and talked and laughed. Everyone seemed to know everybody else. Beck would have fit in. He fit the look of a high-earning executive, so bored with his home life that he went to the local Ruby Tuesday's instead of driving the five extra minutes to spend time with his wife and kids and dog.

Clarissa knew she'd never fit in. Not because she'd go home to her family, but rather because they'd take one look at her and know she was below them. No matter how she tried to change her appearance, her mannerisms, the way she spoke, most folks looked down on her and pegged her as nothing but a gutter dweller.

"What are you thinking about?" Beck said.

Her gaze drifted away from the bar and met his. It was the first time she noticed that his eyes weren't dark brown. They were hazel, with a touch of gray.

"You look like you're about to take that M9 and go take out the bartender."

Clarissa smiled. "Not the bartender. He's my kind of people. The others, not so much."

"Don't get along with your peers?"

"My peers? I've got nothing in common with those folks up there. They wouldn't offer me a drink even if I walked up there on fire."

Beck looked over his shoulder, back at her, shrugged. "For starters, don't use the word 'folks.' And maybe they'd ignore you while they're all in a group. But, I bet individually, any one of those guys would be offering you all the drinks you wanted."

"Right," she said. "Thanks for proving my point."

He held out his hands, smiled and cocked his head to the side.

"Your charm won't work on me," she said. "I've got a post-graduate degree in bullshit."

This elicited a laugh from Beck.

Clarissa glanced beyond the booth. She'd caught the attention of four of the bar's patrons. One pointed at her, said something, smiled. The others did, too.

"Beck," she said. "Let's go."

"I'm just getting comfortable," he said.

"Yeah, well, so are those guys. They'll be over here in five minutes."

He picked up his mug and finished his beer. "Okay, let me run to the restroom first."

"Give me the key, Beck."

He slid out of the booth, rose and walked toward the restrooms, ignoring her request.

The men shifted their attention toward Beck. One nodded at the others. Three of them followed Beck toward the dim hallway with the restroom sign hanging overhead.

Clarissa grabbed the edge of the table. The lone man started toward her. He had short brown hair, a clean-shaven face. His khaki pants and blue polo shirt looked recently pressed. She stuck one foot in the aisle. He took three long steps and blocked her.

"Where are you running off to?"

The whiskey on his breath pervaded the air around her.

"Not the drunk tank, which is where you'll be going after you get behind the wheel of your overpriced car."

"Maybe you should drive me."

"Maybe you should get one of your boys to do that for you." She jutted her chin toward the restrooms.

The guy hiked his thumb over his shoulder and leaned back. "Yeah, they're gonna be busy for a few minutes." He leaned forward and glanced at her hands. "And so is your boyfriend."

She heard a door open and fall shut in the background. She looked past the man in front of her. Beck appeared in the hallway opening. The right side of his face was red. He dabbed at his lip with the back of his hand. No one else followed him out.

Clarissa smiled at the man in front of her. "One thing first."

The guy placed his hands on the table and leaned forward as she set her purse down. She opened it. His eyes grew wide. She wrapped her hand around the pistol, shoved it against the end of the bag, and placed the bag against his crotch.

"Now you're going to get your hands off my table, take three steps back, turn around and go pick your boys up off the bathroom floor."

The guy jumped backward. He turned without looking back first, and came face to face with Beck. Beck brought his hands in tight and shoved them forward. The motion caught the guy in the stomach, and he stumbled to the side and fell onto an empty table.

"Ready?" Beck said.

"What happened to you in there?" she said.

Beck shrugged. "The place is filthy. The floor is literally covered in human waste."

They returned to the Infiniti. Beck sat behind the wheel. Clarissa adjusted the passenger seat and leaned back. She hadn't slept on the plane, and had been up for close to thirty-six hours. The engine roared, then hummed. Beck shifted into first and rounded the front of the building, driving past the restaurant's entrance. The four men stood on the sidewalk. Three of them had taken a beating. One looked like he needed to go to the emergency room. It was obvious at that moment that Beck was not someone to be messed with.

"Does trouble always follow you like that?" he asked her.

"Since I was a little girl," she said. "Pays to be tough, though."

"And to have tough associates," he added.

"That too."

Beck took the I-95 south on-ramp. Traffic had thinned, but Clarissa wouldn't call it light. Beck pressed the gas pedal and weaved through the maze of vehicles.

They crossed the Ben Franklin Bridge. The sun hovered deep in the western sky, dancing with the ripples in the water. The rigid design of the bridge, and the orange glow in the sky behind it, and the red and purple swirling ballet that took place on the river below left Clarissa in a tranquil state.

She closed her eyes. The sounds of the radio and the high-pitched hum of the tires tearing across weathered asphalt faded away.

Chapter 5

Clarissa jerked forward against a stiffened seat belt that cut into her chest. The sounds of brakes squealing flew past her. Her head snapped back against the leather headrest.

"This is your stop," Beck said.

Clarissa opened her eyes. It was dark out. Streetlights illuminated the sidewalk and part of a building next to the car. She looked up the familiar condominium's facade. Only a few of the windows were brightened.

"That's my apartment building," she said.

He nodded. "That's where the directions led to."

Clarissa rubbed her eyes and turned to face the man. "Are you supposed to come in, too?"

He shook his head in response, fixed his gaze on her.

"This makes no sense, Beck. Why did we have to travel all the way down here together if the only reason was to take me home?"

Beck glanced at the rear-view mirror, then back at her. "I'm surprised you haven't figured this out, Clarissa. Or, perhaps you have, and you're looking for confirmation?"

She shrugged. He escorted her, plain and simple. She got off a plane in Boston, and he made sure she got to D.C., and into her building. She knew the city too well, that was why she didn't fly into Reagan or Dulles. Likewise, she would have spotted a tail from a mile away. There was no point in following her home, so they did the next best thing. They put a man they trusted in the car with her.

Clarissa relayed her thoughts to Beck.

"Pretty much spot on, Ms. Abbot."

"So, will you tell me who you really are now?"

Beck smiled and said nothing. Headlights approached and reflected off his eyes. The car passed. Shadows danced from right to left.

Clarissa grabbed the chilled door handle and pulled it toward her. She swiveled in the seat, placed both feet on the ground. Before turning and walking away, she leaned forward and ducked her head inside the car.

"I'll see you around, Beck."

"Someday, maybe."

She flicked the door with her fingertips. He pulled away before it had closed. The engine revved and echoed off the two opposing twenty-story buildings. Beck turned right at the first stop sign. The Infiniti disappeared behind a wall of concrete.

Clarissa walked along the sidewalk toward the lobby entrance. She dragged her fingers along the rough exterior of the building. It felt like heavy-grit sandpaper. Would probably have the same effect, too, if she pressed any harder. The pizzeria around the corner baked their last pies of the night. They must've had the front door open. The aroma hit her hard.

Through the smoky glass entrance, she peered in at the empty lobby of her apartment building. Her key and access card were in a safe deposit box two miles away. She had no way of retrieving them until morning. Clarissa traced her hand along the door and reached for the call button mounted to the side of it. A man answered after two quick buzzes.

"This is Carrie Reese," she said, using the alias the apartment was leased under. "My flight home from Europe was delayed, and I didn't have the opportunity to get my access card and apartment key. Can you let me in?"

The door buzzed and the lock clicked and the cameras moved to focus on her. She pushed the door open. The lobby smelled fresh, looked spotless. A man she didn't recognize sat behind a counter. He had a smile plastered across his weathered face. Wrinkles rose into his bald head. He waved her over. When she reached the counter, he lifted a frail arm and placed a key in front of her.

"For your room," he said. "Nice to have you back, Ms. Reese."

She smiled and grabbed the key. She didn't recognize the guy, but he acted as though he knew her. She brushed it off and walked to the stairs. She hurried up three flights and exited onto her floor, pausing near the stairwell for a moment. She heard no noise and no voices, so she continued down the hallway.

Her apartment had been empty for over a month. As a rule, she kept the refrigerator as barren as possible, making sure to pour out milk and get rid of anything that could mold if she had to go away for an extended period of time. She questioned whether she had done that, and whether she had taken out the trash before leaving.

She opened the door, prepared for an obnoxious smell to greet her. It didn't. The air fresheners plugged into the wall did their job. She crossed the dark room to the open kitchen. There, she felt along the wall for a light switch. The overhead light blinked on, illuminating the space. She pulled the refrigerator door open, grabbed a bottle of water off an otherwise empty shelf.

Something beeped behind her. She spun around, hand on her pistol. A thin black box sat on the counter next to sink. She grabbed it, shook the box and listened to the contents rattle against the inside. The thought that it might be a bomb passed through her mind. She dismissed it. Why go through all that trouble to get her home only to blow her and the building up? Pointless. They didn't operate like that.

At least, not that she knew of.

She used a serrated steak knife to cut the clear tape that sealed the box. The lid slid off with a gentle tug. A new cell phone waited for her inside the box. A blue light in the upper left corner flashed every five seconds. She pulled the phone out of the package and hit a button on the side. The screen lit up. She dragged her index finger across the large face of the phone. There was one missed call. It had come from the 202 area code, locally in D.C.

She tapped the number, then the green phone icon. After a three-second pause, she heard it ringing. She brought the phone to her ear.

Sinclair answered. "Hello, Clarissa."

She was less polite. "Are you going to tell me what's going on, or am I supposed to keep guessing?"

There was a pause on the other end as Sinclair took in a deep breath and blew it out into his phone.

"I do apologize for keeping you in the dark like this," he said. "Let's just say, it was absolutely necessary. You'll have to trust me on that for another eight hours or so."

She walked toward the door that led to her balcony. The vent in the ceiling blew a gust in the direction of the door, causing the blinds to sway. She pulled them back. A full moon hovered in the sky directly in front of her. She slid the door open and stepped outside. The air was warm, humid. She didn't care. Clarissa draped her left arm over the railing and leaned forward, looking down at the street. A car drove past. Headlights spread out in a cone formation, washing over the cracked asphalt.

"What happens in eight hours?" she asked.

"A car is going to come for you. You'll need to be out front when they arrive."

She pulled the phone away from her head and checked the time. It was ten o'clock. She had to be ready at six in the morning.

"Where is the car going to take me?" she asked.

"To an undisclosed location."

"What will happen there?"

"A meeting that will never have taken place."

"Lots of secrecy here, Sinclair."

"Honestly, Clarissa, are you surprised?"

She wasn't. This was her life now, and probably until the day she passed on. In some ways, it suited her well. Always on the move. Always pretending to be someone other than herself. There were downsides to it, as well. They were few, but powerful enough to wreak havoc on her emotional side.

"Anyway," he said. "Get your rest. Gather anything important from your apartment. You won't be going back any time soon."

Any other day, she would have taken that as a threat. Today, she didn't care. Plus, would he have told her to take anything important with her if he intended to kill her?

Perhaps. If she had something he wanted.

And she knew that.

Chapter 6

Five a.m. arrived too soon. Of course, it always did.

The last time Clarissa had glanced at the clock had been after midnight. She estimated it took another forty-five minutes from that point to fall asleep. That was nothing new. Difficulty achieving a restful state had always plagued her. Nothing she tried had worked, so she lived with it.

She shuffled from her bed to the kitchen and started a pot of coffee. The first few drips provided confirmation that she'd soon receive her morning jolt. She returned to her room, headed for the shower. Fifteen minutes later, she emerged, awakened and somewhat refreshed, wrapped up in a white terrycloth towel. Her dark hair hung in strands, draped over her shoulders, chest and back. Cold drops of water streaked down her bare skin before settling into the towel.

In her closet, she pushed aside her clothes, revealing a safe. A keypad with slightly illuminated numbers stared back at her. She entered the security code, pulled the door open, and checked the contents. Inside were a passport and Maryland driver's license. Both had the same false identity. A wad of cash in different denominations totaling around five thousand dollars. And a Glock 17. She wanted to take the items with her and place them in a security deposit box. She couldn't, though. Presumably, whoever picked her up wasn't going to chauffeur her around wherever she wanted to go. She would have to get back to the apartment after the meeting to collect the items. Sinclair's warning that she wouldn't be able to return anytime soon played again in her head. She'd take the chance, knowing if it came down to life or death, she'd be better off with a way out.

She slipped on a pair of compression shorts with a holster in the rear for the M9 Beck had given her. She put on a pair of jeans over the shorts, and a casual shirt.

The coffee had finished brewing. Dark roast aroma filled her room, causing her mouth to water. She hurried to the kitchen, poured a mug and stepped outside onto the balcony.

Faint traces of stars shone above. The moon had sunk below the horizon. The air was cool and the humidity had been kept at bay. It'd return in a few short hours. *Better get used to it,* she told herself. *Summer is only just beginning.*

She sat down at the small wrought iron bistro table in the corner. The seat was damp with dew. She didn't care. Her pants would dry. Clarissa extended her legs over the railing, crossing her left foot over her right. She sipped on her coffee until it cooled, then she polished it off in a couple swallows.

In the short time she sat outside, the humidity rose, making it feel as though the temperature had gone up several degrees. Already her forehead grew damp. She exited the balcony into her apartment. It was cool and quiet and still smelled like a cafe. The clock on the stove indicated she had fifteen minutes left. She walked past it, reached into the cabinet, grabbed a travel mug, and filled it.

The only sound in the room was the air conditioning. She closed her eyes and breathed in time with the rhythm of the system.

When it was time to leave, Clarissa reached behind her back and checked her weapon. The M9 fit snug in the holster. She grabbed her purse and the cell phone and left the apartment. There were two sets of stairs in the building. She walked the length of the hall and took the ones furthest from her. Nothing more than a hunch. *The first of many on this day,* she thought.

No matter how many there were, she only had to be right one time. That was all that mattered.

Downstairs, she passed through the lobby and stepped outside. The sun hadn't surfaced yet. It was dark and muggy. The street was empty. In a few hours, vehicles would be jammed end to end in front of the building.

She heard the car's engine before it appeared. It rounded the corner and approached slowly. Headlights cut through the hazy morning air. The driver cut them off. Clarissa caught a glimpse of the man as the black car came to a stop. He had buzzed dark hair and wore a black suit. He brought the sedan to a halt next to her. The passenger side window rolled down.

"Ms. Abbot?" the guy asked.

She leaned forward, right hand behind her back. "That's me. Sinclair send you?"

He nodded. "Get in."

She reached for the handle and pulled the front door open. She expected the guy to protest and tell her to get in back. When he didn't, she feared the backseat would be occupied with two more men. One she could deal with. Three spelled bad news.

She stuck her left leg in, ducked her head and looked past the front row.

The seat was empty.

She exhaled in relief, sliding into the passenger seat and closing the door. The window rolled up. It got caught near the top. The motor whined for a second, then the window lurched into the weather stripping. Maybe the vehicle had been t-boned, or the driver had slammed into something. She pulled the seatbelt across her chest and latched it.

"So, where are we going?" she asked.

The guy said nothing. He put the sedan in gear and pulled away from the curb. It seemed as though he drove in a large square, heading up 11th, west on Q Street, and then south on New Hampshire Avenue. A few more unnecessary turns placed them on Pennsylvania Avenue, headed toward the White House.

She almost laughed at the thought of going to meet the president. What would President Rhodes want with her? Just her presence in the domicile would spark rumors the likes of which she had never seen.

"What?" the guy asked.

Presumably, he'd seen the look on her face. She stopped smiling, shook her head and said nothing.

The guy didn't press for more. He continued on, stopping when the traffic lights told him to.

Traffic picked up the longer they drove. Maybe that was the point. Why come get her so early, though? She thought back to her items in the safe in her closet. She knew why. Sinclair wanted to prevent her from leaving to take care of something and then returning to her apartment in advance of her ride. Nothing important opened before eight or nine in the morning. By getting the guy to drive her around for an hour or so, Sinclair cut her off. She felt annoyed. It wasn't like she had plans to flee.

Yet.

It all depended how things played out. Though he wouldn't give her a choice, she knew a decision loomed. And it all depended on what she found out today when she met with him.

The man cleared his throat. "Almost there." He lifted his index finger off the wheel and pointed.

She glanced around. They were two blocks from the White House. There were plenty of other government buildings close by. She assumed they were going to one of those. Only, she didn't expect it would be one that practically sat on the White House lawn.

.

Chapter 7

"What are we doing at the Treasury Department building?" she asked.

The sun crested over a building to their left. The bright rays reflected off the windows of another. The man slipped a pair of dark sunglasses over his eyes. He removed his hands from the wheel and straightened his tie.

"It's where I work sometimes."

"Where do you work the rest of the time?"

He ignored her question. "I was asked to bring you in today."

"By who?" Her mind raced. She tried to remember all the facts she had stored in her brain about the Treasury Department. Everything to do with money, managing national banks and federal finances, dealing with tax evaders and counterfeit and other financial crimes. The Secret Service had been a part of the department until March of 2003, when they transitioned to the Department of Homeland Security. As far as she knew, the Secret Service maintained their responsibilities over counterfeit production, money laundering, and other major financial crimes.

None of those things had anything to do with her. Had she unwittingly gotten mixed up in something either in London or before she left the U.S.?

Her chest tightened. It felt like her stomach flipped over on itself. Clarissa drew in a deep breath, held it while clenching and relaxing her thighs and upper arms. The man didn't seem to notice her difficulties breathing. He drove past the building on 15th Street, south of F, turned onto a narrow lane, drove through a small parking lot and stopped in front of a gate. Clarissa calmed down. He rolled down his window and leaned out and punched in a code. The gate lifted. He navigated through the opening. Then they went underground into a fluorescent-lit garage.

"Who told you to bring me here?" she asked.

He turned the wheel and made a tight U-turn into the next lane. There were parking spaces at the end. Half the cars in the place looked like his. The other half was a mash-up of domestic and foreign vehicles, mostly mid-range with a few luxury automobiles here and there.

"I don't ask questions like that, Ms. Abbot. I do what I'm told."

She turned her head and rolled her eyes. She wasn't sure why she hid the gesture from the man. Clarissa had never been shy about letting someone see her true feelings.

"So, what? You're just going to drop me off in the garage?"

"Do you think I'd do that? Honestly, do you? From here you can gain access to the White House if you know what you're doing. Do I seem like the kind of agent that would allow that to happen?"

Clarissa stared at the man. He looked as serious as a stone, and he had the personality to match.

"Sorry. I'll just go along for the ride."

"Thank you." He pulled into a spot, rolled up the window and cut the engine. "Now, we're going to exit the vehicle. You are going to walk in front of me. Never will you stop or turn or run or skip without me telling you to. And if I tell you to run, you better haul ass, 'cause that means something really bad just happened."

"Yes, sir," she said with a touch of sarcasm.

"I don't think this is funny, Miss." He exited the car and waited by the trunk for her.

She did as he said, walking two steps in front of him at an even clip. He led her to an access-card controlled elevator. After a short ride, it deposited them into a corridor lit with yellowish lighting inserted into the drop ceiling. A metal detector loomed ahead. Four armed guards surrounded it. Three of them had an animated conversation. One stared ahead at the approaching couple.

Clarissa glanced over her shoulder. "I should let you know right now that I'm armed."

"Stop," the guy said.

She did.

"Why would you be armed?" he asked

"I had no idea where I was going or what I would do when I got there."

"Who are you and who do you work for?"

"I thought you said it was not your job to ask questions."

The man said nothing.

She turned her head to the left and made eye contact. "It's in a holster behind my back. The magazine is in my front pocket."

He stepped forward and placed his hand on the small of her back.

"Lower," she said.

He lifted her shirt and slid his fingers toward her waistband. His knuckles pressed into her flesh as he wrapped his hand around the handle of the pistol. He quickly lifted it out of the holster. She felt his shoulder drive into her upper back as if he had turned away to shield himself while putting the weapon away.

She reached into her pocket for the clip and handed it to him.

"Go," he said.

They stopped in front of the metal detector. One of the guards waved her through. She stepped into and past the machine as they x-rayed her bag. There wasn't anything in it other than some cash and her phone.

The guy said, "Checking her weapon, an M9, and one magazine, full."

One of the guards took it, unlocked a drawer and placed the weapon in there.

"They really leave the weapon right there?" she asked as they walked away.

"No," the guy said.

She decided against pressing for more information. He already seemed perturbed with her. She had no idea how much longer she would be stuck with him.

Turned out that their time together ended ten minutes later. He led her through a maze of hallways, through break rooms, into one elevator, then down a final hall. She struggled to figure out which direction she faced. He halted in front of a dark wooden door.

"This is it for me," he said. "Go on in. They'll be along shortly."

He turned and walked back the way they had come. He turned a corner and disappeared from sight. She leaned forward and placed her ear against the door. No sound escaped the room.

"You won't hear anything," a woman said.

Clarissa straightened up. To her right she saw the woman approaching. The lady was older, around fifty-five. She had on a black skirt, white shirt and black blazer. Her hair was long and pulled back. Brown and gray were at odds with one another. She carried a laptop bag in one hand, a green folder stuffed with files in the other.

"You must be Clarissa," the woman said, looking her up and down. "You had dark hair in the picture I saw."

"It had been dyed to match—"

"It doesn't matter, Clarissa." The woman reached past her, turned the handle and pushed the door open. "Go on in."

Clarissa glanced around the room before entering. A twelve-foot long wood table was placed in the center. There were four leather chairs to a side, and one at each end. There were no windows. Each wall had two wide screen televisions or monitors. A fake plant had been placed in each corner of the room. Ambiance. Nice touch.

She stepped inside. It was fifteen degrees colder than the rest of the building. She glanced up. There was a vent in the ceiling on each end of the room. She walked to the other side of the table until she felt no draft, pulled out a chair in the middle, then sat down.

The woman placed her bag and the folder opposite Clarissa. She walked to the other end of the room and opened a cabinet. Clarissa noticed a black coffee maker. The woman pulled it out, along with a tin can. She set both on top of the counter. Thirty seconds later, the sounds of percolating coffee could be heard. She eyed a stack of brown paper cups and a dish of to-go creamers.

"Do you know why you're here?" the woman asked, returning to the table.

Clarissa shook her head.

The woman looked away as she sat down.

After a few moments, during which there was no response, Clarissa asked, "Do you?"

The lady's gaze cut back to Clarissa. Her thin lips took on the shape of a smile. "Why else would I be here?"

Clarissa waited, but the woman did not expound upon her answer. What was the point of asking the question in the first place? She decided to let it go. They'd have to tell her at some point, whether the woman liked it or not.

When the coffee finished brewing, Clarissa rose and poured herself a cup. The older woman waited until she had finished, then poured one for herself. She stood in front of the coffee machine, sipping from her cup. It seemed as if the lady would do anything to avoid having a conversation with her.

The atmosphere in the room was heavy. Clarissa felt tense, nervous. Despite the temperature, sweat beaded up on the back of her neck at her hairline. Her palms were coated. She wiped them on her pants a few times.

There was a bang against the door, then it opened. A man entered the room. He glanced in Clarissa's direction and gave her a slight nod. He looked the same age as the woman. He had no hair on the top of his head, but sported a gray mustache. His bushy eyebrows drew her gaze away from his eyes. Following him in was another man about the same age. He had a different air to him. His shoes were built for comfort, but not action. His suit had the appearance of costing a thousand dollars more than anyone else's in the building. There was something different about him.

Behind the man stood Sinclair. He looked the same as the last time she had seen him. Thin, pale, evil. Though, she couldn't recall seeing him in a suit before.

Sinclair walked to the far end of the table and sat down. He smiled at her. She returned the gesture.

"Glad to see you made it here okay," he said.

"Yeah, well, you had those bases pretty well covered, didn't you?"

He shrugged. "You're a wild card, Clarissa. You always will be."

"So what am I doing here? The way I hear it, if I know what I'm doing, I can get into the White House from this building."

The other man cleared his throat. "We don't take those kinds of threats lightly around here. This may not be our building anymore—"

Sinclair lifted his right arm. "I've got this, Banner." He looked at her. "Please, Clarissa, take this seriously. There is something going on and we all feel that you can be helpful in solving this."

She leaned toward him. "When did you get cozy with the Treasury Department folks?"

"You don't know everything about me," Sinclair said.

In part, she took that as a challenge. For now, though, she let it go.

He continued. "And you never will. Besides, these folks aren't part of the Treasury Department. Isn't that right, Banner?"

"Nope, they cut us loose back in '03. We're part of the happy Homeland Security family now."

The older woman cleared her throat, and asked, "Are we ready?"

Banner said, "Waiting on one more person."

On cue, the door pushed open and a man she recognized stepped in.

Chapter 8

"Sinclair," Banner said. "Have you met Evan Beck?"

Sinclair rose, extended his hand toward the younger man. "Yes, of course. You were coming in as I was going out."

Clarissa had never heard any mention of Sinclair working in the Treasury Department. She couldn't picture the man doing so, either. What was he talking about?

Beck nodded at Sinclair, smiled at Clarissa.

"Good to see you again," Beck said.

All stares were fixed on the man. He glanced at Clarissa. She held out her hands and mouthed the word, "Why?"

Why hadn't he told her what was going on if he knew all along? Had he been instructed not to? Did they fear that whatever they were about to ask her to do would have caused her to run the night before?

Of course, all that assumed that he did know what she was doing there. He might be as much in the dark as her.

Beck walked past the other end of the table toward the cabinets on the opposite side of the room. He poured a cup of coffee and took a seat. He kept his focus on Clarissa. She glanced around the room. They all stared in her direction now.

"What?" she asked. "Am I supposed to know what's going on here?"

No one spoke. The older man and woman glanced at each other. Sinclair smiled. Beck stared. She felt her cheeks burn.

"Banner," Sinclair said. "Why don't we get started?"

Banner took a seat. He pointed at himself. "As you heard, my name is Banner. This here," he pointed at the woman, "is Polanski. You've met Beck. And, obviously, you already know Sinclair." Banner glanced toward the other man. The guy nodded at Banner, then shifted his gaze back to Clarissa. Banner said, "This is Senator Patrick Hogan. He's on a few committees and subcommittees. Things we really can't get into here. I'm sure you understand."

Clarissa nodded, said nothing.

"Anyway," Banner said. "He's here to observe and sign off."

Polanski spoke next. "I'll get right to it. We have a mole. Someone has leaked vital information to an outside group that can use that information to hurt one of our interests. Problem is that we don't know who the leak is. But we do know the only place the information could have come from is within the walls, halls, and rooms of the White House."

"Which part? Who would do this?" Clarissa asked.

No one responded.

"You don't know? Or you can't tell me?"

"A little of both," Banner said, meshing his fingers together. "The point is, we need you in there to do nothing more than observe for a few days, a week, something like that."

Clarissa leaned forward. She placed her forearms on the table. "Do you know who it is I'm to observe?"

Polanski said, "We don't. If we did, you wouldn't be here right now." She glanced at Sinclair. He nodded. She added, "You are going to be in a position that you'll have access to everyone and everything that happens in the building."

"Does President Rhodes know about this?" Clarissa asked.

Banner, Hogan and Polanski looked at Beck. The man shook his head, said, "The President has not been made aware yet."

Clarissa studied Beck for a moment. He'd shaved the shag off his face. His hair looked an inch shorter. While the other three looked worn down by life and their job, Beck was clean cut and crisp. Who was he that he would deal with the president directly? Part of the Secret Service? She shifted her gaze to Banner, then Polanski. Who were any of them? Other than Senator Hogan and Sinclair, she knew nothing about the others in the room. She figured they would give her a sideways answer if she asked, so she didn't.

"There are some things you'll need to change," Sinclair said. "Hair style, color, length—"

"I know the drill," she said. "I'm not opposed to any of that. I'm still not sure this is the job for me, though. I'm used to working in more hostile conditions. I don't see how I'll be an asset in a building as heavily guarded as the White House. I mean, doesn't the president have around twenty or so agents nearby at all times?"

"Ms. Abbot," Polanski said. "If this isn't stopped, you'll be square in the middle of the most hostile conditions you can imagine."

Banner said, "And the truth is, you don't have a choice. You try to walk out of this room without agreeing and you'll never see daylight again. We can hold you here as long as it takes. And if it takes too long, and you know what I mean, you can forget going back to the life you used to lead."

The life she used to lead. Clarissa nearly laughed over the thought. She focused her energy on the tone of their words.

"You're threatening me over this?" Clarissa asked, glancing at Hogan. She expected him to look shocked. Appalled, even. He didn't, though. And she found that didn't surprise her. All along she had suspected that people in government knew more than they let on.

Sinclair stood and held out his right hand. "Let's just take a moment here to calm down." He turned toward her. "Why don't you and I take a walk?"

"I think I'd like that."

She rose and walked around the table, toward the door. Beck followed her with his stare, and smiled. She looked away. Sinclair opened the door. It glided silently on its hinges. She stepped through the opening. The hallway warmed her bare skin. They walked to the end of the hall without speaking. Sinclair led her to a stairwell. They made their way to the ground level. Another corridor led them to a door that opened up to a courtyard. Thick concrete interspersed with square sections of grass lay out in front of her.

Shadows indicated that the sun stood behind the building. Clarissa stepped out into the shaded area. It was hot, humid, and still. Whatever breeze there was had been blocked by the walls, just like the sun. She paced along a line, alternating her steps from concrete to grass and back again. Sinclair remained by the door they exited through. She turned and walked toward him, stopping five feet away from the man.

Sighing, she asked, "Do I have a choice?"

He shook his head. "Afraid not."

"What did they offer you to make this happen? And why me?"

He took the accusation like a spear to the heart. "Offer me? Why you? They asked me if we had anyone skilled enough to pull something like this off. They wanted a chameleon, and you, though still wet behind the ears, are one of the best I've ever seen. This is a huge opportunity for you, Clarissa. Don't you see that? This could be your ticket out of danger's lair and into a higher level position."

"No one is going to bring me into their organization."

Sinclair stepped forward. "I brought you into mine."

"I'm not like you, though, am I? I'm not CIA. Contractor. That's what my badge says."

"God, you are a stubborn woman." He shook his hands in front of him while staring up at the sky. "Things change when you do something like this. The people that have the ability to make things happen will do it for you. Look, I'm not going to go into a bunch of bullshit about honor and doing the right thing for your country. You know who I am and how I operate. But you need to consider doing this for yourself. How long do you think you can last playing the games I place you inside? Don't you want something more for yourself? To be more than bait?"

Clarissa remained quiet for several seconds. She avoided Sinclair's piercing stare. A fraction of a breeze blew down. It did little to cool her off.

She asked, "Who is the target?"

Sinclair shook his head.

"You don't know, or you won't tell me?"

He took two steps, stopped in front of her. "I honestly don't know."

She didn't believe him. Still, she nodded, said, "Thank you."

"Are you ready to go inside?"

He had already turned around when she responded.

"Are they serious, Sinclair?"

"About what?"

"I'll never leave the building if I don't do it?"

He looked back at her, nodded once and glanced away.

"And there's nothing you can do to stop them?" she asked.

"Nothing, Clarissa. Like you said, you're only a contractor. Might as well not even exist. Who would miss you, anyway?"

She felt anger claw its way through her body. He'd never talked to her like that, even at the time of their first meeting. She balled her hands into fists.

"That's their take on it, Clarissa. Not mine. I'd miss you, and I know there are others who would, and probably do right now."

She had hardened herself to the point of never thinking of those people, and she didn't break now. She couldn't afford to. Instead, she closed her eyes and pulled humid air in through her nose. She exhaled even warmer air out. It cascaded over the middle of her upper lip.

"Are you ready?" he asked.

"As I'll ever be," she said.

They returned the way they came, down a hall, through the stairwell, down another hallway. She took in more on the way back. Going down, things had been new, unseen. Now she counted the doors between the exit and the stairs. She took note of the number of stairs between floors. On the top floor, she memorized the names on the wall plaques. Not all rooms had one, and she doubted that the ones she saw corresponded to the actual person in the office. Probably memorial names for the room itself.

How many had died in the line of duty since the inception of the department?

Clarissa glanced toward the end of the table when they reentered the meeting room. Beck had left. So had Senator Hogan. Banner and Polanski remained. Neither of them acknowledged her. When both she and Sinclair sat down, Banner rose. He walked to the back of the room, rose up on his toes and sat on top of a filing cabinet.

"What's it going to be?" he asked.

That was the question she'd asked herself over and over again since the moment she stepped into the hallway. The day had not gone as expected. And now, for everything they said they would do to her if she didn't accept, she still wanted nothing to do with the job. All but one thought kept her from trying to walk out. She made eye contact with Sinclair. He nodded and gave her a slight smile. She knew what she had to do.

"I'll do it."

It wasn't the fear of being locked up. There was only so long they could get away with it. They couldn't hurt anyone who meant anything to her. Her parents were gone. There were no siblings. Her friends were out of her life. In the end, she wanted a new start. A chance to be something more than anything she'd been in the past.

Chapter 9

Polanski smiled briefly and nodded at Clarissa, then pulled a stack of papers from the folder she'd set in front of her on the table. The loose stack made a sound like wind through dead leaves while they were being shuffled and straightened. The woman stared down at them, thumbing through and scanning each document for a few seconds before moving to the next. Her lips moved as she read each file. They moved too quickly for Clarissa to determine anything the woman mouthed.

Banner hopped off the filing cabinet. The metal piece of furniture groaned as his weight shifted away. He, too, smiled and nodded, walking across the room toward Clarissa. His gaze diverted away from hers. Sinclair shifted in his seat. Banner continued past Clarissa, and placed a hand on Sinclair's shoulder.

"Thanks for bringing her in," Banner said. "I think she'll be great for the job."

"Just get her back to me in one piece," Sinclair said. "She's a natural."

Clarissa leaned forward, letting her elbows knock against the table. "I'm sitting right here. No need to talk about me like I'm out of the room."

Banner continued on as if she hadn't said anything. "That'll be the end of your involvement, Sinclair. I'll send daily updates. Outside of that, you needn't worry about anything. She'll be cut off from communicating with you until the operation is over."

Sinclair nodded, seemingly unaffected by the news. The guy had a way of acting as if nothing ever bothered him.

"Wait a minute," Clarissa said. "I'm his direct report. Why can't I have contact with him?"

Polanski rapped her knuckles against the table. "Ms. Abbot, we're going to brief you on the details, after that you'll understand the whys of this. For now, let me say that starting tomorrow you'll be under amazingly tight scrutiny, the likes of which you've never seen before."

"Ever lived inside a terrorist's compound?" Clarissa said, then immediately regretted it.

Sinclair leveled her with a stare, and said, "Of course, she didn't mean what she just said."

"Of course," Polanski said. "Anyway, that's none of our concern. The only thing we care about is getting Ms. Abbot ready for tomorrow."

The sound of heavy breathing filled the space. Gazes passed from one person to the next. Clarissa watched Banner. He stared at the far wall. She looked at Polanski. The woman rubbed the knuckles she'd knocked against the table a moment before.

Sinclair stood and walked toward the door. "I'll be going now."

Clarissa rose and followed him. "Can I speak with him alone for a minute?"

Polanski shifted her gaze to Banner. He shrugged as if he didn't care. "Okay, keep it quick."

They left the room, leaving Clarissa alone with Sinclair. He aimed a finger toward the ceiling and twirled it around.

Clarissa shrugged and shook her head.

Sinclair mouthed the word, "Bug." They'd have to be careful what they said.

"I'm not sure," Sinclair said. "But they left us in here rather than us going into the hall. So keep whatever you say quick and to the point."

Clarissa took a moment to compose her words. She had to let Sinclair know that she'd reach out to him if she found herself in danger. After all, she had no idea what she was getting herself into. And, if she could, she wanted to give him an idea of what her job entailed. Obviously, she had to do this without letting anyone who observed the conversation in on the meaning of what she had said.

"Let our associate know that I'll be indisposed for a time, but when the time is suitable, I'll reach out to him so that we can resume our work together."

Sinclair's reaction was delayed. He, too, had to be considering how to handle the situation. After several seconds, he shook his head, said, "Unfortunately, Clarissa, your associate finds himself quite indisposed at the moment, and for the foreseeable future. The chances of being able to relay any thoughts or plans or well wishes to him are quite slim at this time. I'm sure once your assignment has played itself out, he'll be available and you'll be able to speak with him as you wish."

She feared that her words had angered him. He didn't do anything to help her feel otherwise. She paused while thinking of anything else she could say. During that time, Sinclair turned away and reached for the door.

She said, "Wait."

He stopped. "What?"

"Thank you for making this opportunity available to me."

"How do you know it's a good one, Clarissa?"

"I trust you."

Sinclair looked back over his shoulder. She saw the left side of his face. His look was hard, eyes narrow. He didn't make eye contact. "That's everyone's first mistake, Clarissa."

She said nothing else as he exited the room. A hollow feeling formed in her stomach. It wasn't the first time she had experienced it. Surely, it would not be the last. Where this would lead was anyone's guess. Would she and Sinclair work together again? If she failed, what would that do to his reputation? To hers? A few moments later, Banner and Polanski returned, saving Clarissa from her thoughts. Banner spoke first.

"Polanski will take it from here. My number will be listed in the cell phone she gives you later. You report to her. She reports to me. If you can't reach her, then feel free to call me should you need something."

Clarissa returned to her seat as Banner left the room. The door fell shut, latching securely. She glanced toward Polanski.

"Should I call you Ms. Polanski, or…?"

The woman stared at her for several seconds before responding. What was she thinking? Polanski's eyes were narrow and her face hardened. She clamped her lips together tightly. Her nostrils flared out with every inhalation. Clarissa believed that the woman felt inconvenienced, at the very least, with having to deal with her. Perhaps

Polanski had recommended someone else for the job and had lost to Banner. Why else would she have such obvious hatred for Clarissa?

"You can call me Julie." She glanced away, toward the wall where windows should have been. Her head bobbed as if she were shaking her legs under the table. "Frankly, I hate the way they call me by my last name. You can't let them know that, though. Never show weakness. This department has come a long way from when I started in the mid-eighties. But the feeling that it is a good old boy network still permeates the upper echelons around here. You'd be wise to remember that if you get an inkling that this is someplace you want to stay."

Clarissa said nothing, nodded and smiled.

Julie rolled her eyes. "Forget it. You wouldn't last one day here." She pushed away from the table and stood. "Then again, with those looks, you'd probably be my boss within five years."

Clarissa hated comments like that. She'd dealt with them since the time she was a teenager. Accusations flew because of her grades, then due to promotions after a short time on her first grown-up job. Both situations led to her leaving college early, and then quitting a promising career.

"I didn't ask for this, you know," Clarissa said. "I was forced to come down here. You people make it sound like I had a choice, but we all know that's not true."

"Listen to me. I have no idea who you are or what you have done up to this point. The fact is, I don't trust you and I'm against this. I've got about as much say in it as you do. We've got a real problem across the lawn. Their solution is to let you play house in the most recognized home in the free world. Don't for a minute think you are going to breeze through this by flashing your smile and shaking your ass. There is more on the line than you could possibly be aware."

Clarissa rose, walked around the table, stopped in front of Julie.

"I don't know anything at this point because you people haven't told me anything. So get over yourself and stop giving me shit for no reason."

The two women squared off next to the table. Julie's cheeks were red. Clarissa felt hers burn. They breathed heavily, and out of sync. Neither blinked. Neither spoke. How long could they go on? Clarissa wasn't one to back down. Apparently, Julie wasn't either.

Not a great way to start a new job, Clarissa thought, taking a step backward and forcing a smile.

Julie continued to stare. Finally, her cheeks paled and she put some slack in her shoulders and said, "Let's go down to my office so I can begin briefing you on your duties for the next few weeks."

Chapter 10

Julie led Clarissa out of the room and into the hallway. It seemed brighter than it had earlier. Definitely warmer. She glanced up and shielded her eyes from the full barrage of lights that illuminated the space. Through closed doors, hushed voices slipped through. Offices with doors wide open bustled with activity. Fingers danced across keyboards and conference calls echoed off thin walls. Another type of concrete jungle, though tamer than Clarissa was used to.

Stopping in front of the elevator, Julie reached out for the down button.

"What floor is your office on?" Clarissa asked.

Julie said nothing. Clarissa watched the woman's unwavering reflection in the mirrored door. Julie stood close enough that each exhalation fogged up the surface in two small, oblong spots. The elevator arrived and the mirrored barriers slid open. Clarissa waited for Julie to step inside, then followed.

After the elevator began its descent, Clarissa asked, "Are you back to disliking me?"

Julie said, "No. I don't feel like being pestered by questions all day, and undoubtedly that is what is going to happen. At some point, you are going to ask me questions that matter. I'll answer those. But this talking just to fill the empty void surrounding us has got to stop. I'm used to working with strong independent agents who can handle themselves without me babying them all day long."

Clarissa's intention had been to goad the woman along, but she didn't expect to get as upset by the answer as she did. She was not a petulant child. Clarissa considered herself one of the most independent people she knew. She opened her mouth and prepared to lash out when the elevator stopped and the doors once again parted. Two men nodded and stepped on board.

"Going down?" one of them asked.

Everything in my life, Clarissa thought.

"Yes," Julie said, batting her eyes at Clarissa.

Neither of the men pressed a button on the panel.

The elevator lurched and resumed its downward trek, then came to a stop again. It opened up to the long hall that led past security. Was Julie's office on this level? Clarissa couldn't recall seeing any offices on the floor. Perhaps they were leaving.

The men stepped to the side and allowed the women to exit first. Clarissa followed Julie down the hallway. They passed security. The same four guards from earlier were still manning the station. Clarissa reached out and tapped Julie on the shoulder.

"What is it now?"

"They took my handgun when I entered."

"Your personal weapon?"

"Yes." She paused, then added, "Well, no. Beck gave it to me when he picked me up."

"Then Beck can pick it up here if he has the proper paperwork for it."

"What am I supposed to use in the meantime?"

"Why don't you have the one issued to you by your department?"

"I had to ditch everything I had when I left my previous assignment. I have one at my apartment, but it's a backup. I guess I can get it this evening."

Julie stopped, turned. "No. You can't go back there until this is over."

"Until what is over?"

The two men from the elevator approached. They carried on a conversation while moving down the hallway toward the garage.

Julie watched them, eyed Clarissa for a moment, then shook her head. "I'll be able to get you a weapon when we get to my office."

"Where is your office?"

For the first time, Julie smiled after one of Clarissa's questions.

"You'll find out soon enough."

Clarissa decided she'd remain quiet until they reached their next destination. In the garage, Julie pointed toward a black Cadillac. It looked new on the outside. Smelled like it on the inside. She eased into the leather bucket seat and slid the seatbelt over her chest.

Five minutes later, they were on 15th Street, driving north. The crowded sidewalk thinned out the further they drove from the White House. Before long, tourists gave way to business people. The men hurried along in their Brooks Brothers suits. The women, not to be outdone by their male counterparts, wore designer clothing that made them look powerful and sexy. A statement, she supposed. *I can do it all, and then some.* They all occupied space on an empty sidewalk, moving from one meeting to the next with bluetooth devices covering their ears, and Starbucks coffee cups in one hand, and a laptop bag in the other. Some complimented the ensemble with a backpack or messenger back or purse slung over a shoulder.

Julie pulled into a parking lot and told Clarissa to remain inside the car. She did not object. The woman exited, leaving the engine idling and air conditioning running.

Clarissa glanced at the four-story brick building. She had no idea who worked inside. It didn't look official, like the rest of the government buildings in the city. Maybe Julie had a friend inside she had to see. A thought passed through Clarissa's mind that caused her to tense up.

What if it was a setup? Again, a long shot considering the elaborateness of getting her to this point. But that didn't mean that Julie Polanski hadn't gone rogue. Perhaps this was the tipping point, and Clarissa was the first step on the woman's path.

She reached for the glove box, but found it locked. She shifted her gaze from the side mirror to the rear-view, which she adjusted to give her a better view. Every person she saw walking became an instant threat. She considered exiting the vehicle and going inside the building.

Every second that passed was both a blessing and a curse to her. Either nothing was going to happen, or something was about to.

It wasn't until she saw Julie exit the building carrying a white plastic bag that she relaxed.

Julie pulled the door open and sat down. Clarissa smelled toasted bread and melted cheese and an assortment of deli meats.

"Hope you're hungry," Julie said. "These are the best in the city. I got you a foot long. We'll eat at my office. First, we've got to take you to get your hair done."

Clarissa protested, but Julie cut her off. They drove another block north, then parked behind a salon where a chair had been reserved. The woman didn't ask Clarissa how she wanted her hair styled. Instead, Julie told the woman to cut it short and dye it darker. An hour later, Clarissa stepped out of the salon looking like a different woman. She stopped in front of the front window and stared at her reflection. Her hands patted her shortened, black hair. She figured she could make it work. She had no choice.

They returned to Julie's car and pulled out of the parking lot and drove back the way they came, crossing into Virginia. Julie continued on taking them into Crystal City.

Clarissa pointed at an approaching building she recognized. "That's a Secret Service building, right?"

Julie nodded, and said, "That's correct. I've been stuck in that building every day the last five years."

The disdain in the woman's voice did not go unnoticed. Clarissa had heard people speak like that, but never at a job she imagined earned someone recognition and trust.

"You talk as if you hate your job."

"Hate is a bit of a strong word. I love what the job stands for." She glanced at Clarissa. "I dislike the stuff I have to shovel every day, and most of the people I have to answer to. I've passed the point where I'm going to get any further up the ladder than I already am. And I'm never going back to the Treasury Department building. Next stop for me is probably a field office in Oklahoma. You see, once you've been passed over so many times, you come to grips with the fact that this is as good as it is going to get. And, frankly, it ain't that great."

Clarissa didn't know what to say, so she didn't respond. The woman sitting next to her looked pissed off one moment, and defeated the next. Anything Clarissa said might set Julie off, so she turned her head toward the window and stared out at a man pushing a shopping cart full of cans and other various objects. She wondered if the guy really was homeless. What if he was an agent who'd been planted there to keep an eye on things from the street? After all, she could spot a Fed from five blocks away. Surely anyone meaning them harm could as well. But this guy, with his unshaven face, shaggy hair, and soiled clothing, who would bother with him?

"What are you looking at?" Julie asked.

"That guy. He seems out of place."

"Why?"

"Just doesn't look right."

"D.C., NOVA, it's a big area. Lots of money. Lots of jobs gone wrong. Lots of homeless."

"Yeah, but right here? What's to say he's not from your department?"

Julie glanced at her. "You've got a good eye."

"When you're completely on your own at the age of nineteen, you learn how to spot the creeps and assholes. The skill grows as you get better and older."

"I heard about your father, how he died."

"Did you know him?"

"Me? No." Julie shook her head as she turned off the street. "I read your file, and as much of his as I could. A lot was classified."

"The man responsible is still out there."

"You know who it was?"

"I don't know who pulled the trigger, but I know who ordered it."

"Why not tell someone?"

Clarissa laughed. "It's complicated, and I don't want to get into it now. I was barely eighteen when it happened. I've moved on."

"So you say," Julie said, then repeated.

"What's that supposed to mean?"

"When you don't take care of something, it tends to eat away at you until you explode."

"You think I'm going to explode?"

"I don't think anything."

"You don't know me, Julie. No matter what you think, you don't."

Julie shrugged. "We're all the same, Clarissa."

She drove through a dark hole in the side of the building and rolled down her window. A guard checked her credentials, then motioned her forward. The gate rose as the Cadillac inched forward. They drove up one lane, down another, repeating the process six times before finding a spot to park the car.

"Should have come by closer to lunch." Julie smiled briefly.

Chapter 11

Julie Polanski led Clarissa through a maze of hallways connected by break rooms and stairwells. They passed three separate elevators, but the woman refused to stop. And Clarissa didn't ask her to. Perhaps the woman was trying to show she still had it by running up the stairs two at a time.

When they stopped in front of a door with a nameplate that read "POLANSKI," the older woman was out of breath.

Clarissa smiled. "This it?"

Julie glanced over her shoulder at the bronze plate next to the door and said, "What do you think?"

Right when Clarissa had thought they might get along.

"Wait here," Julie said.

Clarissa remained outside the office and watched as Julie took a seat in front of her computer. The monitor was angled away from the doorway. The printer began whirring with activity. Julie spun in her chair, collected her printouts and exited the office, shutting and locking the door on her way out.

"Follow." A single command, as though she thought of Clarissa as a dog.

Polanski wouldn't be the first.

They entered a long, narrow room. Two women were seated behind desks placed side-by-side. The first, a lady with dark hair and even darker eyes, looked up and nodded.

Julie stepped forward, holding one of the forms in her outstretched hand. "Need a badge created with the following information."

The lady took the paper, set it in front of her and began typing. Every so often, she'd reach for her mouse, slide it side-to-side and click on the buttons. "Clarissa Weston," she said. "How tall are you, Clarissa?"

"Five-nine," Clarissa replied. "And don't ask for my weight."

Julie rolled her eyes. The lady smiled and looked from Clarissa to the older woman.

"Is this right?" the lady asked.

"What?" Julie said.

"No restrictions?"

"That's correct. She'll be overseeing all staff activity, therefore she needs unlimited restrictions. Just make sure it's set up so that everything she does is stored in the database."

The lady went back to typing.

Clarissa took a step toward Julie. She knew where her assignment would take her. And now she'd heard that she'd have no restrictions once inside the White House. How was this possible?

"Stored in a database?" Clarissa asked.

"The cards track you as you go from room to room. Allows us to quickly identify anyone on camera, as well as helps us to know where you are at all times. It's for your benefit and protection. God forbid, if something happens, you'll be glad because we can practically rule you out as a suspect."

"Are there any rooms without cameras there?"

Julie looked away and said nothing.

The only sound in the room was the women behind their desks tapping away at their keyboards and clicking their mice. After a few minutes, the lady asked Clarissa to stand on a square gray mat. Clarissa's picture was taken. The woman returned to her desk, swatted her keyboard some more, then rose and handed the newly minted badge to Clarissa.

Julie instructed her to put it on, then led her down another hall.

While walking, Clarissa said, "Didn't trust me enough to give me an alias for my first name?"

"Too dangerous. If someone called for you, and you didn't respond, that could spell trouble for you. This way you'll immediately answer any request made of you."

"I've lived under presumed names for the better part of the last year with some of the most dangerous men you could imagine. I think I can handle this."

"Too late, doesn't matter." Julie turned down a hall that ended at a counter topped with bulletproof glass. Her pace increased. Clarissa didn't try to match it. There was nowhere else to go, so she'd catch up eventually. When Julie stopped, Clarissa did too, remaining five feet behind.

"Yes, Ma'am?" the guy behind the partition said.

"SIG Sauer P229, checked out under my name and assigned to Clarissa Weston."

The guy punched a code into a keypad then stepped into another room. The door slammed shut behind him. Two minutes later he returned carrying a case and a DeSantis holster. The guy set the case on the counter, opened it and tilted it toward them. The P229 chambered for the .357 SIG looked bulky on its own. Combined with the holster, Clarissa wondered how she would conceal the weapon.

After the man closed the case, Julie reached forward and gathered it and the holster, then turned and walked past Clarissa. They traveled the halls without speaking until they reached Julie's office.

"Do I have to use that holster in the White House?"

Julie sat in her seat. The cushion wheezed. "You're not going to be armed inside. However, you'll keep this weapon on you at all other times. You'll enter through the Treasury Department building. A locker will be assigned to you. You'll leave it in there. Make sure you wear a blazer or a windbreaker at all times. That will help with concealment."

"What if I want to take a jog?"

Julie took a deep breath, looked up, and stopped herself before she began, apparently realizing by the look on Clarissa's face that it had been intended as a joke.

Taking a serious tone, Clarissa asked, "Can you tell me about my assignment now?"

"Pretty simple, really. Your job will be to monitor. You'll be introduced as a member of the staff, supervisory level. You'll spend a few days getting to know everyone there, the housekeepers, chefs, and so forth. I want you to use and trust your instincts. If someone seems suspicious, you tell us. We're not sending you in there with a target in mind. Everyone is fair game and should be considered both innocent and as a suspect."

"But only the household staff, right?"

Julie smiled, paused, said, "Everyone, Clarissa."

A rap on Julie's door startled them both. Clarissa looked over her shoulder.

"Come in," Julie said.

The door cracked open. Evan Beck stepped into the square room.

"Are you close to finished? I've only got an hour-and-a-half to spare."

Julie nodded. "Clarissa, Evan is going to take it from here." She pulled her desk drawer open and retrieved a cell phone. She set it on top of the case containing the SIG P229, next to the holster, and slid them across the desk. "He's going to take you to your apartment."

Evan glanced down at her. "You look different." His tone and the look on his face did not leave her feeling as though it was a good look for her. "Anyway, are you ready?"

Ten minutes later Evan and Clarissa crossed the bridge into D.C. in his government-issued sedan. It was a far cry from the Infiniti coupe they had driven in the day before. They didn't speak until they had passed the Treasury Department building.

Beck said, "You'll meet me out front, tomorrow, seven a.m. Understand?"

She nodded and said nothing.

"If you are late, I'll leave you on the street, and you'll have to walk."

This time she turned and caught his eye. "No, you won't." She had no problem calling his bluff.

He smiled, slightly. "You're right, I won't. But I will give you an earful, so make sure you are there at seven a.m."

"Do I get a car?"

He shook his head. "You'll walk."

She searched her memory for apartment buildings nearby. There weren't any she could recall. "Where are you taking me?"

He answered by extending his index finger over the top of the steering wheel.

Two minutes later he pulled up to the curb. Clarissa stared up at the building full of luxury condos. She had heard about the place, and knew that several athletes and famous people had resided in there at one time or another.

"You go inside, tell them your alias. They'll escort you to your apartment. It is one that we lease out and put people in from time to time. No one there will think anything of it. Most of the people here will keep to themselves, so nothing to worry about there." He glanced at the case holding her weapon. "There's a suitcase in the trunk. Put that inside of it."

"Beck?"

He lifted his eyebrows. "Yeah?"

"What's all this about?"

"Polanski gave you the run down, didn't she?"

"Yeah, and it reeks of bullshit."

He shook his head. "I can't tell you anymore than she has."

"If all you wanted to do was watch people, you could do that through all the surveillance footage. It doesn't make sense to pull me away from London to do this."

Beck said nothing.

Clarissa waited for a moment, deciding whether to pursue her line of questioning. The man sitting across from her stared directly ahead. His lips were clamped shut. Deciding to leave it alone for now, she reached for her door handle and exited the car.

Chapter 12

The man at the front counter was quick about getting Clarissa her apartment number and the key. He didn't attempt to make small talk. He only looked at her twice, when she walked up and as she stepped away. After a short elevator ride, she stepped onto the fourth floor, glanced up and down the hall to get her bearings, then located the door with 4F stenciled on it.

She stuck her key into the lock and turned it the wrong way. Before she corrected herself, the door behind her opened. Clarissa spun and faced a woman roughly five years older and a couple inches shorter. Pushing past the lady was a young boy, somewhere in the neighborhood of eight.

"Hi," the woman said, tucking a strand of long brown hair behind her ear. "You must be the tenant of the week."

Clarissa reached for the woman's outstretched hand. "Clarissa."

"Amy," the woman said. "And this little guy is Adam."

Clarissa smiled at the boy.

"How long are you in town?" Amy asked.

"In town?" Clarissa spun a story in her mind. "Not sure yet. I'm doing some consulting, and it is going to be a week-to-week kind of thing."

Amy glanced down at the suitcase on the floor. "I can see you're getting settled in, and I've got a huge stack of errands to run.

Tomorrow night we're having a little social thing up on the roof. Why don't you come as my guest?"

"Oh, I don't know, I'll probably be pretty—"

"I'm not taking no for an answer, Clarissa. I'll knock on your door around nine-thirty. You better be ready." She flashed a smile then reached for Adam's hand. "Okay, we're off. Talk to you tomorrow night."

Before Clarissa could respond, the woman had turned and jogged halfway down the hall. Her son had to sprint to keep up, his feet barely touching the paisley carpeting. Strange, to say the least, thought Clarissa. She normally presented herself in a way that resulted in people leaving her alone. Yet Amy seemed to welcome it. Perhaps she'd forget, and Clarissa could go on with her business. Of course, she could simply not be at the apartment. But Amy had said she would be over around nine-thirty. Clarissa would have to stay out most of the evening to avoid the woman.

Deciding to put off worrying about the invitation until the next day, Clarissa unlocked her door and entered the apartment. The first thing she noticed was the million-dollar view. She presumed the apartment had the price tag to go with it. The furnishings were high end and modern. There were identical white leather couches facing each other. They had wide seats and low backs. Rather uncomfortable looking. A short metal and glass coffee table had been placed in between the couches. The glass top was barren. A modern-looking lamp stood behind the couch furthest from her. A sixty-inch flat panel TV hung from the wall above the white, sleek fireplace. On either side were built-in bookcases. The floor, like the fireplace, looked to be actual marble, white with streaks of silver.

She turned to her left, facing the kitchen. The appliances were stainless steel. The fridge was extra-wide. The stove had six burners. Everything looked new.

"So this is home," she muttered to herself, dropping her bag and setting her purse on top of the kitchen island. She opened each cabinet, pulled out the items within and inspected the shelves. She moved into the living room, checked under the couches and their cushions. She ran her fingers along the edges of the television, and underneath the shelves of the built-in bookcases. She flipped the coffee table over and inspected the frame. She found nothing. But that did not ease her concern that there wasn't a camera or some sort of listening and recording device hidden in the condo.

She continued into the bedroom. It was nearly as big as the living room. A king-size bed was positioned at one end, and an eight-drawer dresser at the other. Past the bed was a sliding door that led to a balcony. She ignored it for the moment, and proceeded to take the sheets off the mattress, checked every dresser drawer, and inspected the closet. Again, she found nothing.

The view through the glass door was expansive. She opened the door and stepped out onto the balcony, which stretched from her room to the living room, where there was another door leading inside. From her perch, she looked to the southeast. A stretch of the Potomac River flowed past. Three small boats floated away from her. The sun hovered high in the sky still. She imagined the view in the morning when the sun came up over the forest beyond the river, then trickled light through the buildings adorning the city's skyline. Soon enough, she'd see it for real.

Chapter 13

Clarissa's cell phone rang at ten till six in the morning. She didn't recognize the number, but answered anyway. It was Beck. He told her she had forty minutes to get ready if she wanted a ride. She figured that would be better than walking on her first day, so she rolled out of bed, showered, started a pot of coffee, and dressed. By the time she left her room the second time, the coffee was close to ready. She poured a cup and checked the time. She had fifteen minutes to spare.

The sky beyond her balcony had begun to fade from deep blue to red and orange. She carried the hot mug across the room and stepped outside. A cool, crisp breeze blew into her face. She didn't smell the city. Instead, the air felt clean. Three large trucks rolled past on the road below. Early morning joggers pounded the concrete on a route that carried them past her building. From four stories up she heard their footsteps climb up the brick exterior.

In the distance, the sun blinked through the furthest trees. It would still be a few minutes before its rays hit her balcony, and she knew she didn't have the time to wait around.

Clarissa went back inside. She found a travel mug in the cupboard, dumped the remainder of her coffee into it, then topped it off with steaming hot brew from the pot. She left the ceramic mug on the counter and tugged on the refrigerator door handle. The fridge, which had been stocked, offered her several quick to-go options for breakfast. She settled on a green apple.

A glance at the microwave clock told her she only had five minutes. Who knew if Beck would wait one second longer than the forty-minute deadline he gave her? Clarissa decided not to push her luck. She holstered her P229 and untucked her shirt to cover the bulky weapon. With her mug in one hand and the apple clenched between her teeth, she exited the apartment. Though the hallway was empty, she had a feeling in her stomach that she would run into Amy. Fortunately, the woman was nowhere to be found.

Clarissa walked quickly down the hallway and reached the elevator lobby. There was a man with a head-full of thick gray hair waiting there. He had on a dark blue suit and expensive leather shoes. He glanced over his shoulder at her, then looked away without acknowledging that she stood there. A ding announced the elevator's arrival. The wide doors parted. No one stood inside. The man entered without offering her the opportunity to go first. Clarissa looked down at the panel and saw that he had pressed the lobby button. She leaned back into the corner and waited for the initial lurch to signal their downward journey.

Twenty seconds later, the doors parted again, revealing a dim lobby that had yet to come to life. A sleepy man propped his chin on his fist behind the counter. He glanced her way for a moment, then looked straight ahead. Long night, she presumed.

"Right on time."

Clarissa turned left and saw Evan Beck standing by the front door. Faux-lantern lights flickered behind him, casting a shadow across the front of his face. It made his eyebrows look thick and his face unshaven. It's how she imagined him looking during his bathroom fight at the restaurant.

"Military brat," she said. "Not a good thing to be late in the house I was raised in."

Beck nodded, perhaps in agreement. She thought about asking if his experience growing up was the same, but decided against it.

"You're all set?" he asked.

"Yup."

"Got your pistol holstered?"

She nodded, following him outside.

"I'll walk you through the routine this one time only. After that, you are on your own."

"Is this a weekend position, too?"

He stepped over an empty water bottle that had been discarded on the sidewalk in front of the building. "Yes, seven days a week until we are finished."

"We? So you're involved in this, too?"

Beck remained silent for a moment. They walked in stride toward his vehicle, parked half a block away.

"You could say I'm involved, but not directly."

That didn't help, but Clarissa expected as much.

They said nothing during the drive to the Treasury building. Clarissa studied the few faces she saw on the sidewalk. The early birds and go-getters walked at a brisk pace while morning joggers threaded past them.

As Beck pulled into the garage, he said, "If you ever plan on walking, go in through the front door. Your badge will get you past security without any problems."

Nothing was ever without problems. "And what if there is one?"

"Then call me, and I'll handle it." He looked over at her. Presumably, he knew that she was going to mention that she didn't know his number. "It's in your cell's contact list. Everyone you need is in there."

She swung her door open and placed both feet on the ground. Rising, she reached into her pocket and wrapped her hand around her phone. It was her only link to anyone who could help now. She had no idea if they were monitoring her personal line. She had to assume they were, and that if she placed a call to Sinclair, they would know. And until she knew more, she couldn't risk that.

Beck walked past the front of the car and headed toward the stairwell. Clarissa jogged to catch up to him, passing between two black government sedans. He led her up two flights of stairs. He had her scan her badge over a card reader. The light changed from red to green and the lock gave an audible click. Beck tugged the door open and waited for Clarissa to pass through. She stepped into a hallway she hadn't seen before. He pointed toward the security desk, manned by two guards. They looked different from the guards she had seen the day before. Although the two men were younger, they had more of an aggressive appearance. It appeared as though they were more than rented badges. These guys could take down a threat.

After they passed through security, Clarissa wondered why he'd taken her that way. "Isn't this area only for Secret Service?"

Beck shook his head. "Certain staff members come this way. Not only is this our office, but it provides a secret, secure entrance to the White House. It is better that some of the staff, not all, come this way. You'll be one of those people."

She nodded, assuming that entering in public would raise her profile.

"In this case, the fewer people to see your face, the better." Beck extended his left arm. "This way."

They stopped by his office. Beck sat behind his desk and checked his computer. Clarissa noted that the surface of his desk was bare except for a large stack of yellow notepads.

From his office, they traveled up a flight of stairs, coming to a stop in front of the ladies' locker room. He handed her a piece of paper and told her that it contained her locker assignment and code. She was to store her weapon inside the locker and wear the outfit provided for her. Her first instinct was to decline. Beck had seen the code, and so had whoever gave it to him. On top of that, the clothes could be bugged. Not could. Probably were.

"I know what you're thinking," he said. "It has to be done this way. Everything is legit."

She entered the empty room, stored her belongings, dressed and exited. Beck leaned against the far wall, waiting for her. He lifted an eyebrow as if to ask if everything was good to go.

"All set," she said.

"Great," he said. "One more thing."

She sighed. "What?"

He pulled a lapel pin from his pocket. She flinched when he reached for her. Extending the pin formed like a bald eagle toward her, he said, "Yes, this is what you think it is. And you need to have it on at all times."

The item she stared at felt light in the palm of her hand. She wondered how it worked. How would they see and hear everything she saw and heard? She also considered what they might do if she covered it up, or outright got rid of it. It was small enough that it would slip right down a sink drain, or succumb to the flush of a toilet. She pulled the back off the pin, stuck it through the lapel of her blazer and fastened it.

"What happens when I need privacy?"

"Press the eagle's head."

She tested it out. Beck's phone beeped. He glanced down at it and said, "And that's how we know."

"What happens then?" A moment after she asked, Clarissa waved both hands in front of her chest. "Forget it. I don't want to know."

"All right," Beck said. "Ready for the fun part?"

Chapter 14

Beck led Clarissa down a narrow flight of stairs. The sounds of their breathing echoed off the walls. The dim lights gave the stairwell an air of suspense. She wondered what was at the bottom. For years, since she'd seen the tunnels at her father's installation as a kid, she contemplated what the tunnels beneath D.C., and specifically the White House, were like. Where did they go? What kind of lights adorned the ceilings? Did water drip down the walls and pool along the corners where the floor met the rounded walls?

"Going in, no one knows anything about you, Clarissa. I'm going to introduce you to a few members of the staff and tell them that your job here is to observe. You'll pretty much have full access. I'll give you a tour and tell you where you can and can't go. Remember, someone will be watching at all times, so don't disobey."

"Is there anyone I shouldn't talk to?"

Beck shrugged. "Don't approach the president unless he requests you do so."

"What about the Secret Service stationed in the house?"

"They know nothing about you. You'll be an employee in there, and they'll watch your every move. Ultimately, those men report to my chain of command. If there is an issue, you just do as you're told and we'll handle it."

His answer satisfied her. As assignments went, this one seemed to be as easy as they came. Spend a few weeks inside one of the highest profile houses on the planet, and study people. She was under no obligation to provide a certain answer. Any answer, for that matter. If she saw nothing out of the ordinary, nothing that concerned her, then her time there would come and go and she'd be sent out on assignment by Sinclair.

At the same time, she couldn't help but hope that she did help them. This post could lead to something new, something better for her. She'd grown concerned that the only way to leave Sinclair's group would be to take another position within the agency. Otherwise, one of his cleaners would show up and that'd be the end of her. They wouldn't do that if she became a part of Homeland Security. She knew that the chances of entering the Secret Service were slim, but there were other opportunities out there, and having the backing of certain people might help.

After five flights of stairs, Beck asked her to use her access card on the reader next to a steel door. She swiped her card in front of the device and saw the light change and heard the lock click.

"Every day, this is your routine," Beck reminded her.

She reached for the door handle and pulled it toward them. The hallway in front of her did not disappoint. She smiled, if only for a second, at the concrete tunnel with yellowish lights lining the ceiling. Her first few steps echoed throughout the tunnel. She wondered why they hadn't done anything to dampen that, given that it could alert one's presence. After a few more steps, the echoes faded. She stretched her fingers out and let the tips trace the rough wall. It felt like worn sandpaper.

"We're heading toward the East Wing," Beck said.

Clarissa nodded. She knew the layout. When she was young, her father brought her and she received an exclusive tour of the place.

It didn't take long to reach their destination. They passed through two security doors, turning after each one, and then reached the final door. Beck explained the entry process, which required her badge and a pin number. This time, a guard on the other side of the door opened it. He verified their identities before allowing passage.

A set of stairs led them up to a final security door. Once through, they stood in an empty office that Beck said was located in the back corner of the Secret Service office.

Clarissa turned in a circle and pointed up. "Oval Office?"

Beck nodded. "And that way," he aimed his finger to the other end of the room, "is the Cabinet Room."

"Will I be over here much?"

Beck walked away from her without answering. He pulled a door open and motioned her forward. From this point on, she knew she would not be able to ask additional questions. He led her through the Secret Service office. The room seemed to buzz, but she saw no one milling about. Perhaps there were men and women glued to monitors watching every square inch of the property, ready to pounce at a moment's notice. She wondered how many agents were stationed there at any given time. She recalled that around two dozen were always around the president, and they had counter-assault teams in place everywhere he went. Maybe she'd learn more about it during her time on assignment.

Stepping out of the office, Beck turned right and started up a flight of stairs. Clarissa followed closely. At the top, they emerged between the press secretary's office and the Cabinet Room. They continued past both, turned right and walked through the West Colonnade. A warm breeze washed her with scents from the rose garden. She glanced to her right briefly to take in the sight of the perfectly manicured lawn surrounded by trimmed hedges and flowers in bloom along the perimeter. She reached out and touched a couple of the thick white columns that lined the walkway.

They entered the ground floor of the main building through the Palm Room. Two thick potted plants guarded the door. It felt light and airy in there. She took notice of the latticed walls and a painting of a young woman in period garb carrying an American flag over her head.

The Palm Room led them to the main hallway running throughout the ground floor of the main residence. Beck rattled off the names of the rooms they passed. He adjusted his path toward a closed door.

"One of my offices," he said, cluing her in that she shouldn't mention who was in the room or what went on inside.

He motioned her forward, but she hesitated, throwing a glance over each shoulder.

"Don't worry," he said, hushed.

She took his word for it and followed Beck inside. The room was empty. Clarissa felt relieved. She wasn't sure why, though. Perhaps she thought that the hardest people to fool would be those who were tasked with seeing anything and everything that went on inside the place. If

Beck had told her the truth, no one inside knew her purpose, not even the Secret Service. Wasn't bringing her into the room a risk?

Beck took a seat at a desk and logged onto the computer. He did not appear to be in a rush to get up and leave.

Clarissa shuffled from foot to foot, waiting for the door to pop open. When it finally did, she felt her face go slack.

Two men entered the room. One paid her no attention. The other, a shorter guy with buzz cut dark hair, smiled at her. She hadn't met many people in the Service, but the few she had had given her the impression that they didn't do that when on duty.

"Beck," the guy said.

"Jordan," Beck said.

"Who's this?"

"Clarissa Weston. She's new on the staff. They missed something on her profile and I'm taking care of it now."

Jordan nodded, staring at Clarissa. "Why'd *she* have to come in here for that?"

"I'm sorry," Beck said, "but did I miss a memo where you suddenly outrank me?"

Jordan's cheeks turned a shade of red.

"She's going to be assigned to McCormick when he returns tomorrow."

Clarissa stiffened. The vice president had not been mentioned before then. What purpose would she serve with the man? Was he the leak they were concerned with? What happened to monitoring the staff? Beck peered at her from behind the monitor. She knew then to keep her concerns to herself. She felt Jordan staring at her, so she turned to face him.

"He warn you about McCormick yet?" Jordan said.

Clarissa said nothing.

"He's gonna like you."

Beck slid the keyboard in front of him and rose. "We can go now."

She didn't wait for him to lead the way. In the hallway, she shot him an angry look.

"Would you have accepted if you knew?" Beck asked.

"Knew what?" Clarissa said.

"That you'd be assigned to the vice president."

She shook her head. "What am I going to be doing?"

"His assistant went on maternity leave last week. It was the perfect opportunity."

"So he's the one you suspect?"

Beck glanced over at her as they passed the library. The doors were closed. She recalled the ornate furnishings and built-in bookcases, wondering if and how the current residents had changed the room. Did each president keep the same books on the shelves? Perhaps they placed their favorites there. Or maybe they rotated them.

Beck led her on his rounds. As he introduced her to his staff, she got the feeling that he was more important than he had let on. She saw parts of the residence that not many ever saw. Though the place was impressive, she couldn't imagine the stress that went along with living or working there permanently. From the top down, it had to take a toll on everyone.

Shortly after noon they returned to the West Wing. Beck showed her McCormick's office. Tomorrow he'd introduce her personally. She noted the two desks in the foyer. One had pictures and other personal items lining the surface. The other was bare. She assumed that workstation was meant for her. At that moment, she dreaded coming in. At least what she believed she would be doing previously would have allowed her freedom to move around. Now she faced the possibility of sitting at the barren desk answering the phone all day long.

"Why don't we call it a day?" Beck said.

She didn't need to hear the suggestion a second time.

L.T. Ryan

Chapter 15

Later that afternoon, Clarissa stood on her balcony, watching the sky change from blue to red as the sun lowered. She'd spent the afternoon reading. Her attempt at keeping the endless questions at bay. Several stories below her, cars jammed the street. A road-rage-ridden driver honked his horn incessantly. The sound echoed between her building and one across the street. After a few minutes, the car had passed and the honking continued. It sounded like a toy horn the further away it went.

She couldn't imagine a life where she would get up, fight traffic, sit behind a desk all day, and then fight traffic all the way home. From there it only got more exciting, making dinner and falling asleep on the couch to the late news, if she managed to stay up that late. Her life wasn't perfect, yet, she felt that she had it better than those stuck in traffic below her.

Sunlight faded, but the temperature hardly dropped. She reentered the apartment, started a pot of coffee, and decided to shower and change. By the time she had finished, the coffee was ready. She didn't care that it was half past eight as she took a sip from her mug. Coffee, and caffeine in general, never had much of an effect on her. It'd wake her in the morning, but beyond that, the effects were minimal. She could drink it up to the moment she lay down at night and still fall asleep within minutes.

An hour into a new book, someone rapped on her front door. Clarissa sat up, startled and concerned. She tossed the paperback onto the coffee table and retrieved her pistol. The weapon brought about a sense of security. She knew that she could handle whoever was on the other side of the door.

She looked through the peephole. Amy leaned her head to the side and smiled.

"I see you in there," the woman said from the hall.

Clarissa slid the deadbolt to the right, tucked her pistol behind her back and pulled the door open, blocking the entrance with her body.

"That's not how you're going, is it?" Amy asked, waving her hand in front of her own outfit.

"Going?"

"To the social gathering tonight. You know, otherwise known as a party. You didn't forget, did you?"

She had. And at that moment, there was nothing she wanted to do less than go to a party full of people she didn't know.

Perhaps sensing her resistance, Amy said, "Don't worry. I won't leave your side. There'll be plenty of eligible men in attendance, too. Now, you look clean, so go get changed and meet me out here in thirty minutes."

"I really just—"

"I'm not taking no for an answer, Clarissa."

She'd become aware of that. Reluctantly, Clarissa agreed. She closed the door and headed to her room. She picked a casual outfit, one that would not reveal the bump of her weapon holstered behind her in a pair of compression shorts. The jeans and blouse fit perfectly, and revealed nothing. Perhaps, if she was lucky, she'd be left alone most of the evening. She could hope so, at least.

When she stepped into the hallway, a teenage girl with short blond hair and thin blue-framed glasses perched on her narrow nose stood in the middle of the corridor. She smiled at Clarissa and reached out to knock on Amy's door.

"You're Adam's babysitter," Clarissa stated.

The girl nodded and said nothing.

Amy pulled her door open, said hello to Clarissa, then welcomed the babysitter into her home, calling her by her first name, Beth.

Clarissa waited in the hallway for Amy to return. When the woman did, she said, "Follow me."

She'd yet to explore the halls of the building. Her time alone had been spent in her apartment, away from prying eyes. Although she doubted everyone in the building was as friendly and inquisitive as Amy. Sometimes it was better to remain a wallflower. This was one of those times. Which was why she had second thoughts about going to the party.

"Listen, Amy. I don't mean to sound—"

"Don't try and back out on me now. You're already accounted for up there. You have to show."

"What does it matter? It's not like I'm going to be here long."

Shrugging, Amy grabbed Clarissa's wrist and pulled her forward. They reached the end of the hall where a seldom-used set of stairs waited. The stairwell deposited them onto the rooftop.

Clarissa took in the sight of the manicured bushes and flowers. Gravel filled in the spaces between the walkways. At the far end, globe lights hung from a solid-frame structure. Smooth jazz played in the background at a volume slightly above the murmur of the fifty-person crowd.

"You know all these people?" Clarissa asked.

"Most," Amy said, nodding. "You'd think a building like this would be stuffy, but it's quite the opposite. Sure, some of the higher-up executive types keep to themselves, but even then, most of them have wives who like to socialize."

Clarissa took in the sight of the crowd, realizing how out of place she was. Her casual clothing looked like something a bum would don when compared to the outfits these people wore. Although she had limited options to choose from, she wouldn't have dressed up to their level even if she could. Things like that mattered little to her.

She felt Amy's hand wrap around her wrist. A moment later she was pulled forward. They stopped in front of the bar. Amy asked for a glass of Chardonnay. Clarissa, a glass of Cabernet. She tried to leave a tip for the bartender, but he declined with a shake of his head, and a wave of his hands.

Amy led her around the rooftop, introducing her to half the crowd. Clarissa placed faces with names and stored them for those awkward elevator moments. When they reached the other side of the crowd, she felt her stomach tighten at the sight of a man she didn't expect to see on the top of her building.

Chapter 16

Beck leaned to the side, his right elbow atop the railing, legs crossed at the ankles. He wore a pair of blue jeans and a dark sports coat. At least she wasn't the only one in denim. The wind lifted his hair. Gray strands reflected the diffused lighting strung two feet overhead. The globe lights swung side-to-side in the breeze. He was engaged in an animated conversation with an older gentleman who appeared to be rather riled up over whatever it was they were talking about.

Clarissa drifted to her left, placing herself in Beck's peripheral vision. Amy's voice trailed off. Perhaps the woman had noticed Clarissa staring and figured she was about to make a move on a handsome stranger. Out of the corner of her eye, she saw Amy take a few steps back.

"I'll grab us a couple more drinks," Amy said.

Clarissa nodded without taking her gaze off Beck.

The older man was the first to notice her. He stopped mid-sentence. Turning to face her, he said, "Help you?"

She said nothing.

Beck turned his head. "Clarissa."

"Beck."

"This is Harold McCain." Beck gestured toward the older man, who stepped forward and extended his hand. "He lives two floors above you."

"Pleasure," McCain said.

Clarissa nodded, shifted her gaze to Beck. "Can I talk with you for a minute?"

"Excuse us, Harold," Beck said, stepping past the man toward a darkened corner of the roof.

When Clarissa was sure they were out of earshot, she said, "What are you doing here? Checking up on me?"

"What are you talking about?"

She had the urge to smack the smug look off his face. "Why are you here, Beck?"

"I could ask the same. You're supposed to stay put at home."

"This is my home now."

"It's mine, too."

She was taken aback by the statement. While not positive, she had a hunch that the condos in the building went for seven figures. There was little doubt that Beck's salary wouldn't cover such an expense.

"It's my sister's place, and she's away for two years. I'm staying here while she's gone."

"What about your place?"

"It all worked out kind of perfectly, actually. I had just lost my place in a divorce settlement."

Sensing the conversation taking a personal route, Clarissa changed the subject. "What should I expect tomorrow?"

Beck shrugged while taking a drink. "He's getting back from an overseas trip. That means lots of catching up. You'll most likely sit outside his office most of the day. I believe he has one meeting that you'll be dragged along to."

"What am I looking for?"

Beck didn't answer. He diverted his stare to a spot over her shoulder.

"Is it him? Did he do something wrong?"

Again, Beck did not respond.

"Beck, this is ridiculous. If you feel I'm responsible enough to handle this post, then you should tell me what I need to know."

"It doesn't work that way, Clarissa." He glanced around, perhaps suspicious that his raised voice had drawn eyes. "Next week we'll all meet with you and ask you some questions. Then we'll do it again."

"What about the pin you gave me to wear?"

He smiled. "That was a lie, a psychological trick. It makes some people more risk-adverse."

She finished her wine and placed the glass on the wide concrete ledge next to her. The whole idea behind the assignment was convoluted now. She thought about asking if she could back out, but knew that was not an option. They wouldn't let her. Even if she tried to run, they'd find her.

"There you are."

Clarissa turned at the sound of Amy's voice.

"I carried that glass around so long I ended up drinking it myself." Amy smiled. Even in the shadows, Clarissa noticed the woman's face looked flushed. "Anyway, who's your friend?"

"Amy, this is…" Her voice trailed as she looked over her shoulder and saw that Beck had left.

"Was is more like it," Amy said.

Staring into the darkness of night, Clarissa could only nod in agreement. Where had he gone? Did he even live in the building? Had the older man been a plant, part of the agency? Glancing around the party, she didn't see either of them. Amy might know if either man lived there, but now Clarissa didn't want to bring Beck's name up. He'd taken off for a reason.

"Let's get you a refill." Amy tugged at Clarissa's arm.

Relenting, Clarissa followed her across the rooftop. They stopped three times. Each time, Amy introduced Clarissa to residents of the building. She didn't really see the point. By the time she got to know anyone, she'd be on her way to her next assignment.

For the next hour, she stayed close to the bartender. Amy had drifted further away, caught up in conversations. Clarissa managed to get away after her third glass of wine.

The bright stairwell offered no shadows to hide in. That didn't settle her fears, as anyone could be waiting for her on the next landing. Once she reached the final one, a new source of worry set in. They knew where she lived, and they could be inside.

Stopping in front of her door, Clarissa drew her P229. She pushed the door open slowly with the pistol aimed in front of her. It moved with her eyes. A reporter on the television covered today's financial news. Clarissa couldn't remember if she'd left the TV on. She had been watching a twenty-four hour news station, though.

She passed through the living area and went to her bedroom. The door was shut. There was no light escaping from underneath. Instead of entering the room, she went back into the living room, opened the glass door and stepped out onto the balcony. She stayed close to the wall, turning only when she reached her bedroom. The curtains were pulled back. Nothing appeared disturbed. If someone were in there, they hid in the closet or the bathroom.

With her gun still drawn, Clarissa reentered the apartment and stepped into the bedroom. She used a flashlight she had retrieved from a kitchen drawer to illuminate the space. In sections, she verified it was empty. Then she checked the bathroom, and finally the closet, using the flashlight to separate clothing while keeping the SIG aimed at chest level.

She nearly squeezed the trigger when her cell phone rang from within her pocket. She answered, sounding out of breath. Her heart beat in her ears.

"Did you make it home okay?"

She paused, recognizing the voice. "Beck?"

"Yes. Are you back home?"

"Yeah, I am."

"If you want a ride tomorrow, meet me at the same time in the lobby."

Chapter 17

At five o'clock in the morning Clarissa lay in bed staring at the dark ceiling. The orange glow of streetlights filtered in through the curtains. The longer she kept her eyes open, the brighter the room became.

Sleep had not come easy the night before. With so many things to consider, Clarissa found herself wanting to run. That would be pointless, though. Eventually someone would find her. And the ending would not be pretty. Her best bet was to do as told, and relay everything she saw and heard.

The thought that she was being set up crossed her mind a time or two. Not in the sense that someone was out to frame her for an act, but rather that the information she would pass on would be used for someone's gain, whether financial or political. And there were four people she had to assume could benefit. Banner, Polanski, Beck and Sinclair.

In her mind, it would take a lot to get Sinclair to turn. Perhaps not on her, but on his dedication to the Agency and the country. She questioned how well she knew the man, though. Perhaps he had lied to her all along. Everything up to this point could have been a set up. Training.

Beck also confused her. She wanted to trust him, believe him, but the way he showed up everywhere left her uneasy.

When it came to Banner and Polanski, the woman concerned Clarissa most. Of course, by the time she considered those two, she realized that it was all or none. If one was in this for gain, then all four were. They worked together.

She waited in the lobby five minutes before Beck showed up. While waiting, she fixed the pin she had been given to her shirt an inch above her heart. Beck exited the elevator and motioned for her to follow him to the parking garage. There would be no timely curbside pick-up today.

A half-dozen times she opened her mouth to say something, and a half-dozen times she closed her mouth without a word. Could he be trusted? Truthful? Until she had some idea of what was going on, she wouldn't be able to tell.

They parked in the Treasury Department parking garage and followed the same procedure as the previous day. Beck escorted her from the Secret Service's office in the West Wing up a flight of stairs and then to the far end of the building.

"McCormick's not in yet," Beck said. "When you see him, give him your name. He's aware that you'll be here."

"Beck?"

"Yeah?"

"What am I supposed to do for him?"

Beck shrugged as if he hadn't given it any thought. "Whatever he asks, I suppose."

She resisted the urge to roll her eyes. Every job she'd ever held, from working in a seedy bar, to the assignments Sinclair had sent her on, had always had a goal at the very least. She was not used to being told to wing it completely. Although, at times, she'd had to on her previous assignment.

Beck walked away. His hard soles echoed off the tiled floor and faded as he descended the stairs. Presumably, he returned to the Secret Service office. Would he spend the rest of his day watching her? Someone had to be. There'd be no way they would leave a woman like her alone with one of the most powerful men on the planet.

Looking around, she took a seat behind the empty desk. The chair was straight and rigid. She'd have to swap it out if the job required her to stay at the desk all day.

With McCormick's office behind her, she stared at the closed door of the Chief of Staff's office. What went on inside the room? Her cheeks grew hot over her embarrassment of recalling little about how the government functioned. What if McCormick put her on the spot? She'd look like an idiot and was going to have to come up with a diversionary tactic to avoid any questioning. Of course, that assumed that the man would pay any attention to her.

After an hour of sitting and staring, she straightened at the sound of several people approaching. The possibilities of who it was narrowed to two as the group neared. Two men in dark suits appeared. They fixed their stares on her. Behind them, she saw the vice president, flanked by two additional agents.

"Name?" the man nearest her asked.

"Clarissa Weston," she said. "I'm filling in as Vice President McCormick's assistant."

She couldn't tell whether her answer satisfied the men. None of them had pulled their P229s. Perhaps she was in the clear.

McCormick stepped forward. Standing a few feet away, she realized he was much larger than he appeared on television. She also understood why she never saw him close to the president. McCormick appeared to stand around six-and-a-half feet tall. Even if the president was above average height, the vice president would tower over him. Not only that, McCormick was younger and considerably more attractive. Not good when you are trying to look like the most powerful man in the free world.

"About time they gave me a proper assistant." McCormick looked down at her, smiling. He extended his hand. Clarissa noticed one of his security detail grimace at the gesture. McCormick nodded as Clarissa reached for his hand. "Nice to meet you, Ms. Weston."

"Likewise."

"Come on into my office and I'll fill you in on what I'm going to need from you."

Rising, she heard someone else approaching. One of his security detail turned. A dull ache washed over her stomach at the site of a fifth agent joining them. It was Jordan, the man who'd creeped her out the day before inside the main residence. She'd sensed the tension between Jordan and Beck, and it had left her with an uneasy feeling about the guy.

Just a feeling, she reassured herself. The man would not be tasked with working inside the highest profile residence in the country, hell, the world, if he hadn't been properly vetted first. He might not be the kind of person she wanted to associate with, but that did not put the guy in the same league as the bastards she routinely had to deal with while working with Sinclair.

Jordan gave her a look, then fell into place with the rest of the detail. These guys looked as though they could handle anything. She figured they wouldn't bat an eye if she removed her shirt. At least not with McCormick around.

The vice president ignored Jordan. He walked to the first of two doors leading to his office, waiting for Clarissa to enter before moving to the next. It placed her uncomfortably close to him. His cologne was overbearing at the distance. She fought to keep from choking on the fumes. She hoped that it would fade as the morning progressed.

The man stepped forward to the next door. His brown hair was lined with silver and had been cut perfectly, hanging a centimeter above his collar and sitting on top of his ear. She guessed his age to be forty, give or take a few years. He was still fresh-looking. By the end of the administration that would no longer be the case.

The thick door swung open and McCormick stepped into his office. He didn't look back. Clarissa assumed she should follow, so she did. McCormick continued around his desk and took a seat. He jutted his chin toward an empty chair opposite him, then looked down at his scheduling calendar. She had figured most people would use an electronic method of keeping track of their day.

"This is the only way I know for sure," McCormick said, glancing up with a smile. "My schedule. They change the damn digital one so often I don't know what end's up."

She returned his smile and said nothing.

"You don't want to hear about that, though. Let's talk about why you're here."

"I was hoping you could fill me in on that, sir."

"None of that sir, stuff. Call me Don." He looked over her shoulder toward the door. "When we're alone."

This time she didn't smile. The tone of his voice left her wondering if she'd be calling out for help at any time.

"I know the real reason you're here, Clarissa."

Her heart beat against her chest. Consciously, she kept her breathing steady and fought against the burn in her cheeks.

McCormick continued. "And I'm not happy about it."

Chapter 18

Clarissa's stomach knotted and her lungs deflated. No matter how hard she tried to suck air in through her mouth, it didn't happen. She grew dizzy. Her heart could have broken a rib or two, it beat so hard. It felt as though she'd been hit in the gut. Here she was, alone with McCormick, and he knew why.

Outwardly, she showed no signs of concern except for slight blushing. No matter how hard she tried, she couldn't stop her cheeks from burning.

McCormick didn't take his gaze off her. He sat five feet away, stoic. It seemed as though minutes passed, but in reality it had only been seconds. He opened his mouth, looked away a brief second, then rose.

She stiffened. He could have anything inside his desk, including a weapon that he could use on her. The Secret Service worked for him. They'd corroborate any story he told, especially without being in the office. Instinctively her gaze darted to the corners of the room in search for a camera. She saw bookshelves, framed pictures of McCormick with dignitaries from around the world, artwork, but no cameras. They were hidden if they existed.

They had to, though. Right?

McCormick lifted a hand, pointing his long index finger at her.

"Look, I don't know what they told you about me, but it's not true. I'm a good man. I've never done any of those things the media accuses me of. I guess it doesn't matter whether you believe me, because my wife does. And that's all I really need."

The pressure on her head and chest and stomach lifted. She didn't quite understand what McCormick was talking about, but it certainly had nothing to do with her being placed in the room by the Secret Service. Or maybe it did, but not in a threatening fashion. Clarissa didn't know exactly why she was there. Could his suspicion be the purpose? She didn't keep up on current events as well as she should, but somewhere in her mind she recalled an article or news report that claimed infidelity on McCormick's part. She wondered if there had been additional complaints.

McCormick continued. "I don't know about Rhodes, but there are others in the party who are concerned about me rising to power over the next year or two. They think I'm a lock, and that scares the shit out of them. So if they think they can just send you in here and get me to do something stupid, then screw them."

"I never believe what I read in the papers, sir," she said. "And I've got no idea what you are talking about right now. I'm here to assist you in any way that you need for the next few weeks until your regular assistant is back on the job."

McCormick leaned back, eyed her. "Why haven't I ever seen you before?"

"I was in England."

"Why?"

"Because that's where I worked." She knew she couldn't keep avoiding the question, and eventually she'd have to provide an answer. Hopefully by that point Beck could give her a solid story to use.

McCormick smiled, looking past her toward the door as it opened. The bottom of it brushed against the carpet, making a whooshing sound. Clarissa half-turned her head and saw Jordan standing in the opening.

"What is it?" McCormick asked.

"We need to get moving."

"Why?"

"Your meeting."

"That's in half an hour."

"We have to take the long route."

McCormick's eyebrows pinched together and his lips drew thin and tight. He nodded slowly, exhaled, and said, "You know best. We'll be out in a minute."

The door shut, but didn't latch. Clarissa studied the man opposite her, his concern making her worried. "What is it?"

McCormick shook his head. "Routine precautions, that's all. Hell, might even be a training thing for them. We'll take a secure route over to the meeting at the Cannon HOB." He looked like he was going to be sick while saying it.

"What meeting?"

"You sure you're really my assistant?"

Clarissa forced a smile. "First day on the job."

"We're meeting with the House Republican Leadership."

"Bet that's a fun one."

"Nothing is ever accomplished. They want what they want, and we don't want to give it to them."

"And vice versa."

He had been moving things around on his desk and stopped after she spoke. "I suppose so. No matter what you think, or what you hear, we all want what's best for this country."

Clarissa had a dozen things she could have said. Instead, she smiled. No point in upsetting the guy.

They both rose and left the office, her in front. She felt naked without the P229, especially since they were leaving the relative safety of the White House. She assumed that the House Office Building would be safe, and they'd have their escort. Still, she worried over not being able to take care of herself.

Jordan watched McCormick until the vice president looked away, then he cut his stare toward Clarissa and smiled. She couldn't place it, but something about the man disgusted her. She continued forward, staying a few paces behind McCormick. Though there was an exit next to his office, they turned and headed toward the main residence. Outside the Cabinet Room they descended a flight of stairs. From there they went into the Secret Service office, entering the tunnels Clarissa had used.

The purpose, she figured, was because they wanted as little time exposed as possible. The vice president's schedule was not made public, although there were things that occurred quite often. The way she understood it, they'd have the meetings in different places to throw off those that might be making plans.

No one spoke during their walk. Everyone moved with purpose. They took a different route than she had earlier, and she wondered where they were going. Perhaps they had an underground network that led from the White House to the House of Representatives building, and other places. After all, everything was within a mile or two. Some faces had to be seen in public. Others did not.

Her thoughts were proven correct ten minutes into their walk. Five minutes after that, they emerged into what she presumed was a deliberately empty office inside the Cannon House Office Building. Clarissa was instructed to wait with Jordan while McCormick conducted his meeting. What was her purpose, she wondered, if she couldn't be involved in the meeting? Did any of the Representatives' aides join them? She had no idea how she was going to win enough of McCormick's trust to find out whatever it was that Beck, Polanski and Banner wanted her to find out.

In the narrow hallway off the main atrium there was no avoiding Jordan's stare. She waited until the sounds of chatter and passing footsteps died down.

"What?"

He shrugged and said nothing.

"Then quit staring at me."

He laughed at this. "Or what?"

Were they at recess in the schoolyard? Clarissa shook her head and stared down the hallway. Let him stare, she thought. She only had to put up with it for a few weeks. She'd never see the guy again after that.

"Who are you?" Jordan said after a few minutes of silence.

She shrugged and said nothing.

"Why were you with Beck?"

"Why don't you ask him?"

Jordan pushed off the wall and took a few steps toward her. "I did, but he didn't tell me anything."

"Not my problem."

Jordan rubbed his chin. "Just kind of odd, you know. Normally, we're informed well ahead of time. But in this instance, they sprung you on us."

She crossed her arms over her chest and leaned back into the wall. "Take it up with your management, I guess. I'm only doing what I was asked to do, fill in for a woman on maternity leave. Surely you guys had to know someone was coming."

Standing in the middle of the hall, hands at his side, Jordan looked down at her. In any other scenario, Clarissa would have readied herself for an attack. But here and now? That wasn't going to happen. If she ran into the man on the street, though, she'd have to be prepared to strike first and fast.

Whether Jordan kept up his staring act, Clarissa wasn't sure. She spent the remainder of the time staring at her phone and pretending to text. In reality she did nothing with it other than swipe through screens and catch up on the news, which left her feeling depressed more than anything else. He left for a few minutes, disappearing down another corridor, then returned without speaking a word to her.

The doors next to her opened. Jordan straightened up. Two agents stepped out. McCormick's voice boomed as he said goodbye to the House Republican leadership. He appeared a few moments later. He glanced down at her.

"Let's get some lunch," he said.

"Sir, we should get you back to the office," Jordan said.

McCormick waved him off. "Get a car out front."

One of the agents left, presumably going for the car. Clarissa wondered if they had reserves at every building.

They walked through the HOB, Clarissa next to McCormick, the both of them surrounded by the team of Secret Service agents. Where would they exit? Not through the front, she thought. Too easy to be spotted. Her sense of direction was mixed up, and it wasn't until they exited the building at the corner of New Jersey and C Street that she regained her bearings. Looking out over the street, something caught her attention. An object or reflection or something from the top floor of the building across the street.

And then the shots rang out and her body hit the ground.

Chapter 19

"He's been hit! He's been hit!"

The words passed through Clarissa's mind like molasses traveling up a tree. Her shoulder stung. So did the side of her face. She felt warmness spreading across her cheek. Her mouth tasted like copper. She traced her tongue across her teeth. They were all there. But her bottom lip had hit the concrete and was, at the very least, cut. Maybe split.

She didn't recall any pain when she heard the shots. Someone hit her and drove her into the ground. That person lay on top of her now. A human shield, she presumed. She opened her eyes to blinding light. Her sunglasses laid on the ground a foot or two away from her face. Her left arm was pinned and she was unable to free it. She wanted to scream out. Jordan yelled first.

"McCormick's down. Two shots. Get the damn car here now."

Clarissa maneuvered her head to get a look at the vice president. He lay with his back to her. A crimson pool formed around his head. It didn't look like his chest rose. She recalled stepping out of the building, the soles of her shoes hitting the concrete sidewalk. The sun reflected against the building behind her, warming the back of her head. She had turned her head right, looking up New Jersey. Then left, down New Jersey the other way, then up and down C Street. There hadn't been anyone waiting for them. Where was the car? Why hadn't it been outside?

The roar of a large engine approached, drowning out Jordan's voice. Brakes squealed. The scent of rubber and asphalt and her own blood filled her nose. The weight on her back lessened. She felt someone's breath on her face.

"Are you okay?"

She nodded and said, "Yeah," but her words were garbled.

The man rose off her. She felt his hands reach under her arms, and he pulled her to her feet. Her head spun. The blood that had pooled in the back of her mouth and throat choked her. She coughed, then spat red onto the sidewalk.

A crowd gathered across the street. Sirens approached from all directions. The oldest of the agents opened the back door. The one who pulled her up shoved her in the car. He joined the rest who lifted McCormick and placed him inside, laying him on the floor. Two of the agents gave him CPR.

Jordan seated himself across from her, staring. He did not smile now. Blood covered the sleeves of his white shirt. He no longer wore his jacket. She didn't see it on the seat next to him. She glanced over her shoulder and saw it bunched up on the sidewalk. She turned back around. McCormick's vacant eyes stared up at her. So did Jordan. He hadn't taken his eyes off her since he sat down.

And she knew why.

She was the odd number here. They'd all been placed and swore an oath to protect the men they served. But Clarissa, who had been sitting in the hall tapping away at her phone, was not one of them. The expression on Jordan's face only served to cement the idea in Clarissa's head. He blamed her, and it wouldn't be long until he pushed that thought up his chain of command.

Clarissa's mind went from trying to figure out what had happened and into survival mode. She considered opening the door and jumping out. Then what, though? They knew where she lived and most likely knew where she'd run. Not only would they be after her, so would the FBI, Sinclair, the NSA, and a half-dozen agencies most people hadn't ever heard of.

Before she could come to a decision, the car stopped. She glanced at the figures standing next to the passenger side of the car. They were dressed in scrubs, and she saw a gurney behind them. The door swung open. The agents in the car assisted with moving McCormick from the vehicle to the waiting gurney. The lead doctor began barking orders. He looked the most senior there with tufts of silver hair poking out from under his cap. There would be no delay. They were taking McCormick straight to surgery.

Clarissa slid across her seat to join the four agents standing next to the car.

"Don't move another inch."

She looked in Jordan's direction. He had his SIG out and aimed in her direction.

"What are you doing?" she asked.

"I could say the same to you," he said. "Or, better yet, what did you?"

She shook her head. "I don't know what you mean."

"How did anyone know that McCormick was there?"

She said nothing.

"Give me your phone."

She didn't move.

"Now," he shouted.

One of the men outside the car looked back. She thought he was going to help. Instead he slammed the door shut. The driver had exited the vehicle. Clarissa found herself alone with Jordan. She clutched the phone tight in her hand. The only thing Jordan had was his weapon, and he wouldn't use it on her. Not here.

He held out his free hand and repeated his request.

"Screw you," she said. "Take me back to Beck."

Jordan rapped against the passenger side window with his knuckles. The door flung open. One man leaned in. Another stood close to him.

"Take it from her," Jordan said.

Clarissa lunged to the other side of the vehicle, but with nowhere to go, the men overtook her and pried her phone from her hands. As they let up, she heard another vehicle pull up beside them. The door next to her was flung open. Someone reached in and grabbed her by her arms. She didn't get a good look at them. They said nothing as they pulled her hands behind her back and held her wrists in place. "What are you doing?" she asked, trying to see a reflection in the window her face was mashed up against.

"I've got her phone here," Jordan said.

"Want to ride with me?" a man asked. She didn't recognize the voice.

"Sure," Jordan said.

"Help me get her in back."

She was yanked back, and Jordan pulled the door open. As the man behind her pushed her forward, Jordan grabbed the back of her head and forced it down. She flew into the back seat, face first. The door slammed shut. She managed to get her foot in at the last moment. The back of the car was dark. The windows were heavily tinted. There was a mirrored barrier window between the front and back seats. The glass was smoky. She saw a ghost of her own reflection staring back.

The car pulled away from the hospital and whipped around a corner, causing her to slide across the seat until the door stopped her. Through the tinted window, she kept track of the streets as they drove past. It seemed that they drove in the direction of the White House. A few blocks short, they turned again, headed toward Virginia. Her mind raced in an attempt to determine their next stop.

The Pentagon? The Secret Service office in Northern Virginia? Langley?

The Potomac looked like black ice as they drove over it. From there, she estimated another five to ten minutes until they reached their destination. What would happen there was anyone's guess. She couldn't help feeling as though she was a prisoner. Thirty minutes passed and they were still driving. They'd exited the highway several minutes prior. The roads here were deserted and lined with trees. The only other military or government instillation she could place at this distance from D.C. was Fort Belvoir, and the Secret Service had nothing to do with the base.

Clarissa's mind went to the place she had been avoiding since she left the plane in Boston. Tears spilled down her cheeks at the thought of what was coming next. They were taking her to a place where there would be no record left behind.

Chapter 20

The car turned onto the remnants of a dirt and gravel driveway tucked between several tall pines. The vehicle bucked and swayed, rolling slowly and crunching the ground underneath. She pressed her face to the window to get a view of what laid ahead. The glass felt cold against her cheek. All she saw were trees.

The brakes made a high-pitched sound as the car came to a stop. She took a deep breath and steadied her nerves. In a way, her breakdown minutes before had helped to ease her tension. She couldn't stop them from whatever action they were about to take. But she could defend herself. And to do so, she had to have a clear head.

The partition between her and the two agents lowered. The first thing she saw was Jordan's pistol pointing at her. He peered at her from behind it, facing her, perhaps with one knee on his seat. The man driving the car opened his door and stepped out. Through her window, she watched him draw his P229 and hold it at his side. He'd lowered his window prior to stepping out, presumably to monitor what happened inside the vehicle.

"This is how this is going to work," Jordan said. "You're going to turn in your seat so that your back faces the door. Then you're going to place your hands behind your back, interlocking your fingers. When my partner opens the door, slide back until he tells you to stop. He'll place a pair of handcuffs on you, then escort you inside the house."

She looked past Jordan at the unassuming building behind him. The wood siding hung off in clumps. The porch sagged in the middle and one corner was gone. The supports were crooked. She saw a hole in the roof and wondered how many squirrels and raccoons and possums lived in the attic.

Jordan gestured with his gun. She turned in her seat and placed her hands behind her back as instructed. With her thumbs she traced the section of her pants where her pistol would have been. If only she'd questioned the decision for her to remain unarmed.

The door behind her opened. A gust of cool wind blew in, lifting her short hair off her ears and forehead. She caught the scent of mildew and dead leaves.

"Slide back," the man said.

She did as instructed until reaching a spot where his outstretched fingers poked her like twigs. With one hand he grabbed her right wrist. She bit her lip to keep from acknowledging the pain his grip caused her. The cold steel wrapped around one wrist, then the other, effectively entombing her. This was not the plan she needed to hatch. *There's still the walk,* she thought. In the open, a new set of rules came into play.

Secured by handcuffs, the man pulled her back by her collar. She did not resist, gliding across the seat until it no longer supported her. She twisted her body so she landed on the ground on her left side. If something had to break, it was better it be on her non-dominant side. The wind momentarily left her lungs. By the time the man pulled her from the ground, she managed to pull in a small amount of oxygen.

Something cold covered her cheek. She twisted while being pushed and caught a glimpse of herself on the car's windows. There must have been a puddle where she hit the ground, because the side of her face, shoulder, and part of her shirt were covered with mud.

Jordan exited the vehicle and made his way to the front while facing her with his weapon drawn and aimed. He glanced from her to a spot past her right shoulder, giving away the location of his partner.

She glanced around, looking for an escape route. With Jordan at the front of the vehicle, running behind it was the most logical plan. But she couldn't look back without giving away her intentions. The shock of the situation interfered with her reasoning and memory. She couldn't recall what the area had looked like when they arrived.

"Don't even think about it," Jordan said. "I'll shoot. Maybe I hit you, maybe I don't. But don't think I won't because I'm afraid of hitting Cooley. We show up to work every day prepared to die."

Clarissa tensed and straightened. The cuffs tightened as her arms pulled away from each other. Cooley's hand hit the middle of her back, propelling her forward. She stumbled, caught herself, and began walking toward Jordan. He backed up, never taking his stare or weapon off her. Instead of the men leading her to the house, they moved to the left of it. Jordan waited for them to reach him, then they continued on, with him maintaining a distance of six feet from Clarissa. It was obvious they were treating her as a threat. One they knew little about.

One they were wise to distrust.

Behind the house was a clearing twenty feet deep. The ground was littered with red and yellow and brown leaves. The trees were thick beyond the yard. Clarissa couldn't tell how far back they went before reaching a road.

They positioned her so she stared at the woods. She heard a lock clink, then a chain dragged through something metal. When they turned her around, she stared into a dark opening where wide cellar doors had been moments before.

Cooley holstered his weapon on his left. He grabbed her by her left elbow, leading her toward and down the cellar stairs. With her hands behind her back, and his weapon on the other side of his wide frame, she had little chance of taking his weapon. She could throw her body and send both of them careening down the steps. But with six to go, she risked injuring them both with little chance for gain on her part.

The cellar doors closed, blocking the bright sunlight. Jordan came down the steps behind her. Her eyes adjusted to a yellow flood of light from bulbs inside wire cages mounted to the ceiling. The area in front of her was small and square. A splintered wooden door sat in the middle of the far wall. It didn't look like anything that would keep anyone out. Jordan passed her and crossed the room. He used his body to shield his actions from view. A moment later he stepped back and pulled the door open.

Cooley started forward, pulling her with him. She stepped into a room that looked nothing like the surrounding property. It felt like walking into a tin can, a roomy one. There wasn't much in there. A desk in one corner with a laptop computer. A steel table mounted to the floor filled up the center of the room. There was an eyebolt on one end of the table, and one on the floor below it. It didn't take a stretch of her imagination that those were used to secure a prisoner.

After they passed the table, Cooley said, "Turn around, away from me."

She turned in place, prepared for a chain to be threaded through her arms. Instead, the handcuffs' lock clinked and her wrists were freed. She instinctively brought them forward and rubbed the sore, red rings around her arms.

The sound of Cooley's fading footsteps indicated he had put a few feet of distance between them. Jordan approached her. He still held the SIG and aimed it at her.

"Go ahead and have a seat," Jordan said.

Clarissa took a step back and positioned herself so that she could see both men. Neither were in reach, and both were several feet away from each other. She high stepped over the solid bench, then picked up her other foot and lowered her body onto the steel seat.

"Place your hands on the table," Jordan said.

Clarissa did, thinking they'd cuff her again now. But they didn't.

"We're both armed, and neither of us have any qualms with shooting you if you move. Got that?"

She nodded. Said, "What am I doing here?"

Neither man answered.

"Jordan, what the hell happened out there? And why are we here now?"

Again, she received no response.

Five minutes, maybe ten, passed. She began to acclimate to her surroundings and the idea that the room would be her tomb faded.

Then she heard the door handle turn.

Chapter 21

When Beck stepped into the tin can, Clarissa didn't know whether to cry or smile. He'd left the cellar doors open and bright light flooded past him. She squinted in pain, looking beyond the man to see if anyone followed him in. There had to be another. Why else would he leave them open? He closed the door to the room before she could see anything else.

With a nod in her direction, he said, "Did she say anything?"

"Nothing," Jordan said. "Asked a few questions, but we followed protocol."

"Okay," Beck said. "You two wait out there and let me handle this."

"You sure?"

Beck drew his pistol. "She can't make it across the table before I can shoot."

It felt as though she'd been slapped.

The men exited, letting the door fall shut behind them. The solid thud led her to believe that the splintered wood was only for show. She looked up at Beck, who glanced away when their eyes met. Tears welled in the corners of her eyes. She tried to hold them back, but it was of no use.

"What is going on, Beck?"

He took a deep breath, exhaling as he took a seat across from her. He set his SIG down on the table to his right. He placed his hand inches from it. The gesture showed some trust, either in her, or in his abilities. Instead of answering her question, he stared at her. She had trouble deciphering the look on his face. He'd been trained to look hard at all times. But there was something else there. Confusion, perhaps.

She took in a sharp breath in advance of asking again.

He cut her off. "Ten people knew the location of the vice president this afternoon. Four were part of the Republican House leadership. Five were sworn to protect him. That leaves you."

There was no doubt what he was implying. Clarissa couldn't believe it. "Are you saying I had something to do with McCormick being shot?"

Beck said nothing. He only stared. His was a waiting game. She knew the more she said, the more he could use against her.

"I only found out yesterday that I would be working with him. How on earth could I have pulled something like this off?"

"Where's your phone?"

"My phone?"

"Your cell." He reached out with his left hand. "The one we gave you."

"They took it."

"They told me they don't have it."

She shook her head. "I...I don't know what to tell you, Beck. They pried it from my hands."

Beck worked the muscles in his jaw. "Dammit, Clarissa. You know how this looks?"

For a moment she had a glimmer of hope that he believed in her. "I don't know anything right now, Beck. We stepped out of the building and I heard two shots. Next thing I knew, I was on the ground. I thought I'd been shot."

"Why?"

"The pain."

"Where?"

"My body, where it hit the ground."

"Who took you down?"

She tried to recall, but the only image that popped into her head was that of McCormick and the pool of blood surrounding his head. She shook her head and shrugged.

Beck pinched the bridge of his nose and leaned his head back an inch. His gaze drifted toward the ceiling. Hers traveled to his pistol. The table was wide, maybe four or five feet. He'd probably reach it first, but she had to try.

Before she could make a move, he slid his hand over a couple inches and placed his palm on the handle of the pistol.

"Were you holding it when this went down?" he asked.

She looked away from the gun, but didn't meet his stare. "Holding what?"

"The phone."

"Maybe?"

"Is that an answer?"

"Why are you doing this to me? You can't tell me there's no footage of this happening."

Beck rose, grabbed his SIG and started toward one side of the room. Once he reached the wall, he turned in a half-circle and started the other way.

"It's blank," he said.

"Blank?"

"Every single camera."

"Who could've done that?"

Beck shook his head. He made another pass across the room. Each step was slow and deliberate, the hard sole of his shoe rapping against the concrete floor.

"How is McCormick?" she asked.

He stopped, turned, said, "Dead." He seemed to study her after, perhaps watching for a tell that would give her away. Only there was nothing to give away. She returned his stare with one of her own, her eyes misting over.

"I…"

"Sorry, Clarissa. He's still alive, but in bad shape. That's all I know."

There was a sharp rap on the door then it opened a crack. Jordan spoke from the other side. "He's here."

Beck pointed at her while heading toward the door. "Stay there."

What was next? Her hands went to her wrists and she rubbed the spots where the handcuffs had dug into her skin. The voices outside the room were soft and muffled. She couldn't make out what they said. Perhaps if she got closer. Clarissa resisted the idea, fearing they would open fire if they opened the door and saw her standing there.

After another couple minutes the door opened. The last face she expected to see appeared.

"Sinclair, what are you doing here?"

Sinclair looked back over his shoulder, nodded and stepped toward her. He held out his hands, then lifted the hem of his shirt.

"As you can see," he said, "I'm unarmed. Just like you. I'm here to talk, Clarissa. I need to know what happened today. If you were involved in any way, I might be able to help you. But only if you tell me everything. Hold back, and that could mean the end of your life."

Still trying to process his presence, Clarissa said, "I only found out yesterday that I'd be assigned to McCormick. Today was my first day on the job. I hadn't even spent fifteen minutes with the guy. We took a tunnel to a meeting. I sat in the hall for it."

Sinclair leaned forward. "Alone?"

"Yes. I mean, no."

"Which is it?"

"I was out there with one of the Secret Service agents."

"And he was there with you at every moment?"

She leaned into the chair and let her head drop back. At one time her hair would have grazed the backs of her arms. Not now. She felt the short strands rise.

"I think so."

"You think?"

"He might've left to take a piss or something. I don't know. The guy's a prick. I tried to ignore him. They've gotta have cameras around the place, Sinclair."

"As I understand it, the footage is gone."

"Even inside?"

He said nothing.

"This isn't something I could have just set up, Sinclair. I don't think someone like you could have. Not in such a short period of time."

"Your phone should have all your calls listed."

She shook her head. "It's gone."

"Gone? How?"

"They took it."

He nodded. "They can still get those records and follow up on every number."

"There's no numbers. I don't think I ever used it."

"Nevertheless, they'll check." He looked around the room, then settled on her. "Hold out your hands."

Narrowing her eyes, she stretched both arms out over the table. He grabbed her wrists in the same spot the cuffs had bound her. He manipulated her arms until her palms faced up. His thumbs clamped down below hers, on her pulse. It didn't take her long to figure out what he was doing. Sinclair had worked as an interrogator for a long time. Some called him the human lie detector. And now he was going to perform an examination.

"Answer yes or no to all questions. Is your name Clarissa Abbot?"

She paused. He glanced up at her. She replied, "Yes."

"Were you working under the name Clarissa Weston?"

"Yes."

"Did your mother pass away when you were young?"

"Yes."

"Did your father pass away when you were eighteen?"

"No." She felt her pulse quicken. Sinclair glanced up at her again. "He was murdered."

A twitch of a smile appeared, then faded. "Were you told yesterday that you would be assigned to work with Vice President McCormick?"

"Yes."

"Were you told the nature of the work?"

"No."

"Did you order the assassination of Vice President McCormick?"

"No."

"Did you tell anyone about the vice president's whereabouts?"

"No."

"Did you shoot the vice president?"

"No."

"Did you see who shot McCormick?"

"No."

She felt his grip relax, and he looked up once again. "Clarissa, did you see who did it?"

"Oh my God," she said.

"What did you see?"

The memory came back to her. They stepped outside. There was no traffic on the street. The smell of the air, thick with exhaust. The cool air. They stepped forward. The shots were fired in quick succession. Before she realized what had happened, someone was on her, driving her toward the ground. But before that happened, she saw something.

Clarissa had seen where the shots were fired from.

Chapter 22

She rode in the front seat of Beck's car. He had pushed the sedan past one hundred miles per hour seconds after they merged onto I-95, and he hadn't backed off since. She relayed the story to Beck, starting when she entered McCormick's office. From there she recounted the trip through the tunnels, waiting in the hallway, then exiting the building. But this time she recalled something she hadn't earlier.

As she scanned north up New Jersey Avenue, something caught her attention. It wasn't a flash, or muzzle blast. And it hovered toward the top of her field of vision, across the street, maybe the top floor of the Longworth House Office Building. It felt as though the blood drained from her head as she realized that the crack that shattered the silence had originated from that spot. She saw the rifle extending through the open window. It wasn't much. A few inches, at most. But she saw it.

"How come you didn't tell me this before?" Beck asked, glancing between her and the road.

"I just remembered it. Such a small detail, it didn't really stand out much at the time."

"What did you think it was then?"

"I…" She paused, staring at the soft red glow coming from the brake lights of the car ahead. Her hand went to the right side of her forehead. "I don't remember thinking anything of it. There's a gap where I don't remember. I think I hit my head."

He slowed down and looked in her direction. She shifted in the seat so he could see the red spot.

He winced, then looked back at the road. "Does it hurt?"

Clarissa was aware of the injury, but she hadn't seen it yet. She reached up for the visor and pulled back the flap covering the mirror. Two small lights turned on, illuminating the golf ball sized spot that darkened her skin. More memories of the event came back to her. Shots fired. Falling to the ground. Hitting the ground. Her head slapped the concrete, bounced up, hit it again.

"You blacked out," he said.

She nodded, although her answer was less convincing. "I'm not sure. Maybe?"

"We need to get you checked out."

"You should have had me checked out."

He said nothing.

"What's the deal with bringing me all the way out to the country?"

He still said nothing.

"Is that the way you do things? Just make people disappear?"

Beck stared straight ahead with narrowed eyes. The skin around the corner of his eye bunched up into tight crow's feet. She turned away from him, looked up. The sky had darkened, threatening rain, maybe more.

"It wasn't my call," he said.

"What?"

"Never mind. Think it through again, Clarissa. Is there anything else you remember?"

She shook her head. "How did this happen, Beck? McCormick decided at the last minute that he wanted to go out for lunch instead of returning to his office through the tunnels. How could anyone have set something up that quickly?"

"You'd be surprised. They had to call for the car, so someone outside the group you were with knew."

"No, no one called for a car. One of the agents left to get it. It was totally spur of the moment, Beck."

He reached toward the center console, grabbed his sunglasses and covered his eyes with them. She noticed a sheen of sweat pool on his forehead despite the cool breeze coming from the vents.

Her words had upset him. Had something she'd witnessed violated protocol? Had she inadvertently implicated someone in the shooting?

"What is it, Beck?"

"Where was the car when you left the building? What street was it parked on? Were the doors open?"

"No."

"No what?"

"The car wasn't there yet. We waited for it."

Beck cut across three lanes of traffic, dodging mini-vans and SUVs on his way to the emergency lane. He slammed the brakes. The tires squealed and the car fishtailed, nearly slamming into the guardrail.

Clarissa's heart pounded in her chest. She caught her breath, said, "What the hell are you doing? You could have killed us!"

Beck seemed hardly fazed. He tore his sunglasses off and tossed them toward the console. His eyes were wide. His nostrils flared with each breath. "Are you sure about what you just told me? The car wasn't there?"

"That's what I said."

"You also said that you hit your head and that there were some gaps." He reached out and grabbed her arm. "Think it through again. Please."

She replayed the events in her mind. "We stepped outside. There was no car waiting. We waited near the curb. The four men surrounded us while the fifth was bringing the car."

"Did you see the car approaching?"

"No. It pulled up right after the shots were fired, though. I mean, it was there right after."

Beck looked away as he processed the information.

"You don't think," she began, then stopped.

Beck waited a second, glanced at her, said, "What?"

"Could the shots have come from the vehicle?"

Beck seemed to consider this. "But what about what you saw protruding from the window at Longworth?"

"That could've been a woman sitting on the windowsill with her purse hanging out."

"What direction did the car come from?"

"It pulled to the curb on the wrong side of the street, driver's side nearest us."

"From the north," he said.

She nodded, said nothing.

"The direction you were looking, yet you don't remember seeing the car approach." Beck leaned back in his seat and eased off the brake.

The car rolled slowly along the shoulder while he watched the side mirror, waiting for a hole in traffic.

Clarissa thought through the events again, this time in reverse. Blacking out, hitting the ground, her grip weak on her phone, feeling the shoulder in the middle of her back. It all happened so fast after those two cracks that changed their lives. Her mind tried to fill in blanks with things she knew hadn't happened.

Then she remembered something that had occurred. The reason she was looking up and didn't see the car approaching.

"Beck, the shots came from the window."

"How do you know?"

"I guess I don't. I know why I looked up, though."

He tapped the brake and the car stopped. Looking at her, he asked, "Why?"

"Because Jordan did."

L.T. Ryan

Chapter 23

Beck didn't bother to park in the Treasury Building garage. They let him through the gates to the White House, and he escorted Clarissa to the doctor's office within.

The doctor was middle aged, in good shape, handsome and quick about examining her. He determined she hadn't suffered a concussion, but encouraged her to call him should she start feeling any related symptoms.

Beck waited outside of the room. When she emerged, he rose from his seat and took a step toward her.

"Everything okay?"

"Seems so. He says it's a nasty bump, but that everything on the inside is fine."

"What about you blacking out?"

"That might have been stress induced."

Beck nodded, shifted his weight from his left to right foot, then gestured toward the hall. "Let's go to my office."

They walked to the West Wing Secret Service office, down the stairwell into the tunnel that ran beneath the White House to the Treasury Building, up four flights of stairs and down a hall that led to Beck's office.

He seated himself behind his desk and hit the speaker button on his phone. Julie Polanski answered.

"I need to meet with you and Banner," Beck said.

"I can be there in fifteen minutes," she said. "You'll have to call Banner and find out what his schedule is."

Beck ended the call, then tried Banner's office extension. The call went to the man's voicemail. Beck left a quick message and hung up.

"How much are you going to tell them?" Clarissa asked.

He swiveled in his seat to face her, placing both hands on his desk. "I'm not telling them anything, Clarissa. You are. Start from the beginning and work your way down. Everything you've told me, tell them. Don't let them intimidate you. They know I cleared you. For now, at least."

"For now?"

Beck shrugged. "Everyone's a suspect."

He tried Banner's number a few more times, but never got through, even when dialing the man's cell. Clarissa figured Banner had plenty to deal with and might be unavailable for a few days.

Polanski's arrival was announced with a clearing of the woman's throat. Clarissa smoothed her shirt and fixed her collar, running her fingers over the pin she'd been told to wear.

"Did you manage to get a room?" Polanski asked.

Beck remained seated. "No. And I didn't get a hold of Banner either. I figured we'd meet in his office since it's bigger than most of the meeting rooms around here. We'll have to make do with my tin can."

Clarissa shuddered at the reference, thinking about the abandoned house and steel holding cell she'd been in earlier that day. She wasn't sure how it would turn out, but this was better than any scenario she had imagined at the time.

Polanski turned at the waist and looked around. She disappeared for a moment and returned with a chair. She wheeled it into the office, then shut the door. Clarissa shuffled her chair a few feet toward the wall to make room. Polanski fell back into it without thanking Clarissa for the seat.

"So what the hell happened today, Beck?"

Beck crossed his left leg over his right knee and stared at Polanski as if pissed that she'd implied what had happened had been his fault somehow. His cheeks turned a slight shade of red. His jaw muscles rippled near his ear.

"Dammit, Beck, don't look at me like that. We're crunched for time. If you've got something, then let me know so we can get moving on it."

"Clarissa was there. I'm going to let her tell you what she saw today."

Clarissa recounted her story starting with the long walk in the tunnel, waiting in the hall alone with Jordan, doing her best to avoid the guy including pretending to play on her phone. She told Polanski how the men reacted when McCormick said he wanted to get lunch. They stepped outside, the light, adjusting, the less than busy street. She looked up, then down, then up again, this time following the gaze of Jordan. She saw something, still unsure of what it was, but it was there. Then there were two shots, a shoulder in her back, her head slamming against ground. She mentioned Jordan taking her phone.

"Damn I wish we had that phone," Polanski said.

"Maybe it's still with Jordan," Clarissa said with a glance toward Beck.

He said nothing.

Polanski said, "We've already swept the scene. First thing we did after McCormick was moved. I already received the item list and a cell phone wasn't on it."

Did the woman doubt her story about Jordan taking the phone?

"But what about with Jordan?" Clarissa asked.

Polanski shook her head.

"What are you hoping to find?" Clarissa asked.

"Nothing, Clarissa. I want to find nothing so I can proceed with clearing you on this."

"Well, if it's not there, then someone must've taken it, right?"

Beck glanced at Clarissa before interjecting himself into the conversation. "I think she's got a point there, Julie."

"That someone took it?"

He nodded.

"Why?" she asked.

"Someone trying to cover something up."

"Cover what up?"

Clarissa said, "Jordan glanced up toward the window where I saw something sticking out."

"And what was it that you saw?"

Clarissa shook her head. "I can't be sure. It could've been a rifle. Could have been—"

"Could have been this or that or any other number of things. It does me no good right now."

Beck said, "At the very least we've got to gather some intel on his communications the past few days and bring him in for questioning."

"He's at McCormick's side right now. Refused to leave. Why would he do that if he was behind killing him?"

"To finish the job?" Beck leaned forward. "Is anyone else with him?"

Julie said nothing.

"Dammit, Julie. Is someone else there?"

"I don't know."

Beck rose and began pacing the rear of the room. "Well you better find out, and I mean now. We need to get a hold of Banner. Any idea where he is?"

Julie shrugged as she pulled out her cell phone and began dialing. Beck continued to pace as she spoke. After she hung up, she answered his question before he asked it. "There's two others there, and there will be at least that many. He won't be alone. I'll make sure of that. In fact, I'm going to go over and relieve him of his duty myself."

"He's not going to respond to you," Beck said. "Doesn't have to. I need to go. Right now what I want you doing is getting Banner on the phone and get the okay to start digging into Jordan's personal life. We need records of everything he's done in the last week. That's just for starters. We might need to delve deeper than that."

Julie nodded. She sat ramrod straight, and seemed to be in agreement with everything Beck said. "I'll start looking for Banner now. He's got to be around here somewhere."

Beck said, "If you can't find him in the next twenty minutes, you pull an override and get things moving."

Julie agreed, then rose and reached for the door.

"What about me?" Clarissa said.

In their haste to figure out what part Jordan had in the shooting, and whether he might finish the job in the hospital, they'd seemingly forgotten about her.

"You'll stay close to me," Beck said.

"So that you can bring me in if necessary."

Beck and Julie both remained silent, confirming her fear that she was not out of the woods yet. They still had to get Jordan's story. And if her earlier hunch was correct that someone had retrieved her phone, she felt certain it had been him.

Chapter 24

Clarissa and Beck left his office a few minutes after Polanski. There were doubts about Jordan. Could he have been a part of it? If so, what else would he do? If the guy caught wind that Clarissa had figured him to be involved, he might come after her. For that reason, Beck thought it best that they leave.

Because they had entered through the White House, they had to leave that way, so they made the trip up and down stairs and through tunnels, exiting through the West Wing.

The sun had started its descent in the western sky, visible as a white ball through the thickening clouds. The stifling warm air was at a breaking point where only a strong thunderstorm could cleanse the atmosphere.

Despite the heat and humidity, Clarissa rolled her window down when Beck started the car. The air washed over her like warm water, lifting strands of hair off her forehead.

The drive was short, and it didn't take long for her to figure out where they were going. Beck pulled into the condo's parking garage. He ignored the empty spaces near the front and pulled into one near the stairwell. The less time they spent exposed, the better.

Walking up the staircase, he said, "Let's go to your apartment."

"You think it's safe there?"

"Only a few of us know you are there. Typically, it is reserved for foreign dignitaries that are going to be staying long term. Most aren't going to think to check there."

"Who is 'us'?"

He didn't answer.

She stopped at the landing half a floor below hers. "Beck?"

He stopped at the top step and looked back at her. "Let me worry about that. Okay?"

Together they emerged from the stairwell into the empty and dimly lit hallway. Clarissa half-expected Amy to step out of her condo with a knowing grin plastered on her face. She couldn't believe it had only been a day since the woman dragged her to that stupid party. Would Beck have been there if she hadn't attended? There was no way to know, of course, but Clarissa couldn't help but wonder if the woman across the hall had been friendly for a reason.

What if someone had put her up to it?

Beck stopped in front of Clarissa's door and reached inside his pocket. He pulled out a key and unlocked the door.

"Do you always carry that with you?" Clarissa asked, wondering why he had the key and if he'd been inside her apartment without her present. What would he have looked for? Could he have swapped anything out? She'd only searched the interior for bugs and hidden cameras upon entering. They might've anticipated that and had Beck return later to plant them. She watched his movements as he entered, looking to see if he focused on any one item or area.

"Make sure that's locked," he said after she let the door fall shut. He moved across the room and pulled the blinds shut.

"What are you afraid of?" she asked. "Didn't you just tell me that only certain people know I'm here?"

"I'm just being cautious. That's all. We'll know within the next two hours if someone is out for you."

She felt a chill form in her lower back and travel up her spine. The sweat on her back turned to ice. She shrugged her shoulders inward to tighten her shirt to her skin.

Perhaps Beck sensed her fear. He crossed the room, stopped in front of her. The day had been tough on him, too. She saw it in his eyes, on his clothes, in his scent. He reached out and placed his hands on her shoulders. She avoided his intense stare. The chills that had been present along her spine now wrapped around her torso.

"I'm not going to leave your side, Clarissa," he said in a voice barely more than a whisper. "You might be the key to unlocking what happened today."

"There are some who might think I had something to do with what happened today."

"And there are others who know your innocence will lead to their conviction."

She wondered if Beck knew who was behind it. Who was it he spoke of? Before she could ask, there was a sharp rap on her door. They both straightened. Beck drew his pistol and aimed it toward the entrance to the condo.

He whispered, "Do you have a backup piece here?"

She shook her head.

"In the closet, far wall, feel along it until you notice the crease. Get your fingers in there and pull. You'll need to enter this code, four-nine-two-seven-six-three-one. You'll find a weapon in there along with a spare magazine and a cell phone. Go get them."

She backed away from him, turned and ran down the short hallway to her room. Opening the door, she saw that she'd left the blinds drawn. The room was dim, though, and the sun still brightened the sky. Perhaps anyone watching her bedroom from across the street noticed her. Most likely they didn't. She entered her closet and felt along the back wall. The thought occurred to her that Beck had set her up. She had nowhere to run should he and whoever was at the door attempt to arrest her. They'd block her only escape route, and no one would be able to see or hear what happened to her.

With her heart pounding so hard it felt as though it were in her throat, Clarissa found the crease in the wall. She jammed the tips of her fingers into it and pulled back. It gave a little at first. She wedged the balls of her index and middle fingers behind the panel and pulled until the entire section peeled off the wall, revealing a safe. She entered the code Beck had given her and opened the door.

The SIG hid in the shadows of the safe. She stuck both hands inside, fingers bent, ready to pull back should something attempt to grasp her from within. In securing both items, she felt a third. Further inspection revealed a stack of cash wrapped in cellophane. The top and bottom bills were hundreds. There had to be at least a hundred of them, maybe more. Beck had to have known it was there. She put the money back and pulled out the weapon, spare magazine, and the cell phone.

Clarissa stayed close to the wall, in the shadows, as she exited to the hallway. From there, she saw Beck standing in the same spot, staring at the door with his weapon aimed at the middle of it.

"It's a woman," he whispered when Clarissa was a foot or two away.

"Amy?"

He shrugged. Did he not know if it was her? Or who Amy was?

"I think she left," he said.

"I'll check." Clarissa tucked her pistol behind her back and stepped toward the door. She stopped a few feet shy. She leaned forward, placing a hand on either side of the peephole. The slice of hallway she could see looked empty. She angled her head to try to see further to the left and right. No one was there. The door across the hallway opened and Amy approached. Her hand rose and grew and filled the cone of vision the peephole provided Clarissa.

After the raps on the door, she looked and back gestured for Beck to hide in the hallway. He shook his head in protest, but left the room when she turned the doorknob.

"Sorry, Amy. I heard you knocking but was in the back." A study of Amy's face worried Clarissa. She looked distraught. "Everything okay?"

Amy tried to answer, but her hollow voice led to tears and sobs.

"What's wrong?" Clarissa asked.

"Rob-Rob-Adam didn't come home from school."

Chapter 25

Clarissa reached for her neighbor and pulled her into the apartment, letting the door close. Amy looked past her. The woman's gaze met Beck's and didn't let go. Beck's face appeared tight. He froze in place.

"Is there anywhere he might have gone?" Clarissa asked. "Clubs, sports, a friend's house?"

"No," Amy said. "Not without telling me first."

"Does he have a cell phone?"

"Yes, but there's no answer."

The whole time, Amy focused on Beck. Her demeanor seemed to change, as though she were frightened of the man. Clarissa glanced back at him. He looked at her for a second, then glanced away. He knew the apartment well enough to know there was a safe, and he knew the combination and contents of that safe. He had to have been aware of the neighbor across the hall. Perhaps he interrogated her before. After all, they placed important foreign visitors in the condo. At least, that was what Clarissa had been told.

"Have you called the police yet?" Clarissa asked.

"No police," Beck said.

Whatever fear had been there disappeared in an instant. Amy's cheeks reddened. She pushed past Clarissa and stormed up to Beck, arms flailing, hitting him in the chest.

"What have you people done with my son?"

Beck raised his arms to deflect her blows. He wrapped his hands around her wrists and held them down by her side.

"What did you do?" she yelled.

"Nothing," Beck said. "My people didn't do anything."

"You told me that if I ever—"

"Think about everything we told you," Beck said, looking past Amy and making eye contact with Clarissa. "You are bound to that agreement."

Amy's shoulders slumped. Her knees went weak. Beck stopped her from collapsing. Clarissa knew this was not a routine missing person situation, or a random kidnapping. Someone powerful had taken Adam. But who? And why?

She reached for the door and locked it. Beck led Amy to the couch and told her to sit. He then crossed the room toward Clarissa. Her initial reaction was to step back. He held his hands out, palms facing her, head tilted to his right.

"I had nothing to do with this, Clarissa. You have to trust me."

"I don't trust anyone. That's how I've made it this far." She glanced at the woman who was once again in tears. "If you didn't, who did?"

"I'm going to figure that out. I might need your help."

"What can I do?"

"We'll cross that bridge when we get to it."

"This is because of me, isn't it?"

Beck took his time answering. "It's because of what happened today."

"Then why the boy? Why not kidnap me?"

"Why do you think she lives across the hall from this unit? Coincidence?" He took a step closer, reached for her shoulders. Clarissa deflected his hands as if they were striking snakes. "We placed her there."

"She works for the Secret Service?"

Beck didn't answer her question.

"Or is she a contractor? You know what, never mind that. Tell me what her purpose is?"

Beck looked over his shoulder. He lowered his voice, said, "She collects information. Someone must think she has some involvement in what happened today, or at least had knowledge of it, but did nothing."

"So they take her son?"

He exhaled forcibly. "I'm not saying it's right, Clarissa. And obviously I don't know that for sure. But, yes, someone might have done it to pressure her."

"Into what?"

"That I don't know. I can only assume, and I'd rather not do that right now."

Clarissa pushed past Beck. She shrugged out his grasp as he attempted to turn her around. Amy stared at the closed blinds covering the windows that looked out over the city. She turned her head toward Clarissa.

"What are they going to do to my baby?"

Taking a seat next to the woman, Clarissa said, "I don't know, but I'll do what I can to help get him back."

"You don't know these people, what they're capable of."

"You don't know what I'm capable of."

Amy forced a breathy laugh. "Oh, I can see what you do best. And every man can see it."

What the hell kind of comment was that? This woman who had befriended her, now insinuated that Clarissa's sole attribute was her looks.

"I'm sorry," Amy said, reaching for Clarissa's hand. "You should see what they have me do when they stick a man they're concerned about in this unit."

"Concerned?" Clarissa shifted her gaze toward Beck, who had approached the couch.

"That's not always the case," Beck said. "Sometimes we just want to keep an eye on people."

"I suppose I'm one of those people."

He didn't hesitate. "Look at your background."

Clarissa rose, stepped forward. "What about it?"

"Your mother died suspiciously when you were what, twelve or thirteen?"

She said nothing.

"And then your father is murdered, no, assassinated. Everyone knows who was behind it, but the man goes free except for suffering the embarrassment of bureaucratic exile."

"Tell me everything you know about them."

"Who?"

"My parents."

Beck took a deep breath, closed his eyes, exhaled. He glanced in Amy's direction. "We've got other things to worry about right now."

"Beck, please," Clarissa said.

"I promise you, when the time is right, I'll help you."

She didn't know whether to believe him. He could be stalling, hoping she'd forget or be too intimidated to ask again. She'd waited over fifteen years for answers about her mother. She knew some of the details surrounding her father's death, but there was a lot left unsaid. She avoided thinking about both of them. Most of the time. In a way, she feared that solving the mystery of both would cause a part of her to die.

Clarissa turned and walked past Amy on her way to the door leading to the balcony. She needed a moment alone, away from Amy's sobs and Beck's judgmental stare.

It had cooled off, and the wind had picked up. But the air was thick. It seemed that the humidity trapped what was worst about living in the city. All the exhaust and gases released by air conditioning units fragranced the air with their putrid smells.

Lights fixed to boats twinkled on the river. They floated along, soon to be replaced by another vessel. The trees in the distance blended in with the darkening sky. She could barely trace their tops. The traffic below moved from stoplight to stoplight, never backing up more than half a block. Soon the nighttime joggers would be out, their reflective clothing shimmering in the headlights and street lamps, keeping them safe.

Or so they thought.

No one was ever safe. Anyone's world could be shattered in an instant, and there was nothing they could do to stop it.

The door behind her cracked open. She looked over her shoulder and saw Amy step out onto the balcony. The woman had stopped crying, for the moment at least.

"I'm sorry for losing it in there."

"Your son is missing. I think you have a right to freak out."

"They won't hurt him."

"Then why take him?"

"To scare me. Get me thinking. See, in a couple hours, someone will be by to collect me. That's how this works. They're wedging themselves into my thoughts now, and they know that by the time they bring me in, I'll say anything to get Adam back."

The twisted nature of what the woman said was not lost on Clarissa. She turned her head slightly toward Amy. "What are they going to ask you?"

"About you." She said it so matter-of-factly that it sent a shiver throughout Clarissa's body.

"What're you going to tell them?"

"The truth? Whatever they want to hear? I don't know. I guess it depends on how serious they are."

"You've been through this before, right?"

Amy nodded, said nothing.

"How serious were they then?"

Amy leaned forward, looked away. "Serious enough that I told them what they wanted to hear just so they'd give me Adam back."

"You know what this is about, don't you?"

"Yes, what happened to Vice President McCormick today."

"Amy, I was—"

"Stop." Amy turned and held out her hand. "Don't tell me anything, Clarissa. I don't need to know. I can't know."

Clarissa debated ignoring the woman's warning and telling her anyway. If not for Beck opening the door with a concerned look on his face, she would have relayed the entire day's events to Amy.

"What is it?" Clarissa asked Beck.

"Julie Polanski just called."

The look on his face was enough to tell her that something bad had happened. "Did McCormick die?"

Beck shook his head. "No. He's in bad shape, though."

"Then what is it?"

"Jordan's gone to ground. Disappeared. No one can find him. His wife, family, none have heard from him."

"Oh my God."

"I think your hunch was right." Beck stepped back while holding the door open and gesturing the women inside.

Before she reached the door, a crack shattered the ambient sounds of the city. Clarissa dropped to the ground. Beck did the same. Seconds passed. They stared at each other. Finally, she said, "You okay?"

He nodded. "You?"

"I think so." Turning back, she gasped. She and Beck made it through unscathed. Amy hadn't.

The woman's lifeless eyes stared up at the light-washed sky. Blood poured from the hole in her forehead, trickling down the side of her face and pooling on the concrete.

Clarissa pulled her pistol and peered over the balcony. The man she saw staring back at her was not who she expected.

Chapter 26

Lunging toward the opening to the apartment, Clarissa drove her shoulder into Beck and knocked both of them inside. Another shot tore through the window, spraying shards of razor thin glass on top of them.

Beck moved her off him, got to one knee and drew his weapon. Another shot was fired. He dove forward.

Clarissa shifted and crawled toward him. She reached out, grabbed his shoulders.

"I'm all right," he shouted, turning toward her. "Did you see who did it?"

Clarissa nodded, her vision clouding with tears.

"Who? Jordan?"

Fear had a grip so tight on Clarissa's throat that she couldn't speak or breathe. The man staring back at her from across the street had frightened her to the point of death once before, only he'd let her live in order to get something out of her. There was no intent of letting her live tonight. In that instant, with him aiming at her and firing, she knew she had no one in her corner.

Beck kicked the door shut with his foot and crawled toward Clarissa. There hadn't been a shot in several seconds, but that meant nothing. He could be repositioning to shoot from another floor up. Or worse, on his way to her apartment.

Perhaps thinking this also, Beck said, "We need to get moving. Follow me."

Clarissa got to her hands and knees and crawled to the kitchen, joining Beck behind the island. They knelt on the floor, facing each other.

"Clarissa, I need you to tell me who it was you saw."

She closed her eyes, took a deep breath. Her throat relaxed as she forced air past it and into her lungs. The hot air that returned blew gently out her mouth. The tips of her fingers were numb. She shook her hands.

Beck reached out, grabbed her wrists, brought her hands down to her knees. He leaned forward. Their faces were inches apart. She felt his hot breath wash over her lips and chin.

"Who was it?"

"Sinclair."

Beck's eyes darted wildly to the right and left. The pace of his breathing picked up a notch. The sheen of sweat on his forehead thickened.

"We need to get out of here," Beck said.

"Where will we go?" She rocked back and got to her feet, remaining in a squatted position so the island blocked her from view.

Beck either ignored or didn't hear her question.

"Why would he do this?" she asked.

"Sinclair goes back some ways with Banner and Polanski. After all, that's how you became involved in all of this. But I can't imagine that he... that they are involved in this."

Clarissa studied him as he spoke. She hadn't seen Beck this disheveled before.

He asked, "Are you sure he aimed at you?"

"Yes. I think so. Why?"

"What if he was there to protect you?"

"You mean he meant to kill Amy and was trying to kill you so he could rescue me?"

Beck nodded, but didn't look sure of himself. What was he getting at? What reason would he have to believe that Banner and Polanski and Sinclair conspired to kill him, but let her live?

"Why would he do that? I mean, that makes no sense unless he thought you were going to do something to me, in which case I would see him taking a different course of action." She went silent for a moment. "This makes no sense. That couldn't have been Sinclair."

Beck rose up a few inches and looked over the top of the island. "Doesn't matter who it was. We need to find a way out of here now. If someone was in that building, then they might be on the street by now, or have someone positioned there."

"You know the building better than I do, so lead the way."

Beck remained low as he headed toward the door. He cracked it open, leaned out and cleared the hall.

Clarissa froze as he called for her to join him. Her instincts told her to shut and lock the door, but then she recalled that Beck had a key. Even if he had set it down inside, he could get another. It would only buy her a few moments. She'd still have nowhere to go. In that moment she questioned how well she knew Beck and everyone else she had been around that week. It could have been him setting her up, involved in what had just happened. The bullet may or may not have been meant for her, but if Beck was involved, then sooner or later there would be one shot with the intent of taking her life.

"We need to go now," Beck called from the hallway.

She had to confront him. That was her only option. But she couldn't do it in the apartment. She needed a place where she had more than one escape route.

Clarissa took a deep breath, held it and lunged for the open doorway. She dove toward the threshold, tucking and rolling into the hall. Beck reached down and pulled her up. She braced for a shot to tear through the drywall and into her back. Nothing happened, though. Sinclair, or whoever it was, must've run after the second shot.

Beck ran toward the stairwell. He opened the door and entered first. The air was humid and fifteen degrees warmer. Clarissa felt her chest tighten. Each breath became more difficult than the last. They jogged down two flights of stairs. Beck stopped on the landing and leaned toward the door.

"Don't move, Beck," Clarissa said.

His head was already turned to the left so that his right ear pressed up against the heavy door. He looked at her out of the corner of his eye, hardly reacting to the pistol she held three feet from his face. Perhaps he'd expected this. Did that make him guilty? Did he lead the way to take her toward danger? To make it seem as though he was trying to help her?

"I need to know what your—"

"I have nothing to do with this," he said.

"Don't bullshit me, Beck."

She took a step forward. The pistol was less than a foot away, close enough he could attempt to disarm her. But in his present position, pressed up against the door, he would have to take a step back to be effective. And that would give her time to shoot. He knew that, which meant he'd only attempt it if guilty.

Or stupid.

"Listen to me," he said. "I had nothing to do with what just happened. I'm on your side. My only responsibility at this time is to keep you safe."

"I don't need a handler. Once we get outside, you go right, I go left. I'm disappearing, and you'll be on your own."

"You don't know the people behind this."

"So you're saying you know who arranged this?"

"No, that's not what I mean. I have an idea, though, and you'll never outrun them. And neither will I, Clarissa. If we stick together, we might have a chance."

She took a step back, said nothing, kept the pistol aimed at his head.

Beck lifted both hands over his head. Shadows covered his face, turning his eye black. He turned toward her, then leaned back against the door.

"Call Julie," Clarissa said. "I want to hear her reaction."

Beck shook his head. "We need to get out of this building. They might already be inside."

"Where will we go?"

"Hopefully across the street. They have a back exit."

"And what if that doesn't work?"

"Then we run until we find a car. I've got a place outside the city, about an hour from here. We can go there. No one knows about it."

"You sure about that? After all, you said they know everything."

He smiled, lowered his hands an inch. "Trust me, no one knows."

Whether it was the way he said it, or the look on his face, Clarissa lost trust in Beck. "Call Polanski."

He pulled out his phone and dialed.

"Speaker," Clarissa added.

He complied. The ringing sound echoed throughout the stairwell. Julie Polanski answered on the second ring.

"We haven't located him yet, Beck." She paused, breathing heavily into the phone. "How're things there?"

"You tell me," he said.

"Tell you what? How would I know? That's why I asked you. Are you two doing okay?"

"Aside from being shot at, we're great."

"What?"

Beck said nothing. He fixed his gaze on Clarissa and held it.

"Beck, what the hell is going on?"

"Someone shot at us. Our friend in the building was hit."

"Did you see who did it?" There was a panic to her voice. Clarissa couldn't help thinking it was because the woman already knew who had shot at them.

Beck said, "No, we didn't see who did it. It was from a building across the street, offset to the right. They fired two shots. One hit, the other missed."

"Jesus Christ." Polanski muttered something either to herself or someone in the room with her. "Do you think it was him?"

"Jordan?"

"Yeah."

"How should I know?"

"Yeah, I guess you wouldn't. Okay, get out of there if you haven't already and come in. We'll make sure you're safe."

Beck gestured toward the stairs with his chin, but Clarissa didn't move.

"Julie," he said, "we're not going to find any surprises when we leave the building, right?"

"Are you insinuating I had something to do with this?"

"I'm just asking a question. I avoided one bullet tonight. I'd like to make it through without dodging another."

"I had nothing to do with this," Polanski insisted. "It had to have been Jordan. Maybe he caught wind that we were on to him and is trying to eliminate what he deems to be a threat."

On to him?

Clarissa wondered what Polanski meant by that. Had Jordan been the real target? Was she only assigned to be an assistant to McCormick because of Jordan? And if Jordan was taking out those he thought were threats, did the vice president really know why she was there? Why the act, then?

"We're coming in to see you," Beck said. He hung up and clung to the phone.

"We're going in?" Clarissa asked.

He shook his head. "I don't trust her."

"What was that about Jordan knowing you were on to him?"

Beck held his hand up. "I'll tell you if we get out of here. Speaking of which, we need to get moving."

He led the way, taking steps two at a time. Clarissa jogged to keep up. They reached the main floor landing. Beck stopped, placed his ear to the door.

"Anything?" she asked.

He shook his head and looked back. "Did you grab your personal cell back there?"

"Yeah."

"Ditch it."

"Not a chance."

"Listen to me, Clarissa. We can't leave this building with that phone. They'll track us. I have clean phones where we're going. I'll give you one there."

She squeezed the phone tight. It was her only link to the world. If Beck was playing her, she'd have no way to call for help. Buying time, she said, "What about yours?"

"What about it?"

"Can't they track yours, too?"

Beck turned, taking a deep breath. He held out his arm and unclenched his fist. His cell hit the floor, clattering and skidding toward the stairs. He took a step forward, lifted his knee high, and drove the heel of his shoes onto the face-up phone, shattering it. He repeated the move three times until the phone laid there in several pieces.

"Happy?"

She wasn't, but she dropped her phone anyway. He stopped her when she went to stomp on it.

"Toss it in the trash on the way out."

Chapter 27

The main floor had been empty. They avoided the lobby and the garage. Beck had figured even if someone wasn't watching his car, they'd track their movements through the GPS. It wouldn't matter if he disabled it.

The building's gym had a door that led to an alley, and they exited there. Clarissa stepped out into the dark, narrow lane. It felt like she cut through the thick, stale air. With Beck leading, they hovered close to the building and headed toward the street. She looked up to her right, her gaze climbing the rows and columns of balconies. From down there she had trouble picking out the window that the shots had been fired from.

What if he was still up there?

The thought was enough to send her racing forward, nudging Beck in the back with her elbow.

"What?" he said.

"Move," she said.

On the main road every person was a threat. The man jogging away from them. The woman pushing a stroller toward them. The four drunk guys carrying on across the street. The bum with the brown paper bag held up to his mouth. None could be trusted. Any of them could be there to shoot or follow or report on Clarissa and Beck. Yet, it was the safest place for them at that moment.

Sinclair's network was vast, but it seemed as though he had worked alone. It made no sense. He was the kind of operator who would have both ends covered. Someone should have been waiting outside the apartment or building in the event that Sinclair had failed. They found no one, though. Had someone else already gotten to them?

Questions raced through her mind again. Why had Sinclair missed her? Was it a set up? If so, who was behind it? She doubted whether she could trust Beck once they left the city. For all she knew, he was the mastermind of today's events.

She quickly ran through a list of ways to escape, people to call on, and places to go. Her options were limited. She had people she could count on to hide her. The problem was that between Sinclair and the Secret Service, they likely knew of them all. And on the off chance they didn't, could she risk an innocent's life?

She had to make a decision right then and there. Trust Beck, or neutralize him and flee.

Alone, Clarissa could move place to place without worrying about the motives of another. She had no problem handling herself. With Beck around, she'd either be concerned for his safety, or worry about his intentions.

Beck walked a half-step in front of her. His footsteps were deliberate and quiet. His head inched left and right, up and down. She knew his eyes did the same. When able to, he avoided the yellow and orange pools of light that splashed the wide sidewalk. He never looked back, but she knew that didn't mean he wasn't aware of what went on behind them.

They approached an area shaded by two tall, pruned oaks. The thick trunks pushed up through the concrete. Even in the dark, Clarissa could make out the wide cracks in the grayish sidewalk. A quick glance around told her that no one was out. The darkness afforded here would give her an extra ten to fifteen seconds. If she intended to do something, this might be her only opportunity.

Her left hand grasped for her now-missing cell phone. The other wrapped around the grip of her pistol. The pistol he'd insisted she kept. He'd made her toss the phone, and for good reason. They could be tracked through it. He'd destroyed his prior to Clarissa ditching hers.

But he let her keep the gun. He didn't even make an attempt to take it from her.

Of course, she hadn't confirmed it was loaded. Or functional.

She pulled the pistol from her waistband. Her arm hung loosely at her side. The weapon brushed against her thigh. The canopy of the converging oaks blocked out all light. She lifted the sidearm, aimed at Beck.

"Stop."

Perhaps it had been the tone of her voice, or maybe Beck thought she'd seen something. For whatever reason, he halted and turned.

"Don't move, Beck."

She couldn't see his face or the expression on it. The two dark masses rising next to his head were enough confirmation that the gun he told her to get from the safe in the bedroom was fully functional and loaded.

"What's this about?" he asked calmly and softly.

"What the fuck is going on, and what do you have to do with it?"

"As far as I can tell, I'm in this as deep as you are. Perhaps more."

"Don't feed me that bullshit, Beck. What was Julie talking about when she mentioned Jordan?"

Beck took a deep breath. Its ragged nature belied his calm demeanor. "This isn't the time or place. We have to get out of here. You saw what they did to Amy. I have no doubt they intend to do the same to us."

His hands dropped an inch and he stutter-stepped backward.

"Not another inch," she said. "Tell me about Jordan. Was he the one you were hoping I would gain intel on?"

"Yes, but it doesn't matter now. Either he knows what is going on, or…" He brought both hands to his head and pulled on his hair. "I don't know, Clarissa. I'm still processing this. But this is not the time or the place to figure this out."

She said nothing, and kept the weapon aimed at his chest.

"If you want to run, then run. Take off on your own. I won't tell them which way you went." He paused, perhaps waiting for her to make an initial decision. She didn't. He continued. "But if you want to live and get to the bottom of this so that you're not running the rest of your life, then come with me. Look, I know you don't trust people, and I understand why. Hell, it's the reason we chose you. But you have to believe me when I say you and I are in this together from this point on. You might make it alone. I probably will. But together, we can figure this thing out and put an end to it."

As she lowered her weapon, the sound of two tin cans slapping against one another preceded a bullet slamming into the tree next to them, sending shards of bark flying through the air.

Beck grabbed her wrist and pulled her forward. They sprinted across the street and took cover in a small alley. Clarissa feared they were trapped, but a soft glow of light at the end of the corridor gave her hope.

"This way." Beck ran toward the light.

She paused, discerning that the footsteps she heard weren't only created by Beck. A man burst forward from the shadowy sidewalk across the street. He was armed with a pistol that had a suppressor affixed to the end. Though his face was hidden by shadows, his short and stocky build made it obvious it wasn't Sinclair racing toward her.

She backed up, watching as the guy ran toward the alley. Had he seen her? She imagined that if he could see her now, he'd shoot, unless there was someone watching. Or perhaps, the first shot had been a warning shot. After all, he'd missed and not shot again. But why would he have done that in the first place? Why not approach her and Beck?

The man slowed up as he hit the sidewalk. Clarissa was far enough back that she lost sight of him. Soon he would be at the entrance to the alley. Dark as it was, he might make out her silhouette as she ran toward the light at the end. Clinging to the right wall, she moved toward Beck. Her arm brushed against the rough brick, wet with streams of condensation leaking from window-mounted air conditioning units. The machines whirred above, drowning out the sounds around her. She had no idea if the man approached from behind. A quick glance back revealed nothing other than the alley's empty opening. The guy could be there, lurking in the shadows with his weapon drawn and aimed at her head.

Beck waited inside, past the open doorway. His pistol dangled from his hand by his side. Clarissa half-expected him to raise his weapon and shoot at her. He didn't, though. At this point, all she could do was trust him. He leaned into the alley, waving her toward him. As she reached the doorway, the footsteps of the man following them echoed off the walls. Beck held out his free hand. When she grabbed it, he pulled her into the building, letting the door fall shut.

Old fluorescent lights behind dirty fixtures cast a yellow glow over them. Glancing around, she saw five Chinese men staring back at her. One held a twelve-inch chef's knife. The others were busy at a fryer, a cook top, or preparing plates.

"What is this place?" she asked.

"Never ate here," Beck said.

"Which way?"

Beck pointed past the cooks, at a swinging door. "Looks like our only choice."

"That's going to lead back out front."

Beck nodded. "Got a better idea?"

"What if there's more than that one guy?"

"Then we do what we have to do. And in case you didn't notice, there was nowhere else to go. That alley is a dead end other than into here."

The cooks watched them, but said nothing. Clarissa figured they saw Beck's gun and decided it best to butt out.

She looked back at the door. "Why hasn't he tried to come in?"

"He won't," Beck said. "Not alone. I'm guessing that he's made the same observation about the alley and is now backtracking to the sidewalk where he can watch that door and the ones leading out to the street."

"Through that door," the cook with the knife said. "Stairs to the roof. Five feet to building behind."

Beck looked from the cook back to Clarissa. He lifted an eyebrow, said, "You up for a climb and a jump?"

She didn't know whether to take him seriously. They had no other choice, though. She nodded, grabbed his hand, and followed the cook across the kitchen. The cook pulled open a narrow door, revealing the darkened stairwell. Beck entered first. He placed his right foot on the first step and looked back at Clarissa.

"You ready for this?"

"Yeah."

Together they raced up five flights of stairs, refusing to stop to catch their breath. She feared that the door leading to the roof would be locked, trapping them inside the stairwell with no way out. She imagined the man, who she now pictured as Jordan, climbing the stairs with three or four others in tow.

They reached the final landing. There were no more stairs to climb. Beck reached out, grabbed the dented doorknob, and pushed. The door did not budge. He looked back at Clarissa. She figured that he was doing his best to hide his fear. He turned away, squeezed the knob, and drove his shoulder into the door. It gave with a loud crack. Beck's momentum carried him through. He stumbled forward and fell, sliding on the gravel rooftop.

Clarissa caught the door before it fell shut. She stepped out into the thick night air, hurrying to Beck's side. By the time she reached him, he already had one foot on the ground.

"Jesus, Beck, are you okay?"

Beck nodded, said, "Yeah, I'm fine. Knocked a bit of the wind out of me, but that's all."

She reached out and helped him up. They surveyed the square rooftop. There were visible gaps to the left and right, too far for them to jump. The street was in front of them. They both turned and walked to the back.

"Think you can make it?" Beck stuck one foot on the ledge, which stood eighteen inches above the roof. "Gonna make it difficult to get a running start. You'll have to hit that ledge just right or you're going over."

Clarissa turned and crossed to the front. Looking down, she spotted the man who had followed them. He stood where Beck had said he would, at the corner where he could see both the alley and the street.

"That him?"

She hadn't heard Beck approach. "Think so. See any others?"

"They could be anywhere."

She looked over at him. He no longer looked down at the man on the street. His gaze traveled along the stunted rooflines up and down the road.

"Then we should get out of here," she said.

"Ready?"

She nodded, then sprinted toward the back edge of the roof.

Chapter 28

Clarissa planted her right foot on the narrow ledge and let her momentum carry her left leg up and over. She saw Beck hit the roof. He tucked and rolled the moment he did so. With her knee bent, she powered upward.

But her foot slipped off the back of the ledge. Her body, rather than following an upward trajectory, started to fall forward. Fast. The momentum was lost. Instinctively, she reached both arms out. There was no time to do anything else. Her hands and wrists slapped against cold, hard concrete or bricks. Pain radiated down her left arm and into her shoulder. She feared she'd broken something. The pain did not prevent her from keeping the roof in a death grip.

The move stopped her fall. Her feet slipped off the ledge and came forward, carrying her body underneath her and into the side of the building. She twisted to the left so that her side caught the brunt of the collision.

"Clarissa," Beck shouted. She heard him scuffle toward her. Felt his hands on her, wrapping around her arms. Saw him lean over. "Are you hurt?"

"I think so." The pain continued through her arm and shoulder, but she didn't care. She'd made it through. Death had been imminent, but she won.

He disappeared behind the wall, but his hands never left her arm. He grunted and pulled, and she felt her body sliding upward. The pain she felt vanished as her left wrist popped into place. A few moments later her head crested the roof. Her body followed. She lay on the ground, breathing heavily, with Beck crouched over her.

"What happened?" he asked.

She rolled over, looked past him toward the gray clouds that raced low in the sky. "I slipped."

"You okay?"

She shook her left arm. "Think I dislocated my wrist, but it's in place now."

"Numb?"

"No."

"Let me know if it feels that way. If there's nerve damage we'll—"

"Beck."

"What?"

"Don't worry about that. Let's focus on getting out of here."

They found a fire escape on the side of the building. It brought them within ten feet of the ground. Neither had an issue lowering themselves and dropping the final few feet. Clarissa spotted a Jeep nearby with no top. Its drunken owner approached, staggering, with the keys dangling from a lanyard.

She tapped Beck on the shoulder. "Look."

They scanned the street. It was quiet. No one was out.

"I'll take care of this." Beck rushed forward and knocked the man out. He got behind the wheel and started the Jeep.

"You can't leave him here," Clarissa said, standing over the guy.

"Why not?"

"He'll call the car in stolen."

Beck opened the door and stepped out. He searched the guy's pockets until he found a cell phone. He dialed 911, then told the dispatch operator that an unknown man was down on the street with obvious head trauma.

Hanging up the phone, he said, "Happy? Now get in. We need to hurry."

As she jogged around the back of the vehicle, Clarissa heard two thuds. By the time she rounded the side and looked over, Beck was on his way to the driver's side. The man lay still on the sidewalk, now with a pool of blood forming around his head.

"What did you do?"

Beck said nothing. He shifted into first gear and pulled away from the curb.

She didn't need him to tell her. He'd told the dispatcher head trauma, so he had to deliver. Beck was her kind of guy, willing to do whatever it took to survive. She glanced back at the man lying still on the sidewalk. Poor guy, she thought. Wrong place at the wrong time. Much like her.

They drove west through the city. She kept up with the streets they passed until they crossed into Virginia. From there, they merged onto I-66 west outside of Fairfax, then took I-81 south. When he exited a few miles later, Clarissa asked where they were going. He told her West Virginia and said nothing else. She wondered when they'd ditch the car. It wasn't equipped with built-in GPS. There had been a unit fixed to the windshield, but Beck got rid of that the same time he ditched the phone, throwing both into the Potomac River as they drove over.

Beck navigated steep switchbacks as they drove through mountainous territory around one in the morning. The air was cooler here, compounded by the fact that the Jeep had no top. Every straightaway they encountered, he'd push the vehicle to fifty or sixty. The gusts permeated every stitch of Clarissa's clothing.

She leaned back and stared up. Out here, she'd be able to see millions of stars if not for the clouds. They continued to race, east to west. She realized that she hadn't kept up with the weather since returning. Was there an early hurricane brewing in the Atlantic? She pushed the thought aside and focused on nothing. Her mind was too tired to do anything else. And her body had caught up. With a deep sigh, she closed her eyes and drifted off to sleep.

Chapter 29

"Wake up."

She heard the words, but ignored the message. His hands wrapped around her shoulders and shook her. She opened her eyes. Beck leaned over her. He looked concerned.

"You all right?" he asked.

She nodded, shrugging free from his hands. She turned her head to her right. A wall of trees rose up from the ground. It was the same to the left. The sky above was dark blue, sparkling with thousands of stars. Either the clouds had passed, or they had driven out of their reach.

"Clarissa?"

"I'm fine. Quit worrying about me." She reached for the door, found the handle and opened it. Sliding out, she asked, "Where are we?"

"Nowhere. At least, as far as anyone else is concerned."

Without Beck blocking her view, she now saw the small A-framed cabin. His secret hideaway. Behind the cabin was another building, a shed or garage perhaps. The structure was bigger than the cabin. She wondered what he kept in there.

Beck ran ahead of her with his gun drawn. She reached for hers, but it was missing. When was the last time she'd had it in her possession? In the car? Had she lost it during her failed attempt at a jump? With no weapon, she remained back while Beck entered the house. A moment later he returned to the porch, gesturing her forward.

"Did you take my pistol?" she asked.

He shook his head. "You must have lost it during the jump. Don't worry, I have more inside."

She stepped into the dark, musty domicile. He followed her in, shining a flashlight that he must've found on his first trip inside.

"It's not much," he said, shining the light around the room and letting it settle on a closed door. "You can take the bedroom. I'll get you a lantern to use, but it's best if we remain in the dark." He switched the flashlight off.

It took a few moments for her eyes to adjust to the dark surroundings. Once they did, she moved toward the bedroom door.

"I'm going to park the Jeep in the garage." He walked toward the open front door.

"Beck?"

He stopped, looked back at her. She saw a glint of light on his eyes. "Yeah?"

"You said something about a gun?"

He laughed softly. "Girl after my own heart. Come over here."

She met him in the corner of the room. He flicked on the light. They stood in front of a gun cabinet, secured with a biometric lock. He placed his thumb on a pad. A second later a click signaled that the cabinet was unlocked. He opened it, revealing a small armory.

"If anyone finds us out here," he said, "they're likely to send a team. Go ahead and grab the MP7 and a spare magazine. That'll give you sixty rounds, or twenty shots on three-round burst, which I'd recommend."

Nodding, she reached for the H&K submachine gun. She ducked her head through the strap and let it rest against her chest. Beck handed her a spare magazine. She thanked him and turned and walked back to the room.

Sleep came easier than it should have. She was out before she knew whether Beck made it back to the cabin safely. Perhaps she didn't care if it ended right then. At least in her sleep she wouldn't have time to process what the end of her life would mean. And she wouldn't have to come to grips with the fact that it'd mean nothing to almost everyone.

She woke to the sounds of birds outside her window. The sun's rays blinded her at first. She covered her face with a pillow, easing it away and allowing her eyes to adjust. She had no phone or watch and was unable to tell what time it was. The scent of coffee filled her room. She assumed Beck made it back last night and was already up.

Exiting the room, she clutched the MP7's grip tightly, aiming it loosely in front of her.

"Don't shoot," Beck jokingly said. He held both hands up, clutching a mug in each. "Coffee?"

She continued forward and reached for the earthy-green mug. The coffee smelled strong and looked blacker than any she had ever seen. The first sip straightened her spine and knocked any remaining sleep from her bones.

Beck laughed. "That's West Virginia mountain coffee."

"You're from here?"

"Me? No. This property belonged to my late wife. She inherited it from a great-uncle before we met. That's how no one knows about it."

"I'm sorry."

"About no one knowing about it?"

"Your late wife."

"It's been ten years."

"Does that make it easier?"

Beck considered this for a moment. "No, it doesn't."

"Didn't think so."

They both were silent for a few minutes. Clarissa glanced around the room. It looked much as she expected it to. Old and dusty. She figured Beck didn't spend much time here. Maybe once every year or two to check up on the place. And she doubted he cleaned when he did so. She couldn't let that bother her. They were stuck here, together, for as long as it took. How long would that be, though? She had no idea, and she doubted that Beck did either. She decided to broach the topic with him.

"When do you think we'll get out of here?"

He set his mug on the counter and placed his hand on either side of it. "Hard to say. I'd like to know something before we go. Getting any info is risky. I've got three clean phones here. They're charging right now. I'll start making some calls."

"What if you call the wrong person?"

"The phones route through a few servers, all of which are off-grid as far as the people we know are concerned. And as far as who I'm calling, none of the people I'll be reaching out to are going to have any involvement in what's happened so far." He picked up his mug and took a sip, then added, "I hope."

She wasn't sure whether to be encouraged by his words, or distraught over them. All that mattered is they were safe at that moment. That allowed her to think of other things.

"You don't happen to have a shower here, do you?"

He gestured with his head. "Out back. It's spring fed and freezing cold, so you might want to wait until it heats up a bit outside. Temps get into the nineties during the day here."

She took a seat at the table while Beck fished out something from the cabinet over the sink. He cranked a handle and switched the device on. Turning a dial, he skipped past music and tuned into a news report.

"*—no new updates are available on the condition of Vice President McCormick, or about the identity of the shooter, although this reporter has learned through confidential sources that the Secret Service and FBI are tracking down two potential suspects thought to have fled to Virginia or West Virginia.*"

"How do they know we're here?" she asked.

Beck shook his head. "They don't. Just taking wild guesses, that's all."

She partly believed him. Perhaps they only had a general sense of where the two of them had gone, if it was them the reporter was referring to. It could have been anyone. She told herself this to calm down. The fact was, at that moment, she grew convinced that Sinclair had not acted alone. He'd been working with Banner and Polanski, maybe even Jordan, since the beginning. The plan all along had been to set her up for the assassination of McCormick.

Chapter 30

Later that day, when the temperature had climbed above ninety, Clarissa walked around the back of the cabin and entered the small enclosure surrounding the shower, which was engulfed in shadows. She stripped out of her clothes and stepped into the freezing spray of water. Beck had a few pairs of his late wife's jeans and some t-shirts boxed up. Surprisingly, they were in mint condition, even if they smelled like mothballs. Clarissa had picked out a pair of faded blue jeans and a light blue t-shirt.

Without soap or shampoo, the only thing she could do was stand there and let the frigid water rinse the sweat and dirt off her body. She spent five minutes in the shower, thinking over the events of the previous two days. Her body grew numb to the cold, but it was too much for her to get comfortable and think things through.

She cut the shower, toweled off and slipped into the jeans. The woman had been the same size and probably within half an inch of Clarissa's height. She wondered what the woman had been like. What had Beck been like ten years ago? How had his wife's passing affected him? She'd wandered around the house with an eye for finding a picture or two, but there hadn't been any. She wasn't sure why it mattered so much. It was probably best to let it go for now.

The sun hovered on the other side of the roofline, leaving most of the yard darkened. She escaped the structure's long shadow, climbing up the slope to the barn. There, Clarissa leaned against warm, weathered boards and soaked in the rays. Within minutes the sweltering heat forced a thin sheen of sweat on her brow.

Beck had left the lock off the barn door. She took this as a sign that she could enter. She pulled back the wide door and stepped inside. Windows along the top of the building allowed in enough light for her to see everything in the room, which consisted of one wide main area on the left, and four stalls on the right. At one time they may have been used for horses or other livestock. But now they housed two ATVs and two dirt bikes. Occupying the main area was the Jeep they drove from D.C., and a late nineties Land Rover.

Rounding the back of a dark green Discovery, she noted that the license plates looked legit. Who were they registered to? She doubted Beck registered them under his name. Perhaps he had set up a company in order to keep the property and the vehicle out of his name. Of course, his employer could find that out, so the name behind the company would have to be different from his own.

She realized, based on the age of the vehicle, that it, too, must have belonged to Beck's wife. Perhaps it had all been registered under her maiden name, or that of some family member's. It did little to ease Clarissa's concern. The people she dealt with could get any information they wanted. Perhaps they'd never had a reason to dig this deep into Beck's life. Now they did.

She exited the garage and jogged down the gravel path to the house. The front door was open to allow a slight breeze inside. There was no air conditioning, though each room had several fans running.

Beck leaned over the kitchen counter. He held up a hand as she entered and finished a phone call. Clarissa walked over to the bedroom door and dropped her dirty clothes and the damp towel on the floor, then she joined Beck in the kitchen.

"Good news?" she asked, knowing by the look on his face it was anything but that.

He shook his head and looked away. "We're the suspects."

"I figured."

"I just don't know who is pushing this agenda, and who might be willing to help us."

"Who was that you were talking to?"

"I think it's better that you don't know, Clarissa. The fewer names you know the better. It's for your own good, and theirs."

"You mean in case I'm caught."

"Or I am," he replied, pausing. "Or they are."

"So what's the plan? We can't stay here forever."

"We can't?"

"Sooner or later they'll figure it out if they haven't already." She walked up to the counter where he stood and leaned against it. "Won't they?"

Beck shrugged. "I've been pretty careful with everything here. None of it is in my name. They'd have to go through several records to find a correlation."

"But that's what they do, right? Take these random strings of information and tie them together until they have the answer they want. They might not figure it out today or tomorrow. Hell, we could be safe here a week from now. But eventually these people are going to figure it out."

"I know, I know. I'm trying to buy us some time until we can get this sorted out. I've got someone looking for Jordan. I think that if we find him, we're clear."

"Then maybe we should find him."

Beck straightened up. "Are you suggesting we go back to D.C.?"

"We're not accomplishing anything out here. Or am I mistaken and you've got a server farm going in there working to hone in on Jordan's location, and figuring out what the hell Sinclair was doing across the street with a rifle aimed at my head?"

"Don't you think if it was aimed at your head you'd be dead right now?"

"Being a sniper was never his specialty."

"Then why was he out there?"

Clarissa shrugged. She had no answer for that question.

Beck said, "How much do you really know about the man?"

She thought back to the various things he and others had told her. "He was an officer in the Army, PSYOPs. Did six years in the mid-eighties, you know, Granada and Panama, then he went into the CIA. There he continued with covert psychological operations during Gulf One."

"All the leaflets and then bombings when the troops didn't surrender?"

"I don't know the details of that. From there he was involved in Bosnia and Kosovo. Not sure what he did there. He moved into interrogation at some point, or maybe he was always there and the other stuff was a lie just to make me feel better."

Beck smiled, said nothing.

"I know he worked with Jack at some point—"

"Who?"

She looked away. "An old friend of mine. He was a Marine and worked as a Fed for a while."

Beck nodded, seemingly fine with her answer.

"Then things with Sinclair get murky. He headed a team that had worked everywhere, and respected no borders."

"When you say no borders?"

"Here in the States."

"How?"

"He controlled a team of assets, contractors, people like me."

"So all black ops?"

Clarissa shrugged and offered no reply.

"What else?"

"The only other thing I can tell you is that he freelanced for crime bosses."

"Doing what?"

"Interrogation."

Beck leaned forward. "Why would he tell you that?"

"He didn't."

"Then how do you know?"

"Because he interrogated me once."

Beck's expression changed as he digested the information. She could see him trying to put the pieces of the puzzle together. Why would

Sinclair have interrogated her at the request of a crime boss? The answer was far from menacing, but no one would believe the story. To delve any further would bring up names of people she wanted to protect, so even if he asked, she'd refuse to answer.

"There's a lot I don't know about you, isn't there?" He paused to allow her time to answer, but she remained quiet. "I'll ask you one more question, and I'd appreciate as honest an answer as you can muster."

"Okay."

"Is there any reason for Sinclair to want you dead?"

Clarissa crossed the room and stopped in front of the front window. She peeled back the curtain. The sun hovered just behind the tops of the trees. Hundreds of rays filtered through the leaves. The house had begun to cool, but there she felt warmed by the penetrating light.

Beck approached from behind. The old floorboards creaked under his weight. She felt slight vibrations with every step he took.

"Clarissa?"

"No, Beck, I can't think of a single reason why. If he wanted me dead, he'd have had it carried out. Hell, he could have phoned in an anonymous tip to the asshole I was staying with in London and told them I was an agent. I'd have never left the compound dead or alive. Or he could have had me killed when I got back here. The first time we met, that's what I thought you were there for."

She looked back to see his reaction. If he had one, Beck didn't let it show on his face. He'd stopped a couple feet behind her. As she turned her head back toward the window, he reached out and placed a hand on her shoulder.

"I could handle him having me killed." She reached up and wiped a tear from her cheek. "But to disgrace me like this? To make those that know me think I had something to do with an attempted assassination of the vice president?"

He squeezed her shoulder and pulled her toward him. She turned and allowed him to wrap both arms around her. It was the first time in months that she felt safe.

"We're going to get to the bottom of this," Beck said. "I'm not going to leave your side until we do."

She pulled away and leaned against the warm windowpanes. "Why are you willing to risk it all to help me? For all you know, I *was* involved in this."

"If I hadn't been at your apartment and saw Amy shot down, and then another shot meant for one or both of us, I might not. I'd probably be out there looking for you. But that, and then being shot at again, perhaps by Jordan, it's obvious someone is setting you up." He leaned his head back and took a deep breath, then added, "Setting us both up."

She pushed past Beck and returned to the kitchen. She searched the cabinets for something suitable for dinner. A box of unopened spaghetti offered the safest option.

"There's also the fact that you remind me so much of Victoria."

She hadn't heard Beck approach. There were no vibrations in the floor. His words caught her by surprise. She could only imagine who he had referred to.

"Your wife?" she said, turning to face him.

He nodded. "Especially with your hair short and dark. She was around your age when she passed. We'd been married four years, together another five before that. We met in college. Hit it off right away."

"What did she do?"

"She was a lawyer. Got a job in the D.A.'s office right out of Georgetown Law School. A rising superstar, they'd said. Despite that, she was going to put it all on hold after finding out she was pregnant with our first child."

Clarissa feared the direction the story was headed.

"Never made it out of the first trimester, though."

She clutched the cardboard box full of spaghetti, squishing it. "What happened?"

"Her car went over a bridge. Plunged into the Potomac. There were people nearby, but it was January and the water was frigid and no one went in to help her."

"Jesus, Beck, I'm..." She didn't want to say sorry, but nothing else came to mind.

He shook his head. "You'd think with the time that's passed it would get easier. In some ways, it does. But I've never been able to shake the feeling that it wasn't an accident."

"You think someone killed her?"

He nodded.

"Who? Why?"

Beck hiked his shoulders an inch. "Could have been a case she was involved in. Could have been because of me. Hell, could have been the D.A., pissed that she was leaving." He smiled slightly after making the statement. "Kidding there, of course. I don't know, and I guess I'll always have to live with that."

Clarissa had nothing to offer, and saying sorry didn't feel right.

"Anyway," Beck said, "go ahead and start dinner, and I'm going to get the Land Rover ready for tomorrow."

"What's tomorrow?"

"We're heading back to D.C."

Chapter 31

They ate dinner in silence under the dim light that hung over the kitchen table. The spaghetti was stale and there was no sauce or butter to mix with it. But they needed food and both Clarissa and Beck ate it without complaining.

After they were finished, Clarissa rinsed the plates off in cool water. Beck took a cell phone into the bedroom and shut the door. She wondered who he was calling, and why it had to be done in private. The first assumption that came to mind had to do with him setting her up. She pushed that aside, though, and recalled an earlier explanation. It was better that uninvolved parties knew little about each other.

She left the plates in the sink to dry and went outside. The temperature had dropped close to forty degrees. Her skin prickled in the cool breeze. Thousands of stars twinkled overhead. To the north, clouds gathered. She wondered if they'd head her way, or were they remnants of the storm that had passed?

A dog barked in the distance. She couldn't tell from how far away. They were some distance up the mountain. The sound could have originated from the valley and rose up to her position. She heard it again. This time another dog responded.

She knew little about the area and wildlife that lived in the woods. It couldn't be all that different from North Carolina, or any more dangerous that the urban jungle of New York City. Out here, a black bear, bobcat, wolf or coyote would pose the biggest threat. But, for the most part, they'd keep their distance. A bear might come up if given the opportunity to root through trash, and an encounter would be less than ideal.

"Nice night."

She spun, ready to attack, and saw Beck standing in the open doorway. She hadn't heard him approach.

"You okay?"

She pulled in a cool breath and allowed her chest time to relax. "Fine. You surprised me."

He dipped his head and stepped outside, brushing past her. Looking up, he said, "A few times I've witnessed as many as a dozen deer come out of the woods and feed on the front lawn here. Usually happens later in summer."

Perhaps that was what the dogs were barking at, she thought. And at that moment, a series of barks erupted from below them and echoed up the mountainside.

"They've been doing that since I came out here," she said.

He spun around and headed right at her. "Get inside."

"What? Why?"

"The only dogs on this side of the mountain belong to an old coot down by the river. I've never heard them bark at anything. And even if they were barking, we wouldn't hear it quite like that."

Her heart pounded against her chest as she stepped inside. Beck pushed her another foot further, then slammed the door shut and drew the blinds closed.

"Who'd you call?" he asked.

"Call? No one, Beck. I've been around you all day."

He walked past her as though he hadn't heard a thing she said. When he returned, he had three cell phones. He powered each on and tapped at the screens. She assumed he was checking the call history on each. Not that it mattered, because if she had used them she surely would have deleted any records.

Beck set the phones on the table and pulled his pistol from his waistband. "You promise me you didn't call anyone and tell them our location?"

"For Christ's sake, Beck. I didn't tell anyone. Why would I?"

The door rattled. They both turned toward it. Clarissa waited for it to either burst open or for it to be shredded in a hail of gunfire.

"Wind," Beck said, rubbing the side of his head with his palm.

"Don't you think you're overreacting?"

He shook his head. "If anything, I'm under reacting. I ought to have you tied to a chair until I get this thing figured out."

She fought back the urge to run. "Do you think it's the dogs reacting to something foreign in their environment, or another set of dogs?"

He cut the lights, then walked past her to the door. A cool gust of wind hit her in the face as he cracked the door open. Beck leaned forward, his forehead resting on the jamb.

"Something's wrong. Go to the bedroom and get that MP7. But stay low."

"What is it?" she asked.

He took a deep breath, looked back at her. "It's nothing. And that's a problem."

She said nothing.

He continued, "Not a sound, not even crickets or cicadas. There's something out there."

"You see anything?"

"No." He took a deep breath, then added, "Look, it might just be a bear. But let's be safe about it. Okay?"

Leaning over, she darted toward the bedroom. Beck had closed the door. She stopped in front of it, knelt down and turned the knob. As the door groaned open, she heard the first bullets slam into the front window, spraying shards of glass across the room.

"You okay?" she shouted.

"Get the damn gun," Beck called back.

She glanced back. Unable to visibly verify Beck's state, she threw herself into the room. Rounds pelted the front of the house, slamming into the thick wood siding with a thud or shattering windows. Glass continued to rain down from above. Clarissa kept her body on the ground and used her arms to brush broken glass aside.

She had stashed the MP7 under the bed where she slept. If something would have happened while she slept, all she would have had to do was roll over and retrieve it. Though the room was small, it felt like a distance wider than the Grand Canyon separated her from the weapon. Her only objective was to reach it.

The assault tapered off. Whoever was out there would either approach and take over the house, or burn it to the ground. She strained to hear voices, but they faced either a single man, or a team who didn't need to communicate verbally.

As she reached for her weapon, the lights cut off. Clarissa stifled herself from calling out for Beck. With the windows shattered, saying anything could give her position away.

She rose to her knees and wrapped the MP7's strap around her neck and shoulder. Instinct told her to remain low. The men they faced were more than likely equipped with night vision. The only thing she had on her side was faint moonlight once her eyes adjusted to the dark.

"Find it?"

She spun, aiming the gun in front of her.

"Easy," Beck said.

"You can see me?"

"Don't move. I'll come to you." Glass clinked as he shuffled across the room toward her. He told her to hold out her hand. After she compiled, he placed something cold and heavy in her palm.

"What is it?"

"Night vision. Only a monocular, but it'll have to do."

She let the MP7 hang on its strap and fit the monocular over her left eye. Beck appeared in front of her in hazy green.

"You see anyone out there?" she asked.

"No. But I didn't try too hard either."

"So you're pinning your hopes on us winning a standoff in the bedroom?"

Beck pointed to his left. "The closet, actually."

Chapter 32

Clarissa hadn't noticed the trap door in the closet floor. As she lowered herself into the hole, she hoped that the men assaulting the house wouldn't either. Beck followed her down and moved past her toward the center of the structure. She followed him, only pausing to wipe thick strands of a spider's web from her face.

Beck stopped and pointed toward the back. "We're going to come out next to the shower. From there, I want you to stay low and run straight back. It's less than thirty feet to the trees. Get in there and wait for me."

She glanced up, wondering if the noise she heard had been one of their attackers walking through the house. She considered firing around through the floorboards, but decided against it, knowing it would give their position away.

Beck freed the crawlspace access and surveyed the area behind the house. He looked back at her, said, "It's clear."

"What are you going to do while I'm waiting back there?"

"Take care of our visitors."

"No, not alone."

"It has to be alone. Together, we're liabilities to each other."

She tried not to take it as a demeaning comment. Fact was, Clarissa didn't work well in a group or team setting. Her time with Sinclair had been spent as a solo operator, and she performed best that way. Still, she couldn't fathom the idea of Beck taking on whoever was out there alone.

"I don't care," she said. "We have to stick together."

Beck pulled her forward by her elbow. "There's no time to argue about this. Now go."

Clarissa emerged from the dark hole into the chilled night air. She expected to look up and see the magnificent country sky above the tree line. Instead, wispy gray clouds raced by. The crickets and cicadas were nowhere to be found, either. Their rhythmic bellowing had been replaced with a crackling sound. Clarissa became rooted to the ground, as, at that moment, she realized what was happening.

"Go," Beck said, emerging from the crawlspace.

"Fire," Clarissa whispered. "They're burning the house down."

She expected to see Beck's face grow more concerned than it already was. He surprised her by smiling.

"What?" she asked.

"They obviously think we're inside, because they are giving their positions up if they are anywhere near the house." He rose and looked left then right. He pointed past her. "You head that way. Shoot anyone you see."

She took off running toward the end of the house, glancing back once to determine Beck's actions. He had gone the other way, running just as she did. Cautiously, she approached the corner and whipped around it with the gun aimed in front of her and the monocular over her left eye. It was clear. The area beyond the house was lit up as though it were a mall parking lot. Staying in the shadows, she moved forward and away from the burning structure. The air was thick with smoke, but it did not hamper her vision.

She saw three men standing in front of the house. They held their weapons loosely, aiming at the building or ground in front of them. The blaze lit their faces up, making them look like kids in front of a Christmas tree the night before the big morning.

Clarissa figured that Beck had reached about the same point on the opposite side of the house. He wouldn't wait, and neither should she. Raising the MP7, she secured the butt to her shoulder and wrapped her left hand around the barrel. She verified the weapon was set to three-round burst shots. Firing three 9mm rounds almost simultaneously would increase her chances of inflicting a fatal wound on her first target. She sighted her target, the man closest to her and exhaled slowly.

Before Clarissa depressed the trigger, the man in her sights fell to the ground. She heard the crack of Beck's non-suppressed weapon at the same time. Without hesitating, she adjusted and aimed at the next man, who had crouched into a defensive position. Less than three seconds passed from the time her first target fell to the moment she squeezed the trigger and hit the next man in the shoulder, neck and head, nearly a straight line.

The third man fell a moment later.

Clarissa waited in the shadows, watching where the front lawn met the trees. Was there anyone waiting in the woods? Three seemed to be an odd number of assailants. She had expected up to four men, but in a grouping of one, two or four. Where had the fourth man gone?

Beck must have been thinking the same thing because she had yet to see him. She glanced back on the off chance that he had circled back around. They hadn't discussed tactics, and the things he'd been taught had likely been different than those she'd learned. His job entailed protecting a single target. Hers was all about destroying a single target. Perhaps, she thought, that would make them the perfect team.

After several seconds of no movement, she saw Beck step into the light of the fire. She began to notice the intensity of the blaze and moved further to the side, not yet ready to step into view.

Beck approached the group of men. He knelt down next to the first one and checked for a pulse. He slid over to the other men and did the same. Then he checked them, presumably for identification or communications equipment.

As she started to approach him, Clarissa caught something out of the corner of her eye from just beyond the tree line. She spun toward the movement and called out, "Beck!" In her peripheral vision, she saw Beck look up at her, then follow her gaze away from the house.

Her yell had startled whoever it was hiding in the woods. The man panned left and right with his rifle, stopping when he reached Beck a second time.

Beck dove to his left, taking up behind one of the men they had killed.

Clarissa let him go and focused on the fourth member of the kill team. She dropped to one knee, brought the MP7 up again and aimed. Before she could fire, the man did. She hesitated, waiting for Beck to scream out in pain. The fact that he didn't left her fearing the worst.

She brushed her concerns aside and squeezed the trigger. At least one round hit. The man behind the trees fell backward.

Emerging from the shadows, Clarissa glanced toward Beck. He was up on his feet and heading in the same direction as her. They stopped at the base of the lawn and stared down at the man gasping for air.

"Randy," Clarissa said.

"Who?" Beck said, not looking away from the dying man.

"He's a cleaner. Works for Sinclair."

Beck took a step to the side, using a thick oak for cover. He lowered his night vision goggles and scanned the woods. Clarissa did the same.

"How many does he normally work with?" Beck asked.

"He works alone."

Beck pointed at the pile of bodies in front of the blazing house. "That doesn't look like alone." He looked back at the man gasping for air. "We're running out of time here."

Trusting Beck to watch out for her, Clarissa stepped forward and knelt next to Randy. "What are you doing out here? Why'd you shoot up the house then set it on fire?"

The dying man's lips curled into a smile. The flames that danced behind Clarissa cast insidious shadows across Randy's face. It looked as though he tried to say something. She leaned forward to listen. All that she heard was his choking on his own blood.

"What'd he say?" Beck asked.

Shaking her head, Clarissa replied, "Nothing. He's dying. There's no incentive for him to tell us a thing."

Beck stepped out from behind the tree. He joined Clarissa by Randy's side.

"Answer her," Beck shouted, presumably convinced that there were no more agents in the area.

Randy said nothing.

Beck pressed the barrel of his gun into one of the bullet wounds on Randy's torso. A guttural scream erupted from the man.

Clarissa felt nothing for the man lying on the ground in front of her, but she reached out for Beck and attempted to pull his arm back. Beck jerked away from her, rose and walked toward the house. She got up and chased after him.

"He's not going to say anything, Beck. He knows he's dying. There's nothing in it for him."

Beck looked up, shook his head. "Four of them."

"Sinclair knows me, and I suppose he knows enough about you." She looked back. Randy's unmoving eyes and unheaving chest indicated he had expired. "How did they find us?"

"You got rid of your phone, right?"

"Stripped the SIM card and battery and disposed of it using three different trashcans."

"There's no way they could have traced this back to me."

Clarissa's stomach knotted. "The pin."

"What pin?"

"The one given to me to wear in the White House. Could they have tracked us here using that?"

Beck shook his head. "The technology isn't there. To communicate with satellites, that pin would need to be close to the size of a cell phone."

She grabbed her wrist, still sore from the possible dislocation she suffered when jumping rooftops. Her fingertip grazed the chip that had been inserted when she started working for Sinclair. "What about this?" she asked, offering him her hand.

He looked from her hand to her eyes. "This some sort of game? I'm not in the mood."

"They put a chip in me."

Again, he shook his head. "Same thing as with the pin. That's good for accessing an area of a building. In your case, I'm assuming Langley or some other CIA owned or sponsored facility. But tracking you through GPS? Impossible with today's technology."

They walked over to Randy's corpse. Beck searched the body and found nothing other than a cell phone. Clarissa reached for it.

"I'd like to make a call with that."

Handing it over, he nodded and said, "Not here, though. Not until we figure out how they tracked us."

She directed her gaze past the smoldering cabin, toward the barn that, fortunately, was set far enough back that the flames had not reached it. Then she realized how Sinclair had tracked the two of them.

Chapter 33

Clarissa pushed past Beck and headed toward the barn. The fire's intense heat caused her to widen her path past the house. She squinted against the blaze as she raced by.

Beck joined her in front of the barn door. Together, they tugged it open.

"What are you doing?" he asked.

"The Jeep. That's how they found us."

"I disabled the GPS. There's no way."

"Unless he had an anti-theft system installed."

Beck raised his arms and grabbed fistfuls of hair while cursing under his breath. A few seconds passed, then he lurched into action, popping the hood and practically climbing on top of the engine block.

Clarissa rounded the front of the vehicle in time to see him yanking wires and a device away from the Jeep.

The device dangled from Beck's left hand. "You were right. How could I not have considered that?"

Shrugging and shaking her head, Clarissa said, "I didn't either." She took a step forward, stopping in front of him. "But how did they know? Of all the vehicles stolen, how could they have known we took this one?"

Beck seemed to consider this. "They must have based it on our last known location. Something like that. We should have switched vehicles. Dammit, I was so stupid."

"That's a hell of a risk, don't you think? To come out here, guns blazing, setting fire to a house, all on guesswork?"

"Says a lot about your boss, doesn't it?"

She didn't know if he meant it as an insult to her, but Clarissa took it as such. She jerked back as though he'd slapped her across the face. "For all we know he's working with your people. For all I know, *you* might be working with him."

Now Beck looked like the one who'd been slapped. "Don't you ever insinuate that I did anything to violate the oath that I took to protect this nation's leaders. Do you know what I can do to you? What I can have done to you?" He lifted his weapon for a second, held it mid-air, then tucked it behind his back.

She shuffled on her feet, readying herself to turn and sprint through the opening. The woods were close. In the dark, he had no advantage over her.

The redness drained from his face. His eyebrows relaxed. "I'm sorry. I shouldn't have shouted or threatened you like that. I don't like not knowing what's going on."

She reached out and grabbed his arm. "I don't either."

"You were going to make a call?"

She looked down at the cell phone, then pointed at the anti-theft device. "That thing still active?"

He nodded.

She dialed Sinclair's private number. Only members of his team had access to it. It was the number Randy would use to report back to him. Sinclair answered midway through the second ring.

"Is it done?"

"Tell me why," Clarissa said.

There was a pause that lasted a few seconds, although to Clarissa, it felt like minutes.

"Where's Randy?"

"He can't come to the phone right now."

"Are you okay, Clarissa?"

She didn't respond.

"Did they extract you?"

"I extracted myself."

"Please tell me they got Beck. Clarissa, if he's still around, you need to get away from him."

She glanced at Beck, then turned away. "What are you talking about?"

"He's gone rogue. He is the one behind the shooting. I was trying to kill him at your apartment because we had intel that said he was going to do you."

"Yet here I am, still alive."

"Because he knew he had to change tactics after I missed."

"You didn't miss. You killed Amy."

"An unfortunate mistake, and for that, I apologize."

"What about her son?"

"What son?"

She paused, waiting to see if he would offer any more information. "Who else is involved in this?"

"So far all I know is Beck and Jordan."

"Have you gone to Banner or Polanski?"

Sinclair forced a laugh. It sounded like a dying man's gasp for air. "They're trying to pin this on you."

"So you think they're involved?"

"No. I just don't think they are willing to accept that their people had something to do with this."

The idea had some merit, though Clarissa wasn't sure she considered it plausible.

"Get to D.C.," Sinclair said.

"Can I even get around? Aren't I a suspect in this thing?"

He took a sharp breath, then said, "You're in the clear as far as the shooting goes, but there are some who will be on the lookout for you."

Beck had told her the opposite only hours before. At this point she was only slightly more inclined to believe Beck. She would have to exercise extra caution inside the city limits. Every cop in the city would be on the lookout for her. The fear that Beck was leading her to a cell passed through her.

"Okay," she said.

"Meet me tomorrow morning at the cafe at the corner of 14th and Clifton."

"Why there?"

"Did you have someplace else in mind?"

She said nothing.

Sinclair said, "I want to discuss this, then get you into hiding. So figure out a way to dump Beck and get there."

"Why don't I bring him?"

"Don't play games with me. We found you once. We can do it again." He ended the call.

She lowered the phone, an older flip model, and broke it in half. Then she removed the battery and SIM card. The crackling of the fire outside was the only sound. She turned around and saw Beck opening the door to the Land Rover.

"We should get going," he said.

"If they found the house, don't you think they know about the Land Rover?"

"We know they are aware of the Jeep. I think our best chance is this."

As he turned his back to her, she wrapped her right hand around the MP7's grip. She had no reason to believe Sinclair. But his words permeated her thoughts.

When Beck turned around, his gaze instantly became fixed on the weapon aimed in his direction.

"You're not involved in this, are you?"

He held his hands six inches from his side, palms facing down. "We went over this already, didn't we?"

"Answer the question."

"What's gotten into you?"

She squeezed the trigger and fired three rounds into the rear wall. "Dammit, Beck, answer the question."

He slammed the door shut and hurried toward her. She didn't give any ground. He stopped a foot away.

"The only thing I'm guilty of is helping you. And by doing so, I'm in this as deep as you are. If they decide that you're guilty, I'm going down with you. Got it?"

She studied his wavering eyes, looking for any sign of him being less than truthful.

"Don't you think if I had something to do with this I'd have already killed you, or at the very least, turned you in? Give me one reason why I would have brought you out here if not to help you?"

She lowered her weapon and let it go after the strap had taken over supporting its weight.

"I can't," she said. "I'm sorry, Beck. I had to ask. Sinclair said something, and I…"

He looked her over, then said, "Yeah, well, we all make mistakes." He turned away and hopped up into the driver's seat. "Get in if you want a ride back to D.C."

She joined him inside the Land Rover and settled in for the four-hour trip, hoping that he'd get over her accusations along the way. Beck was the only ally she had. Without him, she'd be dead or imprisoned by now. She didn't want him to think she didn't appreciate what he'd done for her. At the same time, he had to go through his own process of accepting what had happened so far. Eventually, she figured, he'd reach a point where he understood her reasoning behind questioning him.

A few hours into the ride, after she slipped into sleep, he tapped her arm. She opened her eyes. Evenly spaced reflectors placed on the road flew past, dimming to nothing as the vehicle drove past them. She pried her cheek and forehead off the cool window and looked over.

"I wanted you to know I've still got your back on this. We're going to get this figured out."

Her confidence in his words waned, but she smiled anyway. Up to this point he hadn't done anything to harm her. Either he was telling the truth now, or he planned to lead her into the wolf's den and abandon her.

Chapter 34

They arrived in D.C. minutes before rush hour kicked off. It wasn't even eight o'clock in the morning, yet the air felt thick and humid. The sun stared down at them as Beck headed east on N Street. The plan called for Beck to drop off Clarissa so that he could follow up on leads without putting her at risk of capture. People were after her, not him. At least, not that they knew of. Clarissa had the street smarts to stay out of trouble. She also had her own network she could reach out to for assistance.

Beck turned into the dark opening of a parking garage. After stopping to collect the time ticket, he drove until they reached the third level and parked in between two large SUVs. A knee-high jersey wall separated them from the outside. The view stretched down a side street, but Clarissa wasn't sure which. She hadn't been paying attention when he pulled into the structure.

She reached for her door handle. Beck told her to wait. He reached into his pocket and pulled out a cell phone.

"That's a clean phone," he said, handing it to her. "I'm the only one with the number. When I call you, I'll hang up after two rings, then call back exactly thirty seconds later. If you get in a bind, there's an easy way to turn on the GPS." He paused to show her. "With that, I can track you."

"Can I call out on it?"

Beck shook his head. "Get a disposable for that. I guarantee you that everyone you know is being monitored. You make a call, they'll have your location and someone to it in a matter of minutes. Got any cash?"

"It was with my clothes in the cabin."

He pulled out his wallet and handed her a wad of bills. "That should be enough to get you through the day. Remember, one call per phone. If you need to make another, get another disposable." He then handed her his pistol in exchange for the MP7. It was easier for her to conceal than the submachine gun. "Be extra careful out there. Every cop has the Service's picture of you."

She nodded and reached for the door.

"Clarissa?"

She looked back over her shoulder. "Yeah?"

"If you don't hear from me by sunset, assume the worst and disappear."

She hesitated, then smiled. "It's the longest day of the year. Sure you want me to wait till the sun goes down?"

Beck smiled. "Make it a judgment call."

She exited the vehicle without another word between them. The stale, warm air enveloped her. Walking away, she considered exercising her judgment call right then. Why not trash the phone and go? Beck could take care of himself, and so could she. He'd be better off without her around. He only had to account for his location the night before. She had no doubt that the man could come up with something on the spot. Presumably, he had a story ready to go.

Footsteps echoed off the concrete surrounding her. It seemed as though they came from the stairwell. Behind her, she heard a car approach and then turn down an aisle. Beck, she figured, leaving the garage. Though they'd be within a one- or two-mile radius of each other throughout the day, seated in the car was the closest they would be until the ordeal was over.

She stopped outside the stairwell and waited until the man in the grey suit passed. He paid little attention to her as he descended. A sheen of sweat coated his forehead. She wondered how he'd manage to make it back up later that afternoon, when the temperature and humidity were both north of ninety.

After several seconds she made her way down to the ground level. Foot-traffic along the sidewalk was moderate. Enough for her to blend in, but not so much she couldn't wind her way through if she had to take off running. The mix of people in the crowd was enough that her outfit of jeans, a t-shirt and a Nationals hat didn't cause her to stand out. She found two women dressed similarly and fell into line behind them.

Clarissa kept her head on a swivel for the next five minutes. The doubt she had in Beck lingered, and she wondered if the phone he'd given her had been a setup. Beck's pistol pressing against the small of her back provided some comfort. Upon inspection, the weapon was loaded. Why would he hand it over if he meant to stab her in the back?

Two blocks away from 14th street, she faced the decision she had to make. Meet with Sinclair now, or deal with him later. At least the meeting would be in a public place. She presumed so, not knowing for sure what was at that location. Either way, they'd be inside a cafe, or out on the street. There was only so much he could do. Even threats of violence would have little impact. He'd have to get close enough to sedate her.

She knew all too well that he was capable of doing so. Staying out of reach had to be her top priority. That could prove tricky in a restaurant. Of course, she could conceal the pistol under the table, reducing the chance that he would try something.

Was meeting him the right decision? What would she gain from it, assuming she made it out of there alone and alive?

Turning onto 14th street, she glanced to her left. She barely recognized the reflection of the woman wearing a ball cap staring back at her. The short, darkened hair that poked out from under the hat and the effect it had on her face was enough to throw her off. Could it buy her time with Sinclair and his men?

Instead of meeting with Sinclair, perhaps she could tail him for a while to see where he headed next.

She trudged on toward Clifton Street, resolving to make a decision before she reached her destination.

Chapter 35

The darkened windows of Federico's gave Clarissa little clue as to what was going on inside. The sign on the door said closed, but something told her that would not stop Sinclair from entering. The man had friends on both sides of the law, as well as those who hovered somewhere in the middle. Chances were that whoever owned the little Italian restaurant also delved into shadier businesses.

She remained across the street. There was nothing to obstruct her view other than the occasional passerby, which meant Sinclair, if he was inside the restaurant, had the same view of her. She could only hope that her short hair and the baseball cap were enough of a disguise.

The lights flickered on inside Federico's. She managed to catch a glimpse of the first row of tables inside the restaurant, but nothing beyond that. Knowing how Sinclair and other agents thought, he'd be in one of the rear corners, close to the kitchen door. That allowed him to see the entire floor and have a quick escape route available.

Clarissa placed her right hand behind her back, wrapping her hand around the pistol's grip. She steeled herself to cross the street and enter the building where Sinclair waited. She planned to take command of the situation and get the answers she needed to clear her name. However the dominos fell after that did not matter.

But she couldn't push herself forward.

What are you doing?

Sinclair wouldn't be alone. The men on his team all had several years more experience than her, and there would be at least three of them. The moment she stepped foot inside, they'd have control over her. She would not leave the building unless they allowed her to.

She willed the phone in her pocket to ring. It didn't. Looking to her left, she spotted a group of businesspeople walking toward her. She wouldn't fit in, but that didn't matter. Anyone watching her would be less likely to approach while she was surrounded by others. It didn't mean they wouldn't, or that they would stop tailing her. But it'd buy her time, and that was what she needed.

With the group a half-block away, the glare from a door opening across the street caught her eye. She diverted her gaze to Federico's and saw a dark-haired man she recognized staring back at her. He lifted his right arm and gestured her forward. She looked back at the group, now a hundred feet away. When she looked back at the man, he shook his head, patted his waistband, then pointed up. She didn't have to follow his gesture to understand that Sinclair had placed at least one man on a rooftop.

Clarissa stepped in front of the oncoming herd of Brooks Brothers-clad men. The sounds of their footsteps bounced off the building behind her. If they had only been thirty seconds ahead of schedule, she could have slipped into their group and disappeared.

That wasn't to be, though.

A car passed perilously close to the curb. She had to step back in order to avoid colliding with the side mirror. There was enough of a break in the traffic after that for her to cross the street at a decent pace.

The man waiting in the open doorway nodded, then jutted his chin toward the inside of the restaurant. She had to turn sideways to pass him. He brought his hand down and brushed it against her ass. Clarissa spun, ready to strike. The guy leaned back, laughing.

"How you doing, Hon?"

Turning away, she said nothing. Her gaze traveled from one corner of the restaurant to the other. The first rear-corner table was positioned next to the hallway that led to the restrooms. Sinclair was not there. She found him sitting on the opposite side, leaning against the wall in a corner booth next to the kitchen entrance.

"Did you check her?" Sinclair said, watching Clarissa approach.

"Oh yeah," the guy at the door said. "She's clean. Firm, too."

Clarissa ignored the man's comments, happy that he hadn't noticed the pistol at the small of her back. She couldn't believe that Sinclair would allow such a mistake to go unnoticed, so her plan was to position herself in front of the door to the kitchen, keeping her back away from the men. If any of them approached, she'd draw her weapon.

It was then that she realized aside from the man at the door, she hadn't noticed any others. The guy had pointed up, so she assumed that there was one on the roof, perhaps two. Why would Sinclair not have a team inside the restaurant? It made no sense.

Unless he truly meant to help her.

In which case, Beck had been the one lying.

Clarissa stopped in front of the table. A color-changing LED bulb that had been fixed inside a used wine bottle hung in front of her at eye level. The light changed Sinclair's hair color for blue to red to green and yellow.

"Sit," he said, gesturing to the empty booth across from him.

She hesitated. Taking a seat would place her back to the entrance. She'd have no idea what was going on outside. It would also make her vulnerable to the man behind her. He could come up and force himself into the booth next to her, wedging her against the wall. There'd be no way out.

"Sit," he said again with decidedly more force to his tone.

She turned and backed up, placing herself against the back of a booth on the other side of the entrance to the kitchen.

"How'd you know I was out there?" she asked.

Glancing at her wrist, Sinclair straightened and shifted in his seat. He gestured toward the empty seat once again.

Clarissa looked to her right. The other man had stopped halfway between the booth and the entrance. He had one hand wrapped around the opposite wrist. His other hand was empty. Sinclair hadn't produced a weapon either. She resisted the urge to check under each table in the establishment.

She said, "If you don't mind, I'll stand."

Sinclair drew in a deep breath, paused, exhaled. He nodded and said, "Suit yourself, Clarissa. But you should know I'm here to help you. I can only imagine how you've been poisoned against me."

"Maybe firing a sniper rifle at me had something to do with that."

He sucked in his bottom lip for a moment. "I apologize for doing that, but you have no idea what Amy and Beck were prepared to do to you that night."

"I left with Beck. Why am I still standing here if he planned to kill me?"

"I didn't say kill."

"His team had me dead to rights in some abandoned house turned into an interrogation room thirty miles from here. Why let me leave there alive?"

Sinclair leaned forward. His cheeks flushed and his nostrils flared. Despite the anger on his face, he kept his tone even. "They had to make it look legit, Clarissa."

"Who is they?"

"Beck and his partner."

"Dammit, Sinclair. Who is his partner?"

Sinclair said nothing. He reached under the table. Clarissa's right hand inched backward. He retrieved his bag off the floor. She felt a cold sweat form on her neck. She knew what he kept in the bag. Her gaze flicked to the man standing fifteen feet away from her. He showed no inclination of moving. When she looked back at Sinclair, he held a piece of paper in his hand.

"What's that?" she asked.

"Take a look," he said, placing the paper on the table and sliding it toward her.

Clarissa took a step forward and glanced down. A picture of Beck's face was positioned in the upper right hand corner of the paper. Next to it, printed in all-caps, was the word *WANTED*. She didn't need to read the rest to know the reason.

Sinclair reached into his bag again. Clarissa jumped back, checking to her right. The man still hand't moved. Sinclair glanced up at her, smiling.

"No need to worry. If I was going to do something, it'd already be done."

He pulled out another sheet of paper and placed it next to Beck's wanted poster. This time she didn't step forward. She didn't have to in order to recognize her own face.

"You said I wasn't wanted."

"I lied."

The gun in her waistband felt cold against her sweat-lined back. The reassurance it provided kept her pushing forward.

"Why?"

Sinclair clasped his hands together. "How else would I have gotten you here in order to help you?"

"You could have come to me."

"I tried. You killed my man."

She struggled to keep from smiling. There was no remorse over killing Randy.

"Men," she said.

"The rest meant nothing to me. He chose them. Probably criminals from around here or somewhere else. Although, if their bosses knew what they were up to, you might have other problems coming your way."

"I can handle those guys."

"Apparently."

She said nothing.

"You want to walk out that door?" He gestured toward the front of the restaurant. "Then go ahead. But don't ask me for help after you're caught." He paused, presumably waiting to see if she'd leave. "In a few minutes we can all leave together. I'm going to take you someplace safe, somewhere you've been before, until this is all over."

She couldn't tell by his stare or the look on his face if his intentions were nefarious.

His cell phone, which he'd placed on the table when he went for his bag, began to ring. He glanced down on it before answering.

"Yes, Julie," he said. "Right. Right." A long pause ensued. Clarissa could hear nothing of the other end of the conversation. "Well done. I'll let you know what comes of Clarissa if we find her. Everything I've heard tells me that she had nothing to do with this, though. I'm sure once you break him down, he'll confirm this."

Clarissa knew what would follow.

Sinclair placed his phone on the table, face down. He smiled for a moment. "They caught Beck. Actually, he went to them. They took him down before he managed to shoot anyone. They think he was going for Banner and Polanski. They fear he was aiming higher than that, which leaves major concerns because they still don't have his partner. They don't know the identity of his partner. As you could see, I'm doing everything I can to assure them it is not you. In the end, I know it'll be Jordan."

She was unable to hold back the tears. They slipped from the corner of her eyes and fell down her cheeks. The tracks left in the wake felt cold in the steady stream of air conditioning blowing from the vent overhead.

Sinclair said, "Don't feel bad, Clarissa. He fooled everyone, including me. I could have never guessed he'd be behind something like this. Granted, I don't know him that well, but Banner vouches for him, and that's enough for me. Was, I suppose."

This can't be happening. Why didn't he kill me when he had the chance?

"You're lucky you made it this far. I guess he knew that if he didn't return with you, that'd make him look guilty, since they knew he left with you."

She refused to wipe away the remnants of her tears. "They did know, didn't they? And so did you. How, Sinclair? How is it you knew we took that Jeep?"

He shrugged. "What Jeep?"

"We found the anti-theft tracking system that had been installed."

"Pity you didn't locate that sooner. You might still be at the cabin, and he'd still be your hero."

"I don't need any damn heroes in my life."

Sinclair flashed a smile and quickly stifled it. "Anyway, even if you did, it wouldn't be a vice president killing one." He slid toward her. "We should get going."

She resigned herself to leaving with Sinclair and seeing where things went.

Then the phone in her pocket buzzed twice.

Chapter 36

At once it felt as though her throat had closed and her lungs swelled up to twice their size. Her heart pounded against her chest. Her brain felt light, and her vision darkened around the edges.

Beck wasn't guilty and they did not have him in custody. How else could he call her?

And Sinclair had no idea she knew. Clarissa couldn't give any sign that she did.

Sinclair reached the end of the bench seat and placed one hand on the table and the other on the back of the booth. Rising, he told her he'd be back in a moment.

His cologne hovered in the air for several seconds after he passed. She didn't turn around to watch him. Instead, she kept an eye on the other man to see if he gave anything away. If there was someone else inside, he'd look in their direction.

His stare never wavered from her.

Her throat loosened. Air rushed in through her mouth, steadying her body. She counted the seconds, which seemed to stretch on for minutes.

"I'll let it ring twice," Beck had said, *"And then hang up and call back thirty seconds later."*

Her initial shock had clouded her judgment. How much longer until the next call was to come in? It didn't matter whether she reached a count of fifteen, twenty, or thirty. Anything in close proximity would be good enough.

A door behind her banged open.

The man in front of her looked toward the other corner of the restaurant.

She heard Sinclair's footsteps from the hallway leading to the restrooms.

The phone vibrated against her leg once again.

Slowly, she stuck her hand inside her pocket. She felt along the phone and pressed the first button she found. The vibrations stopped. Had she only managed to silence the phone? Or had she accomplished her goal and answered it, allowing Beck to hear everything that happened. He'd told her that he could find her with the phone. If he knew something was wrong, he'd come for her.

"We should be going," Sinclair said, still out of her view.

She pulled her hand out of her pocket, leaving the phone inside, and reached behind her back. A few seconds later she gripped the pistol.

She turned and saw Sinclair heading toward the front door. He stopped next to the other man, looked back at her.

"Going?"

She shook her head.

Sinclair smiled and forced a breath that sounded something like a laugh. "Now is not the time to mess around, Clarissa. We need to leave."

She brought her hand around and aimed the gun in his direction. His smile faded.

"What the hell do you think you're doing?"

"Veering from the plan."

His voice rose with anger. "This is not the time to go rogue on me, girl."

"On the floor."

He reached for his bag with his free hand.

Clarissa extended her arm. "I wouldn't do that."

He held her gaze for a few moments, presumably to gauge how serious she was about shooting him. His eyes relaxed, indicating he didn't deem her a threat. He took a step toward her.

"Stop." She locked in on him.

He kept moving toward her.

She adjusted her aim and fired, hitting the other man just below his right knee. The guy screamed as he fell to the floor. Sinclair halted and spun around. He looked back at Clarissa, eyes wide, and reached his free hand into his bag.

She fired again. The shot went wide, but it caused Sinclair to dive into an empty booth.

The man on the floor had stopped flopping around like a fish and had retrieved his weapon. He fired wildly. She felt plaster coat the back of her neck after his shot slammed into the wall.

Clarissa spun and lunged toward the kitchen door. Hoping it wasn't locked, she drove her shoulder into it and allowed her momentum to carry her into the kitchen. She angled her body so that she landed on her left side. The impact knocked the wind from her and she lost her grip on the pistol. It slid across the floor. A cook with a thick black mustache stopped it with the insole of his shoe.

Sinclair yelled something from the dining room. As the door flapped between open and shut, the sound of his voice rose and fell. She glanced back. He was out of view. She clawed her way up to her hands and knees. The cook leaned over and reached for the pistol.

"Don't," she said.

The guy's forehead crinkled into a dozen jagged lines as his eyebrows bunched up. He lifted his gaze toward hers. With his hands inches from the pistol's grip, he froze.

Clarissa dove forward, grabbing the gun and knocking the cook off his feet. The other cooks in the kitchen howled their disapproval. A scan of the kitchen with the pistol shut them up.

"How do I get out of here?" she asked, rising to her feet.

No one said anything.

She glanced toward the door that separated the kitchen from the dining room. Two feet blocked the light at the inch-wide gap between the door and floor. For whatever reason, Sinclair remained there. She thought of the man on the roof. Was he on his way down to seal off the rear entrance, trapping her?

Raising the pistol, she said, "How do I get out?"

A tall and wide black man standing in front of a boiling fryer pointed to the far end of the kitchen. She saw nothing but a wall there.

"Behind the wall," the guy said. "There's a door that leads to the alley. "If you go right, it dead ends. You gotta go left, then either way at the brick wall."

Before turning to leave, she said, "Can you guys block that door?" The man nodded. That was enough for her. She sprinted toward the rear of the room and saw the hallway leading around the back wall.

A splinter of light filtered in through the cracked rear door. She slowed down, studying the narrow opening for signs of someone waiting there. There were no shadows. The only thing she smelled on the draft coming through was trash, presumably from the dumpster next to the back landing.

Clarissa positioned herself in front of the door. She held her pistol with both hands, extending her arms straight out. She lifted her right leg and drove her foot forward, connecting with the door and whipping it outward. Metal clanked against metal. The door returned toward her, slowing to a crawl on rusted hinges. She stepped forward, nudged it open again. The area behind the restaurant was clear. At least at ground level. There could be a man lurking on the roof.

Recalling the cook's instructions, she ran to the left, staying close enough to the building that her shoulder scraped the rough brick. Glancing up, she spotted awnings and overhangs. They provided enough cover that the man on the roof would have to extend his body out and over to get a shot. Which meant she could return fire. His weapon likely provided more accuracy than hers. He'd be forced to take cover, though.

She approached what looked to be a dead end. On three sides, brick and concrete rose into the sky fifty feet or more. Twenty feet away, she saw alleys leading left and right. Left would bring her back to the street the restaurant was located on. She angled to the right and hit the alley's pavement at top speed. Small dumpsters and metal trashcans lined the narrow pathway. She dodged them and trash on the ground. Two sparring cats took off in different directions as she approached them.

Clarissa fought every urge to look back. The street was close. She had no idea what she'd do when she reached it.

Chapter 37

The black sedan that screeched to a halt in front of her looked like any of the other hundreds of government vehicles she'd seen in her lifetime. Facing the passenger side, she lifted her pistol as the driver's door swung open. Nearby, a woman screamed, resulting in dozens of stares zeroing in on her. How many had thought to aim their phones in her direction and snap pictures or record what happened next?

The car's windows were tinted black. Though the sun shined through the front windshield, she couldn't make out the outlines of anyone inside the car. Whether it contained only the driver, she didn't know.

Enough time had passed that it could be Sinclair inside the vehicle. But leaving his position and searching for her in a random spot seemed unlikely. Of course, she'd taken another of his men out and escaped. His thinking might've been anything but rational.

Time seemed to stand still as she waited for the driver to emerge from the car. A split second would be all the time she would have to make a decision. The odds were heavily in favor of her firing. She aimed the pistol over the roof of the car, in the area where the person's head would emerge from cover.

At once, the world sped up. She became aware of the people diving into stores and office buildings. Cars sped away or braked before coming too close. The busy area turned into the middle of nowhere.

A man yelled her name. His voice came from her right. She didn't have to turn to know that Sinclair had left the restaurant and tracked her down. He did it on foot, though, which left few options as to the identity of the car's driver.

The man on the other side of the car emerged and rose to face her. Her first instinct was to shoot. But she forced her finger away from the trigger.

"Get in," Beck said.

Thunder cracked from the other end of the street. The bullet slammed into a meter ten feet away from her. Glass shattered and sprayed through the air.

She looked toward the source of the sound. Sinclair lowered his weapon and ran toward her. Had he missed on purpose in order to gain her attention? His gait was off. It seemed as though he favored his right leg. There was no visible injury.

"Clarissa, get in now." Beck lowered himself and ducked inside the car.

She took one last look at Sinclair, who had halted and raised his arm in the air. She reached out and pulled the front door open. She paused at the sight of Jordan sitting in the passenger seat. He unlatched his seatbelt and turned away from her.

Another shot rang out. The passenger door's window exploded into thousands of tiny fragments. They reflected the sun's light as they fell to the road.

Jordan climbed between the front seats toward the rear of the vehicle. Clarissa didn't wait for him to make it all the way back. She lunged into the car, knocking into the man and sending his lower half into Beck. It seemed to have no effect on Beck, though. He shifted into drive and pulled away before Clarissa had a chance to close her door.

"Get down," Beck said.

Clarissa wasn't sure if his comments were directed at her, Jordan, or both of them. She leaned forward. A second later, a third shot was fired. Beck flinched forward. The bullet missed the car. Rising up, she had no idea where it had landed.

Beck jerked the wheel hard to the right at the first intersection they came to. With no seatbelt to restrain her, Clarissa lurched to the left into him. He remained unfazed as he held the wheel steady and forced the car around the corner.. Crowds gathered behind the safety of the buildings. Several people pointed at the careening vehicle. Beck straightened out the screaming tires and gunned the engine, blowing through a red light. Clarissa clamped her eyelids shut, flinching at the sound of a horn fast approaching her side of the car. The impact never came.

Halfway down the next block, she forced her eyes open. They continued on another mile, then Beck changed course, heading west, away from the city and toward I-495. When they reached River Road, he eased back in his seat. She followed his lead.

"What happened back there?" Beck asked.

Clarissa shook her head. "How did you know? How did you find me?"

He reached into his pocket and pulled out a cell phone. It matched the one he'd given her. "When you didn't answer my call I knew something was wrong. Like I said, I can track you through this."

His mentioning that reminded her of something that happened inside the restaurant. "He knew I was out there."

"Who? Sinclair?"

"Yes."

"Outside the building?"

"I was on the other side of the street. With the hat and short, dark hair, there's no way he could have spotted me from a hundred feet away through windows and foot traffic."

Beck shrugged. She couldn't tell by the look on his face if he was following her or not.

"Beck, he can track me. Like you with the cell phone, he has a way of tracking me."

"What?"

"The RFID chip. When I asked how he knew I was out there, he didn't answer, but his stare shot to my wrist. I know you said that the technology for GPS isn't there, but—"

Beck interrupted. "But RF technology could pinpoint your location to a couple miles." He stared into the rear view mirror for a few seconds too long. "Which means he might still have you on his radar."

She looked down at the raised lump of skin on her left wrist. Beck's hand blocked her view. He extended a pocket knife to her.

"Are you serious?" she asked.

He said nothing. Didn't need to. The look in his eyes was enough.

She took the knife from him. "Is it sterile?"

Jordan leaned forward and produced a lighter. "I'll sterilize it for you."

Clarissa looked back at him, then at Beck. He nodded. She retracted the blade and held it out for Jordan. An inch-long flame sprouted out of the lighter. Jordan waved it under the knife. The fire enveloped the steel blade, heating it to the point it glowed red.

Clarissa held the blade close to her skin. The heat it produced burned her without making contact.

"I can't stop, Clarissa," Beck said. "If you can't do it, then Jordan will have to."

She glanced back in time to see the guy in the backseat smile. For whatever reason, he'd take pleasure in giving her pain. There was no way she could accept that.

With a deep breath, she brought the blade to her skin and pulled back, slicing her wrist open a quarter-inch deep. She grimaced at the pain, and the muscles of her arm, chest, stomach and legs tightened. She made no sound, though. The RFID chip was visible. She placed the knife in her lap and grabbed hold of the chip with her right thumb and forefinger. With a tug, the device pulled free from the layers of skin and fat it had been embedded into.

"Throw it out," Beck said, using the arm controls to lower her window.

She clutched the tiny device. "This can get us into places, Beck. Places we wouldn't be able to reach otherwise."

"And they'll know we're coming. It's not worth it. Throw it out before they get too close."

She closed her eyes and reached her hand outside. The wind rushed against her closed fist, forcing it upward. She forced her arm further back, then released her grip. The chip blew away from her palm, and with every second that passed, they distanced themselves from being found by Sinclair.

Chapter 38

An hour later they exited I-70 near the I-81 junction in Hagerstown, Maryland. The location was close enough to D.C. that they could get back if necessary. It also placed them far enough away that they weren't likely to be spotted by a random cop. Depending on the situation, their faces could end up all over the evening news. If that happened, no place would be safe.

Beck pulled into the parking lot of a local motel chain. He went inside to get a room, leaving Clarissa alone with Jordan.

She shifted in her seat, placing her back against the door so she could keep an eye on the man. He sat opposite her, in the back seat. His gaze drifted to the pistol she held in her right hand. The wound on her other wrist had stopped bleeding about thirty minutes earlier. It probably needed stitches. By the time she would be in a position to get them, it'd be too late. It didn't matter, though. She could handle a scar.

Several times during their five minutes alone, Jordan acted as though he had something to say. He'd draw in a sharp breath of air, open his mouth, look at her, then glance away. Beck hadn't filled her in on his presence. When she took a moment and thought about it, she was still surprised that he was in the car. And as much as it seemed he wanted to tell her something, she had a desire to ask him why he was present.

The door to the motel's office opened. Beck stepped out, clutching a key card. He walked toward the car with his head on a swivel, scanning the parking lot and road beyond for any sign of a threat. He took the seat behind the wheel and drove them around the back of the long rectangular building.

Entering the room, he said, "We won't be here long. Just need an hour or so to discuss things, regroup, get cleaned up. It's been a long twelve hours."

Clarissa found herself nodding in agreement. Her brain and body were starting to catch up to the events of the past few days, and fatigue overtook her. Not only that, but the question of how many times she could cheat death entered her mind.

She found the bathroom and took a quick shower. The warm water running off her body did little to sequester the thoughts that ran through her mind and the replays of the events of the past few days. She cut the water and grabbed a towel. After drying off, Clarissa put on the same clothes she had worn since the evening before. It was all she had. After they were safe and their names were cleared, she'd make finding a change of clothes a priority.

Beck and Jordan were seated at the small table against the rear wall. The sliding door behind Beck was open. The breeze that blew in was warm and smelled of exhaust.

"Are you ready to tell me what's going on?" she asked, alternating her gaze between the two men.

Beck leaned back in his chair and wrapped his hands around the back of his head. The move eased Clarissa's tension. In doing so, he non-verbally told her that he intended to do her no harm, and neither did Jordan. If Beck felt threatened by Jordan, he would never expose himself in such a way.

"Jordan's the only one I encountered today," Beck said. "First, I went by your old apartment building. There were four spooks out there. They didn't notice me. Of course, I made it hard for them to do so. But it was clear why they were there. I'd guess there would be one or two around anywhere you might go, including any banks you have a relationship with. After that, I went by my building, being more cautious because they would be looking for me there. The guys they had positioned there were tougher to spot, and I only saw two. But that makes me think there were at least two more there."

"Who is behind this?"

"It's a good question, and one that I don't readily have an answer for. Jordan, however, has some information. I'll let him tell you his story and we'll go from there."

Anger flashed across Jordan's face, quickly rescinding. Clarissa got the first inkling that he wasn't there freely, and Beck had somehow brought him in against his will.

"When you said that he's the only one you encountered," she said, "what did you mean?"

Beck shifted his stare in Jordan's direction. "I figured out where he was hiding."

"You weren't supposed to be there for this," Jordan said. "When we planned it, his assistant would be gone, and the next would be starting the following week. Threw me for a loop that you were there at all when I found out a day ahead of time. Of course, McCormick didn't care. 'Just some'..." Jordan paused, glanced away. "'Bitch,' McCormick had said. 'She won't get in the way.'"

Clarissa said nothing and nodded for him to continue.

"The way these things go down, when there's an attempt, no one on the street can tell anything. We react so quickly, surround our guy. Even the shooter wouldn't know for sure if he hit or not."

The man paused to sip from a paper cup. Clarissa took a few steps forward and sat down on the edge of one of the twin beds, leaving the other between her and the men. She looked toward Beck, who focused on Jordan.

Jordan continued. "So, I was against this going down, but the day went as planned. Only thing was, you were there waiting for us outside of McCormick's office."

The conversation he'd had with her that morning took on new life. Perhaps he had meant what he said, about her being there for a certain reason. Or maybe she'd misread him, and he thought her purpose was for something else. Whatever he'd taken from it, he had no problem with her joining them.

"We took the tunnels, as planned," Jordan said. "Then he had his meeting. I kept my eye on you. I had my doubts from the beginning. You were somewhat unprecedented, but, because of Beck's involvement, I didn't put too much stock into thoughts that you were there because of what was going down."

"So that's why?" Clarissa said, directing her question to Beck. "No one would tell me what was going on, but you knew what Jordan was up to."

Beck said nothing. He held up a single finger and gestured toward Jordan, who picked up with his story.

"The call for lunch was part of the plan. That wasn't for your benefit, if that's what you're thinking. We did that in case anyone else was listening in. We didn't want anyone to think that we directed him out there for any reason other than to get in the car and go to lunch."

Clarissa said, "But the shooter knew he was out there. Wouldn't that be indictment enough?"

Jordan shook his head. "Crazy person gone crazier defense. As far as anyone would be concerned, so long as the shooter went uncaught, he or she was only in it to shoot the first person that looked important. Could have been McCormick. Could have been the French Ambassador. Didn't matter. Get it?"

"I suppose."

"So the…" He paused and looked at Beck. "So, the person we had up there, ace sniper. Could make the shot from max distance. The plan was to use a low-caliber round, put it through the shoulder."

"McCormick was okay with this?" she asked.

Jordan nodded. "His idea. Hell, he picked the shooter."

"What the hell was the reasoning behind all this?"

"The election."

"Presidential?"

"Yeah."

"That's a couple years away."

"Groundwork starts now. And the president, in his second term, had already made it clear to McCormick that he was not going to throw any weight behind the vice president. He would push for an outside candidate for the party's nomination."

Clarissa shook her head. "If I've got this right, McCormick arranged for his own assassination attempt because he wasn't getting the nomination?"

"Not exactly," Beck said. "It seems that McCormick was under the delusion that surviving an attempt would raise his sympathy levels with the public, making it impossible for the president to not support his bid for nomination."

"And if he didn't," Clarissa said, "he'd ruin his Party's chances of winning the election. I just saw something about his approval rating dipping. Failing to rid the hot hand would be political suicide then."

Beck nodded.

Jordan said, "Pretty much. But then it didn't go down as planned."

Clarissa had seen the damage up close. Sure, she'd been tackled and perhaps that had clouded her memory, but the hit McCormick had taken had been far worse than what Jordan explained should've happened. And that was what bugged her about his version of the events.

"The shot wasn't as we planned. The bullet that hit McCormick was meant to be fatal," Jordan said.

"Your guy turned on you?" she asked.

"He'd never do that."

"Then what happened? Why'd he try to kill McCormick?"

"It wasn't our guy that fired the shot. He was in the morgue when this all went down."

Chapter 39

The sunlight hit Clarissa directly in the face as she rose off the edge of the bed. It felt as though the wind picked up. A warm burst blew through the room. Pages of a notepad on the dresser rose and fell.

She looked at Beck. He was staring back at her, perhaps to gauge her reaction to Jordan's story. She didn't have one other than surprise. She thought she knew where it was all leading, and that they'd only have to find the rogue shooter in order to clear their names. With Jordan knowing the identity of the assassin, that wouldn't be hard to do.

But this? If Jordan's guy was already dead, who was behind it?

"So it's safe to assume that you didn't know your shooter was dead and in the morgue at the time?"

"I had confirmation from him when we were in the hall," Jordan said. "Remember when I walked away? That was why."

"It takes more than ten minutes to end up in the morgue. You had to have had some kind of encryption set up with this guy, right?"

Jordan nodded. "I did. He and I were the only ones who knew it. Which means that—"

"Someone tortured it out of him," Clarissa said. "What do we know of the condition of his corpse?"

"Nothing. No one has been allowed to see it."

Beck said, "So, basically, what we are looking at is that someone outside of Jordan's circle knew about the plan and decided to call an audible. We're talking about someone capable of taking a trained sniper, someone with Spec Ops training, torture them into giving up dates and locations and pass codes, then getting someone into a Federal building, pulling off the shot, then escaping or blending in."

Clarissa sat down on the corner of the bed, across from Beck. "Sinclair."

"Seems the most obvious choice in terms of taking over and completing the job. He hunted us down. Found you again."

"But why not put an end to it back in D.C.?"

Beck shook his head. "I didn't have control over the situation. Plus, my only backup at the time was him." He gestured toward Jordan. "Think I trust him with my life at this point?"

Clarissa knew he didn't, and neither did she. She remained focused on Beck, attempting to read his body language. He gave away nothing. His posture, hand placement, facial expressions, nothing told her if he was with or against her. She couldn't shake the feeling that he was somehow involved, though. Why did it continue to creep up on her? Everything he'd done up this point had been to help her. Why waste all that time and energy to turn on her in the end?

"How would Sinclair have known?" she asked.

Beck looked toward Jordan, who shrugged.

"I don't know the guy," Jordan said. "No one on my team knows him. Is there a chance he got to one of them? Perhaps. But none of them were in on this. He must have found out some other way. Every conversation I had with McCormick was in private and out of range of any listening device. I'd assume he took the same precautions with the other guy, but, in the end, I can't be sure."

"Beck, I have to ask, what were you told about my presence at that meeting?"

Beck shifted in his seat, then, looking at his watch, rose. "I think we've been here long enough. It's best we move. We can continue the conversation in the car."

They headed toward the front door. Clarissa led the way. She heard a thump, followed by a body falling to the floor. She spun around with her pistol drawn. Beck stood over Jordan's limp body, a blackjack dangling from his right hand.

"I think we got everything out of him." Beck leaned over and took Jordan's SIG, then tucked it in his waistband. He hooked his arms under Jordan's and dragged him over to the table where he set the man down on the floor again. The base of the table was thick, with four wide feet, all mounted to the floor. Beck pulled Jordan's arms around the base and handcuffed the man.

"You're gonna leave him here?"

"We can't bring him with us, and I want him where I can find him. I'll have someone out here soon to watch over him."

They left the room and hurried to the car. Beck backed out of the parking spot and found the exit.

"Where are we going?" Clarissa asked.

"Back to D.C."

"Are you crazy?"

"Remember what you asked me back there? If I knew why you were at that meeting?"

She nodded while watching the cars behind them in the side mirror.

"I wasn't told much at all. One of them knew what was going on, though, and they duped us all."

"You mean Banner or Polanski?"

Beck nodded. "That's why they called Sinclair." The car rolled to a stop at a red light. Beck looked over at her. "Clarissa, did you do anything to upset him?"

"Upset him? No. Not that I'm aware of."

"What were you doing before you came back to the States for this assignment?"

"I was in London. Living in a fortress of a house that belonged to a terrorist group."

"Did you do anything to benefit them?"

The question offended her. "I did my job."

Beck seemed to sense her objection to being questioned. "I'm only trying to figure out why he'd turn on you like this."

She nodded involuntarily. "So am I."

The light turned green, and Beck took his foot off the brake and accelerated quickly. He directed the car to the highway on-ramp and merged in with the other vehicles. They remained silent for a few minutes. Clarissa rolled down her window and let the warm air circle through the car.

"Why me?" she asked.

"They needed a fall guy," he said. "It's the reason your name was floated as a possible suspect at first. When Jordan went to ground it looked bad for him, and your name got lost in the shuffle. I'm sure it'll float back up if the heat gets too high."

"I was never there to uncover any information, was I?"

Beck shook his head. "Now we've got to figure out which of them set this up."

That wouldn't be easy. Both would say the same thing. Neither Banner nor Polanski would admit to proposing the meeting. Only one would be telling the truth. Their hope would be a trail of some kind. A quick email or voicemail. It might come across as innocuous, but when looked at through the eyes of intent, the meaning would be obvious.

"You're good at judging people, right?" Beck asked.

"That's debatable."

"It was part of your job, though. So, tell me, what's your read on them? Did either stand out?"

She thought back to the initial meeting and the time afterward. She only spent a little time with Banner. He seemed hurried, bothered almost, by having to take part. That alone presented evidence that he wanted to be as far away from the situation as possible. She relayed her thoughts to Beck.

"What about Polanski?" he asked.

"She's a different animal. There was a ton of resentment toward everything about the Service. She showed nothing that indicated she liked me, or even wanted me there. But more than that, she seemed to hold a big grudge for being passed over for higher-level positions."

"I've heard her gripe before. Most recently after I was promoted. It wasn't even something she would have done, but seeing me get moved up had a negative effect on her."

"What would she have to gain?"

"By having McCormick killed?" he asked.

She nodded.

"That's what doesn't make sense. It isn't like that cleared a path for her to move up. Even if someone was fired as a result, it wouldn't have opened a position she would be in line for."

"Was McCormick ever involved in any of those hiring decisions?"

Beck squinted as he thought it over. "Not that I can recall. He really hadn't been involved in much at all. The president was considered a strong candidate six years ago, so the Party didn't see a need to nominate an equally strong or stronger vice president candidate. They went with a younger guy. One they could groom to take over eight years later. McCormick hadn't even been in politics that long. Thinking about it, it must've been a whirlwind for him."

"That rules out revenge against him, then."

"Assuming it was Polanski," Beck added.

"No revenge. No hope of getting a promotion. No sure connection between her and Sinclair as far as I know."

Beck nodded, said nothing.

"So where's that leave us?"

"Confused." He tapped on the steering wheel for a few moments. "Unless her goal was to get Banner fired."

Chapter 40

They arrived in Arlington, Virginia a few hours later, after stopping in Frederick, Maryland to ditch the car in a free parking garage and pick up a rental. While in Frederick, they also purchased new cell phones, with the purpose of using them one time and discarding them.

At four in the afternoon, the sun remained high and bright. The heat wave continued to drag on, making it feel like August in June. The rental's air conditioning fought to keep up. It spat lukewarm air at them. For a while it made more sense to leave the windows down.

They drove by Julie Polanski's cookie-cutter house in a subdivision off Washington Blvd. There were no security signs in the windows or planted in the flowerbed. The six-foot privacy fence would do little to keep them out.

The neighborhood screamed middle class. Despite the later hour, there were few cars in driveways. That didn't mean people weren't home, though. Clarissa and Beck had to make a decision.

"We can go in now and wait for her," he said. "That'll give us time to try and break into her computer and check her files, physical and digital. It's that, or we wait until nighttime."

"We'll have better cover then."

"Yeah, but it'll be after nine p.m. By then it's dark out."

She recalled the solstice again.

"I say we go now," he said. "Park on the street behind this one and make our move."

"Okay."

Beck turned right at the next street. There were no houses facing them, only the sides of four large homes. Even better, there was a narrow alley that ran behind the two rows of houses. The car wouldn't fit, but it was more than large enough for them to run down.

He slowed the car down to get a better look as they passed. "Utility right-of-way."

They turned left at the next street and parked two blocks further in front of an empty lot. Beck looked around, then nodded for Clarissa to exit.

She stepped out of the car and met Beck at the rear bumper. He took her hand and started walking.

"We need to make it look like we're a couple out on a walk."

Her nerves got the better of her. A thin layer of sweat formed on her palm. She wanted to pull her hand away. When she tried, he squeezed harder.

They turned on the side street, and again at the narrow utility right-of-way alley. She counted the houses until they reached Polanski's.

"This one," she said.

Beck nodded. He tugged on the gate. It didn't open. Peering through the crack between the fence and gate, he said, "It's got a heavy-duty lock. "We'll have to go over." He turned toward her. "Be quick about it."

She reached up with both hands, grabbed the top of the fence and pulled herself up and over, vaulting a few feet away and landing on her feet. She crouched and surveyed the yard. Her right hand went behind her back and rested next to her pistol. No need to draw it here and alarm anyone who might have seen her jump over the fence.

"Clear?" Beck asked from the alley.

"Clear," she said.

A moment later his head appeared over the top of the fence. He tried to remain low while swinging his right, then left leg over. He dropped to the ground and joined her.

"Watch the neighbors' windows," he said.

"I am." And she had been. There'd been no sign of movement since she first looked up.

Another minute passed. "Let's check for an alarm and then get inside."

They ran to the power meter and found the connection for phone and internet. There was nothing to indicate an alarm system was present. Beck cut the feeds running inside anyway.

From there, they found an unlocked side door that led to the garage. The room was mostly empty, ten degrees hotter than outside, and smelled like paint thinner. They walked straight to the door leading into the house. Beck reached for the knob. It was locked. They both found it odd that Polanski would leave the exterior door unlocked, but not the interior.

"Stand back," Beck said, holding both arms out and backing up. He took a stutter step forward, then drove his right foot into the door near the knob. It cracked and bowed, but didn't open. Again he backed up and repeated the process. This time, when the sole of his shoe connected with the door, it snapped and popped open, whipping hard to the right on its hinges.

Clarissa moved to the left to cover the opening while Beck regained his balance. He entered the home first. A long, narrow hallway led from the garage to the kitchen area. The vent in the ceiling piped frigid air down. She wasn't sure if it felt so cold because she had been outside in the heat so long, or if Polanski was part penguin. She caught a glimpse of the thermostat, noting it was set on fifty-eight degrees.

Apparently, Beck had seen it too. "Always thought she had ice running through her veins."

Clarissa ignored his comment. A more pressing thought had come to mind. "Beck, does Julie have kids?"

He stopped, turned his head to the left and glanced back at her. "Don't think so. I've never seen a picture of one on her desk or anything like that. She's never brought a family to any of the functions we've held."

His comment became relevant.

She said, "You just said she's cold as ice or whatever. Maybe she likes to keep her office informal."

"Yes, perhaps. Keep an eye out for photos, kids' clothes and shoes, stuff like that."

They were in the kitchen. Clarissa glanced at the microwave. The digital clock readout reminded her that school was out.

"If she does, they'll be here soon, if not already."

"Don't worry," Beck said. "It's not like they're going to pop out with guns and knives and try to take us on."

"Okay. But they might've called the cops already."

"Bikes."

"What?"

"Did you see any bikes in the garage?"

"No. What difference does that make?"

"Who would have kids and no bikes?"

Clarissa shrugged. "My best friend growing up didn't learn to ride a bike until we were in high school."

"Okay, whatever then. We'll be careful. Fair?"

They continued through the house. The downstairs consisted of four large rooms with stairs running through the middle. The dining room was formal and looked unused, as did the living room. They completed the square in the family room. There was a single couch, coffee table and television. Clarissa didn't see any family photos or other effects to suggest that Polanski had a family.

From the family room they went back through the kitchen and dining room, then upstairs, checking the lock on the front door first.

Though the house looked like it had been built within the past ten years, the stairs could have been ripped out of a two hundred year old home. They creaked and popped with every step either of them took. If they had come at night, that would have been a dead giveaway. They wouldn't have gotten near the woman before she armed herself and dialed nine-one-one.

Upstairs they found four bedrooms. Only two of the rooms had beds. One of those looked like it had been untouched for several months. Polanski's room was neat and organized. The bed made. The furniture bare and dusted.

Clarissa searched through the drawers looking for anything out of place, but found nothing. Next, she investigated the closet, pushing aside clothes on hangers to investigate the wall. There was a chance the woman had a safe. If she had damning evidence, that would be where they would find it.

But Clarissa found no evidence of a safe installed in the closet. It didn't have to be there, though. The house was at least three thousand square feet. Lots of places to place things never meant to be found.

She left the room and found Beck sitting behind a computer in a bedroom being utilized as an office. Without looking at her, he nodded as Clarissa entered the room.

"Find anything?" she asked.

"Nothing. Computer was unlocked. Julie's not a dumb woman. If she had something on here, she'd require a password at minimum as first line of defense. They've got people that can crack or bypass that easy enough. From that point, the files would be encrypted."

She nodded, having been brought up to speed on these things during her indoctrination into Sinclair's group. And being on the move, Clarissa always carried and used an IronKey USB drive.

"Do you think she'd keep it on the computer?" Clarissa asked.

Beck removed his hands from the keyboard and looked at her. "Something portable?"

"Makes sense. It's what I do."

Smiling, he said, "I've been out of investigation too long. Things have changed a lot in the last half-decade."

"So what now?"

"We wait."

Chapter 41

Clarissa stared out at the street through the spaces between the white plantation blinds. Little kids on bikes raced up and down the street. People on their way home cautiously passed them doing ten to fifteen miles per hour. A few ditched their work gear and returned outside with their dogs or in their running shoes. Why anyone would exercise outside on a day like this without being forced to, was beyond Clarissa.

She spotted Julie Polanski's car a half-block away. Unlike the others, Julie gave the playing children little consideration. She honked her horn. Through the sun's reflection on the windshield, Clarissa saw the woman gesturing wildly at the kids.

"She looks like she's under major stress," Clarissa said.

"The vice president was shot. That stresses everyone in our department out."

"But aren't you picked because you can handle it?"

He shrugged. "Things change, I suppose." He paused a beat, then added, "Let's head downstairs. Go for her after she enters."

They waited until the car pulled into the driveway, then exited the room and went downstairs. Beck positioned himself next to the front door. It would shield him from Polanski's view as she opened it.

Clarissa waited in the formal living room, using the wall to hide her presence. She remained close to the wide opening. As soon as the door shut, she'd whip around the partition and force Polanski to the ground.

She heard the sound of a key being inserted into the lock and the latch sliding open. The door cracked as it moved the first inch. That, combined with the rickety stairs, led Clarissa to believe the house had settled considerably since being built. The door whooshed as it opened. She pictured Beck's position and wondered how close the door would come to hitting him. Would Polanski notice if it did? It didn't come to that. A moment later, the door hit the jamb and then clicked shut. Polanski's heels cracked against the tiled entryway.

Clarissa took a deep breath, held it. She performed a quick scan of the area in front of her for the tenth time, ensuring there were no mirrors or other reflective surfaces that would give her position away. Secure in the feeling that her presence had gone unnoticed, she burst forward and around the wall.

Julie froze, dropping the mail in her hands. A magazine and three envelopes fell to the floor.

"Hands up," Clarissa said.

Julie's mouth worked to form words. She managed to create a few sounds, but nothing coherent.

"Hands up," Clarissa repeated, then added, "And down on your knees."

Julie's eyes widened. Her cheeks reddened. Her hands and fingers, limp a moment ago, tightened and bent into claws. "What the hell are you doing in my house?"

Clarissa diverted her stare away from the woman for a moment to get a read on Beck. He stood in front of the door, blocking both the door and the stairs as escape routes.

In the few seconds Clarissa wasn't looking, Julie sprung forward. Twenty years Clarissa's senior, the woman moved as though they were the same age. Had she thought about it, Clarissa might not have moved in time. But instinct took over.

With the woman charging like a wild animal, Clarissa leaned back to her right, turning at the waist to bring her left shoulder back. Both arms, connected at the pistol's grip, went into the air. Polanski didn't adjust fast enough. The woman's left shoulder caught Clarissa in the side, but the impact was not enough to take her down. Off balance, Polanski stumbled. Clarissa brought her elbows down, driving both into Polanski's back.

The older woman grunted and crashed to the floor. Beck raced up and pulled both her arms behind her back.

"Cuffs?" he said to Clarissa. It seemed something he should have considered earlier.

"No," she said. "I can look for some zip ties or something."

Polanski rolled her head to the side. Her face was red. Her gazed was fixed on Clarissa. "Don't bother. I'm not going to fight you. I know why you're here."

Beck let go of the woman's wrists. He rose and moved back toward the door. Clarissa took that as a sign to move back, so she did, stepping over the woman and blocking the hallway to the family room.

Julie pushed herself off the floor and used the wall to get to her feet. Her clothes and hair were disheveled, and her makeup smeared. One second she looked pissed, and the next defeated.

"What led you to me?" Polanski asked, looking over her shoulder at Beck.

"Logic," he said.

"Then your logic is shit."

"Perhaps, but my chances are fifty-fifty."

Julie forced a puff of air through closed lips.

"Am I wrong?" Beck asked.

"Depends on what you're accusing me of," Polanski said.

"We just want some answers to some questions."

"What if I can't answer them?"

"Then I'll assume you're withholding information from me. And that won't be good." He took a step forward. "Would it?"

Polanski said nothing. Her expression never changed, and she made no gestures that gave her away.

"Why don't you start by telling us about your relationship with Sinclair?" Beck said.

"We've used him in the past for some of our larger financial crimes. At times we needed more of a, I suppose you could say, criminal element in the investigation. He was good at providing that."

"Did this ever occur when I was in the unit?" Beck asked.

Julie Polanski shrugged and offered no answer. Clarissa caught a glimpse of an eyelid twitch and presumed that the answer was yes.

"What personal contact did you have with Sinclair?"

Julie turned and leaned back against the stair railing. She looked up at the ceiling. "Not too much. We always kept contact minimal. A meeting would be arranged in Richmond or Charlottesville in Virginia, or Martinsburg in West Virginia. The meetings were brief, usually in a coffee house. We'd use a magazine to exchange information in the old days. Secure USB drives with data self-destruct mechanisms the past five years."

"So you met with him?" Clarissa asked.

"A few times," Julie said.

"What kind of relationship did you have with him?" Beck asked.

She took a moment to respond. "Minimal."

Clarissa thought the delay indicated there was more to it than that. But searching Polanski's face for any micro-expressions revealed nothing.

"Amy was shot," Beck said, altering the direction of the interrogation.

For the first time, Polanski cracked. A layer of mist coated her eyes and her lips trembled. She took a deep breath, exhaled, and said, "I heard."

"She came over, upset. Her son was missing."

The hardened look returned to Polanski's face. "We received intelligence that indicated Amy was involved in the attempt on McCormick. Her son was taken into custody and is being held now. It's for his protection. Whoever took out Amy might go after him if they think it can benefit them."

Clarissa said, "We—"

Beck interrupted, "Where is the boy?"

"You're as much a suspect in all this as I am," Polanski said. "You think I'm going to reveal his location to you?"

"You know neither of us had anything to do with this. I didn't even know why we were having that meeting when you brought Clarissa on board. I was told who she was, who she worked for, and where to pick her up. That was it."

Clarissa recalled their meeting at the airport. "You said you knew Sinclair."

"Did I?" he said. "Or did you interpret that I did. I only did what Banner told me to do."

Her suspicion of Beck rose again, despite how she tried to divert it away. She wanted to believe in the guy. They'd been through a lot together. It still made no sense that he'd bring her along this far. Unless he planned to turn on her as a last resort. She backed off and allowed him to complete the questioning.

"Can't trust any of us, can you, Clarissa?" Julie smiled for the first time. "You'd think the people tasked with protecting leaders and solving major financial crimes would have more integrity than this."

"Screw you, Julie," Beck said.

"It's not me, Beck," she said. "And you've wasted a lot of time by coming here. He already knows about the incident Clarissa had with Sinclair today. And he's making preparations to move on all of us."

Beck turned toward the door. Grabbing the knob, he looked back at Clarissa and Polanski. "Banner."

Julie Polanski nodded.

Chapter 42

It seemed hotter outside than before they entered Polanski's house. Clarissa didn't think that was possible. Perhaps the humidity had risen to one hundred percent. Whatever the cause, she was relieved when they reached the car. The air conditioning kicked on immediately. The cold air was a shock to her lungs as she forced it in and out in shallow, quick breaths.

Beck navigated the residential street, keeping his speed in check. There were kids all around. Clarissa wondered why so many were outside on such a long hot day when they surely had computers and gaming systems in their climate controlled homes. Maybe a pact had been formed among the neighborhood parents.

Her thoughts turned to the information Polanski had given them. Without giving Banner up, she had told them he was responsible. But how did she know about the meeting with Sinclair earlier that day? Had Jordan managed to get free and contact her? Had Sinclair contacted her? Clarissa supposed it was possible that Sinclair was operating under the assumption that no one suspected him.

They exited the neighborhood and headed toward the sun, which was lumbering in the western sky.

"You think it's a good idea to leave her?"

"She's not going anywhere. And if she tries, I'll know."

"How?"

Beck didn't respond.

Traffic on the opposite side of the road backed up as far as she could see. The vehicles moved at a snail's pace compared to the fifty miles per hour Beck had the rental cruising.

"What if she makes a call?"

"Then she does. It doesn't matter. I'd bet anything that Banner already knows. He knew where we were last night. He knew what happened earlier today. He knew you escaped with me. He's probably got multiple teams out now looking for us and Jordan. I wouldn't doubt that, if Julie calls him, he'll send someone over to take care of her."

"You mean kill her."

Beck nodded.

"We should have brought her with us."

"If something happens, she'll have brought it upon herself. She knows that."

She said nothing, but he must have noticed the shocked look on her face.

"Listen, Clarissa. Don't think she didn't know something about this. Whether she was involved, I can't say. But at this point, she's aware something's not right, and she hasn't done anything about it. For her sake, I hope she sits and sulks all night and comes clean in the morning. Any attempt to jeopardize what we're doing is only going to result in her demise."

Clarissa leaned back in her seat and turned her head toward the window. Her unfocused eyes watched everything pass by in a blur. Much like the past few days had. She found herself wishing she was still back in London, living among the terrorist cell she was gathering intel on. At least she could grasp that enemy and their intentions.

"Where are we going?"

"Banner's house."

"You think that's safe?"

"Depends on whether he's expecting us."

"You think he will be?"

"Yes."

In rush hour traffic, the drive to Banner's home near Fort Belvoir, Virginia took close to an hour. The sun still shone from high in the sky, three hours until it would be extinguished amid a smattering of red, orange and purple.

She knew they had arrived when Beck turned into an older residential neighborhood. The homes were a mix of ranch and colonial style, with all-brick exteriors. The lots were large and wooded. Every home had an ornate door. Every back lawn was enclosed by a chain link or wooden privacy fence.

Beck pulled to the curb. He placed the transmission in park and left the car idling.

"What's the plan?" Clarissa asked.

"His house is at the end of the road. We'll go over a slight hill, giving us a view of what's waiting down there."

Clarissa glanced around, using the mirrors to see behind the rental car. "We can't trust what we see, though. If he knows we're coming, there'll be cops, or FBI, or agents waiting. They'll be hidden."

Beck nodded slowly. He removed his hands from the steering wheel and placed them in his lap. The pistol he'd taken from Jordan bulged at his hip.

"Banner is a family man," he said. "If he's aware of us coming, then most likely he would have taken his wife and kids and left to get them someplace safe. In which case, we'll be dealing with him tomorrow somehow."

"But he'd still get someone to the house."

Beck grabbed the gearshift and placed it in drive. The car rolled away from the curb, up a slight hill. Clarissa saw the entire street from the top. Beck pointed out Banner's house. A white Lexus and black Infiniti were parked side-by-side in the driveway. The trunk of the Infiniti stood open.

Clarissa scanned the road and remaining driveways looking for signs of government or police vehicles. Nothing stood out. The street seemed like any other. There were a few kids out playing. A couple hand-in-hand, walking a dog. A woman jogging toward them.

The front door to Banner's residence whipped open. An older blond-haired woman stepped out. She was thin and dressed in slacks and a short-sleeved blouse. She walked quickly to the Infiniti and reached inside the trunk. When she returned upright, she held a brown paper grocery bag with each arm. She left the trunk open and went back inside the house. The storm door shut, but the red front door remained open.

"He doesn't know anything," Clarissa said.

Beck nodded his head. "He wouldn't risk Audrey's life." Beck took his foot off the brake and let the car roll down the hill. "That woman is our best hope, Clarissa. If we threaten her in front of Banner, he'll crack. Trust me."

She didn't like the idea, but saw where he was coming from. Many people were able to withstand personal torture, but watching a loved one suffer was where they drew the line.

He pulled up to the curb a few houses away and cut the ignition.

Audrey emerged from the house, oblivious to their presence. She went to the back of her vehicle and reached inside.

Beck and Clarissa exited the rental car. They moved on foot toward Banner's house.

Audrey pulled the first bag out and set it on the ground. She leaned back in and grabbed a second bag, which she placed next to the first. Clarissa expected the woman to close the trunk. Instead Audrey reached back in and pulled out a large box. She set this down, rose and closed the trunk.

Clarissa and Beck reached the driveway. Audrey turned around, stopping in place when she saw Beck. Confusion spread across her face.

"Why don't you let me help you with that, Audrey," he said.

"What are you doing here, Beck?" she said. "And who is this?"

By the time Audrey shifted her gaze back to Beck, he'd drawn Jordan's pistol and aimed it at the woman. Her mouth dropped open.

"Grab the bags, then turn and slowly walk toward the front door. We'll get the box."

Audrey nodded and did as instructed.

Clarissa moved forward and picked up the box. Despite its size, it felt light. She resisted the urge to shake it to see what it contained.

Beck moved ahead of Clarissa in order to control Audrey's movements. They entered the house together. A gust of wind washed Clarissa with hot air moments before she crossed the threshold into Banner's home.

Clarissa recognized Banner's voice coming from another room. "Did you get that package for me?"

Beck wrapped his hand around Audrey's mouth so she couldn't reply. The move was not without risk. She could have attempted to scream as his closed hand touched her lips.

"Audrey?" Banner called out. "You in there?"

Beck leaned forward and whispered something in Audrey's ear.

The woman spoke. "I'm carrying too much. Can you come help me?"

Banner's approaching footsteps reverberated through the floor as he approached from the other room.

Beck placed the barrel of his pistol against Audrey's head. A soft whimper escaped her mouth. Beck looked at Clarissa and mouthed the word "gun."

She drew her weapon and aimed at the empty space in front of them.

When Banner appeared, he seemed to take them all in at once. His eyes darted left and right.

"What the hell is going on here? What are you doing with my wife, Beck?"

"You know why we're here. Where are your kids?"

Banner clenched his fist and took a step forward. Clarissa matched him, arm extended, pistol aimed.

"Not another step," she said.

He lifted his arms and held his hands in front of his chest. He still wore his work trousers and a white button-up shirt. But he'd removed his holster and was presumably unarmed.

"Tell me where they are or I'll break your wife's thumbs."

Banner nodded. "They're down the street at a friend's house."

"When do you expect them home?"

"Around eight or nine. Whenever it gets dark."

Beck said, "Here's how this is going to work. I've got all night. You have until they get home to give me what I need. If you don't, then Audrey dies and I start with them."

"You son of a bitch, Beck. So help me God, you are going to pay for this."

"No, Banner. You're going to pay for what you did. The vice president, man. How could you sign off on his death?"

Banner's cheeks turned bright red. "What are you talking about? I didn't sign off on a damn thing."

Neither man spoke for several seconds. They played a high stakes game of chicken. Clarissa knew Beck didn't want to speak first because anything he said would direct the conversation. They had to wait for Banner to come to them, then they'd know which way to take things. Problem was that Banner had been trained the same way. The man went way back with Sinclair as far as Clarissa knew. They'd crossed paths somewhere, likely outside of the Service.

Banner appeared to calm down. In a subdued tone, he said, "Look, Beck. I don't know what someone told you, but I had nothing to do with any of this. Part of me is glad to see you, because when you disappeared, I thought you had left because you were involved. But you're here, and, as misguided as your presence is, together we can figure this thing out."

"Figure this out," Beck said, pushing Audrey's head away with an open palm and adjusting the pistol so that if he shot, his hand would block the majority of the carnage headed his way.

"Christ, Beck! Don't!"

Audrey cried. Her knees went weak. Beck never let go of her head.

"Tell me what I want to hear."

Banner collapsed forward and fell to his knees. With outstretched arms and tears streaming down his cheeks, he pleaded for Beck to spare his wife's life.

"I don't know anything. I swear it. I don't."

"Your kids are next." Beck adjusted and squeezed the trigger.

Banner closed his eyes and continued pleading for Audrey's life. She simply cried.

Clarissa watched on, unable to move.

The click that followed silenced everyone.

Chapter 43

Clarissa unclenched her eyelids and scanned the three other individuals in the room. Diffused sunlight lit the area, reflecting off the brass pendulum bob of the antique grandfather clock.

Banner had fallen face first onto the floor. His hands clasped together behind his head. Choked breaths mixed with fits of sobs.

Audrey lay on the floor as well. But the pool of blood Clarissa expected to see wasn't there. The woman rolled over and scooted toward her husband. He looked up when she grabbed hold of his hands. Neither of them spoke. They embraced in a tear-ridden hug.

Beck took a step back. He looked at the couple on the floor, then at Clarissa.

She felt as though she was going to pass out.

Banner rose to his knees. Pointing at Beck, he said, "You crazy bastard. I'm gonna hang your ass for this, Beck."

Beck reached into his pocket, pulled out the SIG's magazine and inserted it. He lifted the weapon and aimed it at Banner, who retreated while shuffling his wife behind him.

"I'm sorry I had to do that. I had to know. You'd have given up anything you had rather than watch your wife die." He tucked the pistol in his waistband and gestured for Clarissa to do the same.

Banner got to his feet, then helped Audrey up. She wanted to leave, but Beck wouldn't let her. She needed to remain close by. Instincts or not, Beck could be wrong about Banner.

"Tell me what the hell sent you charging in here," Banner said.

Beck and Clarissa told the story from the beginning, starting with Clarissa's account of the shooting. The details left Banner looking upset, but he urged them to continue. Beck detailed the attempt on their lives at the apartment where they had placed Clarissa. When told of Amy's death, Banner became visibly upset.

"I chose her for the position," he said. "Christ, and now she's dead."

Beck said, "She came over because her son never came home. She was distraught, but hadn't contacted the police."

Banner asked, "Do you think she knew what was going on?"

"If this was truly an inside job, I do. And whoever's behind it knew that she would come to me, being so close." He pointed at Clarissa. "Both of our apartments are on the same side of the building. He — the shooter — would have known where to look."

"You think she was killed for a reason, then? He didn't miss Clarissa and hit her."

Beck nodded. "Back to the boy. Do you have any knowledge of where he might be?"

Banner shook his head and said nothing.

Clarissa followed Beck's lead and mentioned nothing of what Polanski had said about taking the boy to protect him. Perhaps there had been some truth in what she had said. If there had, lies were so intertwined that she couldn't help but feel that Adam was in danger.

She continued with the story, detailing their escape from the building, and the city. When told about the attack at the cabin and the identity of the attackers, Banner looked surprised.

"Christ, this places Sinclair in the middle of this thing."

"What do you know of his and Julie's relationship?" Beck asked.

"There's some things that are classified, but what I can tell you is that they've worked together in the past. They don't go back as far as Sinclair and I do, though. I've known him since the eighties. I know he's been in some bad stuff before, but nothing like this."

Clarissa continued with her version of the events, stopping at her encounter with Sinclair in the restaurant.

"That paints a bad picture of him," Banner said. "Why would he do this?"

"That's my question," Beck said. "What does he have to gain from taking McCormick down?"

"Nothing," Banner said. "McCormick was a kid when he went in, and even if he ends up president, Sinclair's ops are so black, he won't deny them. There's nothing political for Sinclair to gain from this."

"What about Julie?" Beck asked.

"How do you mean?"

Clarissa said, "When I was with her a few days ago, she complained a lot about being passed over for positions. Things like that. Was McCormick ever in a position to keep her from being promoted?"

"You were there before you came here, weren't you? Her house?"

Beck extended a hand. "Just think about Clarissa's question. Can you think of any reason she'd want McCormick removed from office?"

Banner shook his head. "He had nothing to do with her, where she'd been, or where she's going." He dropped his head back and took a deep breath. "But I denied her latest request to apply for a position heading up a field office. It would have been a step up for her, but a pain for us to deal with."

They stood in silence for a few moments as their stories settled with one another. Clarissa couldn't escape the feeling that leaving Polanski like they had would come back to bite them. But what was the connection with Sinclair? How did Jordan fit into this? It meant Polanski had to have known about his plan in order to set hers into motion.

And despite everything that had happened, a part of her still wanted to trust Sinclair. Perhaps he was the only one on her side. All she had to do was recall the events in the restaurant to shake those feelings.

The fatigue, questions, constant movement, it all made her head hurt.

Banner shook his finger and pointed at a spot behind Beck and Clarissa.

"What?" Beck said.

"That box," Banner said.

"What about it?"

"I got a message to pick it up. Didn't think much about it at the time. In fact, I sent Audrey to get it. That's the only reason she got home so late."

Beck turned around and walked toward the cardboard box. He looked surprised at its weight when he lifted it into the air.

"What's in it?" Beck said.

Banner shrugged. "No clue."

"Who told you about it?"

Banner cleared his throat. "Julie Polanski."

Chapter 44

Beck tore the box open and pulled out several crumpled up strips of thick brown paper. He stopped and squinted at the contents. Clarissa resisted the urge to look in the event that the box had been a ruse devised by Banner to distract them.

Beck pulled out a folded piece of paper. A single strip of tape held the paper together. He tugged on it, freeing the edge. A thumb drive fell out and bounced on the floor.

"What's that?" Banner said.

"USB drive," Beck said. "Where's your computer?"

Banner turned and took a step down the hall.

"That's far enough," Beck said. "Tell us and Clarissa will get it. And not a company machine, either."

Banner told her where to find Audrey's laptop. Clarissa ran into the living room and retrieved it off the coffee table. When she returned, Beck was reading off the paper. All she heard was him saying Polanski's name.

"What is it?" she asked.

"It's a note from Polanski that says Banner is as good as dead."

"What?"

"Laptop."

Clarissa and Beck huddled together. He inserted the USB drive. She had expected some sort of security they'd have to bypass. But there wasn't any. The drive contained a single folder. Inside the folder were several scanned documents saved as images. Beck opened the first.

The document showed proof that Banner had signed off on McCormick's plan.

Clarissa glanced over at Beck. He continued to stare at the image on the screen.

"Let's see the next," she said.

"What is it?" Banner said.

They ignored him while Beck pulled up the next photo. It contained a scribbled note, hard to decipher. Beck looked up and pointed at Audrey.

"Come here."

The woman clung to her husband. Banner urged her to step forward. As she did, Beck took the laptop and spun it around.

"Is this your husband's handwriting?"

Tears ran down Audrey's cheek. She couldn't deny it now. "Yes, but it looks, I don't know, stressed."

"What do you mean?"

"Hurried."

"Like something done in a meeting that should have never taken place?" Beck stared past Audrey at Banner.

The man shook his head. "I don't know what that paper says, because I didn't write it."

Audrey read the parts of the note she could make out. It wasn't much, but the words "McCormick" and "terminate" were enough to indict Banner. Somehow he was involved.

Beck sent Audrey back to her husband and had Clarissa cover them while he continued looking through the documents.

"Some of these are old, and unrelated, but I know they're true. She's got you on more than this, Banner."

"Think about this, Beck," Banner said. "If what you're holding was true, why would she send it to me? Wouldn't she use it to fry me?"

"I suppose she would. Unless you had something on her, too. Nothing says you aren't both involved in this." Beck set the laptop down and retrieved Jordan's SIG. "One of you knew Jordan's plan and told the other. Both of you had something to gain, whatever it might be, so you formulated your own plan to kill McCormick. But you had to bring someone in to carry out the act. But that person had to have something involved as well, so you used one of his best assets."

Clarissa said, "And who better than Sinclair? The guy's been operating outside the law for so long he doesn't know what's legal anymore. And he's got people in place everywhere. Including the House Office Buildings." She didn't know for sure, but wanted to see Banner's reaction. He gave her nothing, though. "And with me there, the only outsider aware of McCormick's plans, you had the perfect scapegoat."

"You two are sick in the head. You know that?" Banner stepped forward.

Beck raised his pistol. "That's far enough."

"Despite those doctored papers, you've got no motive for me to do this. I can retire at any time. I'm not going to advance any further. No other agency would want me, and I don't want them. I could care less if McCormick becomes president. No one's gonna unscrew this country as far as I'm concerned, so let him have at it. Once I retire, we're taking off for the islands anyway." Banner squeezed his palms against the sides of his head. "Just tell me why I'd do this, Beck?"

"No, you tell me."

"I didn't do anything."

"Tell me why you did it."

"I didn't."

"Tell me why, Banner. Tell me or so help me, I'll kill Audrey."

"We're back to this?"

Beck said nothing. His tension visibly eased over the next few seconds. Had the conviction behind Banner's words won out? Or did the information contained on the thumb drive prove him to be guilty?

Two cell phones chirped. Beck reached his free hand into his pocket.

"That's mine," Banner said. "I should get it considering everything that's gone on the past two days."

Beck nodded. "Clarissa, keep your gun on Audrey. If he says anything out of line, shoot her."

Though she had no intention of shooting the woman, she aimed her pistol in Audrey's direction.

Both men answered the phones. Clarissa tried to keep up with each side conversation.

Banner's conversation was simple and to the point. He said, "Oh, Jesus, you're kidding me." After a short pause, he added, "Let me know the details when you have them. We need to know who did it." He bowed his head and let his arm fall.

"Hang it up," Clarissa said.

Banner lifted his head far enough to make eye contact with her. He turned the phone toward her and used his free hand to end the call.

"Now drop it and kick it over here," she said.

He followed her instructions. She stopped the phone with her foot, then lifted her leg and drove her shoe down onto the phone three times.

Banner's face turned red, but he remained silent.

During this time, Clarissa missed most of Beck's call. The look on his face revealed he had learned something new. Perhaps something damning to the man across the room. Beck hung up and slipped the phone back in his pocket.

"What'd you find out?" Beck said.

Banner's lips and face were tight. He struggled to breathe. His ragged breaths pushed through flared nostrils in spurts. "Give me a minute."

Beck looked at Clarissa. "My guy's been working on Jordan since we left. He got some information out of him."

"What?" she said.

"Jordan told Polanski about McCormick's plan."

"Why?"

"He was sleeping with her."

"What? Why?"

"He'd heard there would be an opening soon. A position he could move into." Beck paused and shifted his gaze to Banner. "My position."

Banner looked away.

"We'll get back to that." He turned toward Clarissa. "So, he thought he could score a few more points with her by telling her about the plan.

He thought, with the way this was going down, he would save McCormick and they'd pin the shooter. The reason he was so unsure of you is because he didn't know who'd planted you, McCormick or us, and what your purpose there was. He'd entrenched himself so deeply in the plan he couldn't back out. To do so would have landed him in jail for twenty years minimum as a co-conspirator."

"Julie Polanski is dead."

Chapter 45

Clarissa and Beck turned toward Banner. The man steadied himself against the wall and brought a hand to his face. He leaned forward, letting out a sob.

Around them, shadows danced across the floor. Clarissa grew concerned that Banner's kids were going to walk in. When nothing happened, she attributed it to a passing car or a breeze strong enough to sway tree branches.

"What happened?" Beck said.

"Her neighbor heard a shot. Ran over. The front door was open. Julie was seated next to it. Gun in her hand. Blood and brains on the wall behind her."

"Did anyone else see anything?"

Banner shook his head. "We don't know. Oh, Jesus." He paused to gather himself. "I should have put a stop to this as soon as they brought it up."

Audrey distanced herself from her husband by taking two steps back.

"Who brought what up?" Beck asked, his tone flat and calm, as though he were a psychologist talking to a patient. He had to keep Banner talking.

"They came to me with this crazy plan. At first I told them they were crazy, and not only that, McCormick was crazy for doing that to himself. But with their idea, it'd eliminate McCormick and give me a chance."

"Who came to you with the plan? Polanski and Jordan?"

Banner looked up, shook his head.

"Give you a chance for what?"

"I would retire, and then he'd offer me the Chief of Staff position. The job's a bitch, but it'd give me a start in what I've wanted to do for so long now."

"Did McCormick promise you the Chief of Staff position if he was elected president?" Beck asked.

Banner continued to babble, lamenting the death of Julie Polanski.

"What did McCormick promise you?" Beck asked.

Banner shook his head. "Not McCormick. Jesus, put it together, man."

Shadows crossed the floor again. Clarissa took a step back. She heard a slight jingling sound. Then the grandfather clock's glass shattered and a bullet struck the pendulum, causing a tinny ring.

Two more shots were fired. The sound that followed was unmistakable. The shooters had hit Banner in the back of the head, and Audrey in the side of hers. They collapsed amid pink clouds of blood and brain, which descended upon their still bodies.

Beck grabbed Clarissa and pulled her into the kitchen. The room was closed off to their left and right, but the opposite end of the room faced outside and a window provided a view in. He pulled her toward the sink and they both fell to the floor, facing the room where Banner and his wife lay dead or dying.

"What the hell just happened?" she said.

"Looks like Julie wasn't the only one who had to be taken care of."

"Sinclair."

"He's either behind it, or he's next." Beck scrambled to his feet, turned and rose. "I don't see anything out here, and it doesn't sound like they've entered the home."

"We should check," she said. "They might know we're in here and are setting us up."

They exited the kitchen and took their time walking past the still bodies on the floor. Clarissa avoided Audrey's lifeless stare. As they stepped into the next room, she spotted the holes in a window. If they were being set up, it'd be the worst frame-job ever. The shots obviously came from the outside. Of course, because of everything that had happened, Clarissa and Beck would be handed over to the government and none of the evidence would matter.

With Clarissa covering him, Beck opened the back door and stepped outside. The large backyard held no secrets. A six-foot privacy fence surrounded the property.

Sirens approached from the distance.

"We need to go," she said.

"They might be waiting for us out there," he said.

"Doesn't matter, Beck. The cops are going to be here any minute now."

He nodded, reached for her hand and together they ran toward the fence. He let go of her when they reached it so they could climb over. Every muscle in her body tightened as she exposed herself to the shooters.

But nothing happened.

She dropped to the ground and looked around. The wide grassy lot was empty. No house. No shooters. Of course, it might not be that easy. She knew that.

Beck gestured to the right and they ran that way. They wouldn't be able to get the rental. Eventually, someone on Banner's street would point out that it didn't belong. The police would track it back to Beck eventually, even though Clarissa doubted that he'd used his name when securing the vehicle. At that point, their faces would be all over the evening news, and the twenty-four hour networks, too. They had to find Sinclair and put an end to this.

Beck pulled up his phone's map application. "We're in a different neighborhood. They don't share the same ingress and egress. None of the streets connect."

"They'll look back here, though. We've got to get moving."

He took a last glance at his phone, then began running. Clarissa followed. They worked their way through the neighborhood until they reached a major road. The sun was low enough that it hung behind the trees across the street. That did nothing to suppress the stifling heat and humidity. Her shirt was soaked with sweat. It'd only get worse, she presumed.

"There." Beck pointed at a city bus lumbering toward them. He then spotted the bus stop and they jogged toward it.

No one else waited, and at first glance, the bus had few passengers. The bus's destination sign read Reagan Airport. They couldn't get through security, but they could get a car, and the airport could be a useful place to meet with someone trusted.

Seated at the back of the bus, Clarissa and Beck talked things through. Banner's last words indicated that McCormick was not involved in the plans that Banner and Polanski made. It also seemed that Jordan was kept out of the loop. He thought he'd end up a hero. Instead, the vice president would be killed on his watch.

"How could I not see this?" Beck said. "It has to be Hogan."

Clarissa recalled the man who had been in for part of their initial meeting. Banner introduced him as no one special. A guy on various committees and subcommittees. He was more than that.

"Hogan was the reason. He was the man the president was going to tap for the nomination. Once he found out what was going on, I guess through Banner or Polanski, he put his weight behind the assassination. For Polanski's part, she'd get promoted."

Clarissa said, "And Banner would be his Chief of Staff."

Staring straight ahead, color drained from his face, Beck nodded and said nothing.

"What about Sinclair, though?" Clarissa said. "What does he get out of this?"

Beck shrugged. "You know him better than I do. You tell me."

Clarissa turned toward the window. Streetlights flickered on. The sun hovered inches over the roofline of a strip mall, ducking behind the lone two-story building as the bus drove past.

"He never talked to me about things he wanted. He often treated me like a daughter, but only in how he looked out for me. That's what makes this so unbelievable. He's already tried to have me killed at least twice. I mean, I can look at the incident at the apartment and say that he did intend to kill Amy and you. But at the house? No doubt that Randy was sent to take care of me there."

"So we know what Banner and Polanski had to do with this. We can see why Hogan would be involved. In his mind, he might've believed he had no choice. The response to McCormick would soar after surviving an assassination attempt."

"But has Hogan mentioned anything about entering the race?"

Beck nodded. "Briefly, and from what I understand, he has the backing of President Rhodes."

Five minutes later the bus pulled to the curb of Reagan National Airport's departures terminal. Clarissa and Beck joined the few remaining passengers and exited onto the sidewalk. Without luggage, they looked out of place. It was the end of the week, though, and anyone looking might figure they were departing on a weekend getaway. Besides, the only scrutiny they would receive would be the first few steps. After they passed the ticketing counters, no one could figure them for who they were. They'd look like passengers who'd arrived early and preferred to wait near the main lobby rather than at their gate.

Travelers waited in snaking lines in front of the check-in counters. The airport cops walked or rode by, paying little attention to Clarissa and Beck. If they were going to be taken legally, the word would have been put out by now. She wondered when and if that would happen. At what point would Sinclair say he couldn't complete the job, and that they should involve federal and local law enforcement?

After passing through the first line of defense, Clarissa spotted a clothing store. She pointed it out to Beck. He handed her two hundred dollars and told her he had a call to make while she picked out a new outfit.

She drew the wrong kind of attention from the woman behind the counter. It wasn't until she passed a full-length mirror that she noticed her face matched the stains on her jeans. She smiled at the woman who now followed her around the store. The lady offered no help, only judgment.

Clarissa found a new pair of jeans, undergarments, and a couple t-shirts. Everything was overpriced, but she had the cash, and the change of clothes was necessary. She purchased without trying them on, fearing that the store employee would follow her into the dressing room to prevent Clarissa from stealing something.

Exiting the clothing store, she scanned the long hallway, looking for Beck. He was nowhere to be seen. She figured he'd found a private place to make his call. The sensitive nature of the information he'd discuss required it.

She found a restroom and located an empty stall. There she changed. As she exited the stall, she bundled up her old clothing and tossed them in the trash, then washed her hands, arms and face with warm water.

Beck was nowhere to be found when she left the restroom, so she headed toward the main lobby and found an empty seat. Every person that passed had to be considered a threat until they proved otherwise. Under normal circumstances, the weapon she carried would put her at ease. But in the airport, it caused her to tense enough to make her feel nauseous. Little she could do about it, though, so she focused on her breathing and tried to keep her muscles loose.

After fifteen minutes of waiting, she reached for the cell phone Beck had given her earlier. Using it would make it useless moving forward, but she had no choice. However, as she pulled it out, she realized the contact list was empty. Beck hadn't given her any of the other numbers.

Had she been abandoned?

Or worse, set up to take the fall?

Chapter 46

Clarissa's heart pounded against her chest as she got up and moved toward the doors they had come in through. The crowd coming toward her was almost too much to process. Dozens of faces looked at her, past her, as they shuffled forward like the undead, boarding passes in hand and nothing to do but wait for their flights. She fought through the crowd on her way to the exit.

Nothing could be taken for granted. If the man she'd spent the last two days running with had turned against her, then she had nowhere else to go. She had no family. The only people she considered friends had been abandoned for her job with Sinclair. They'd take her in now, but she had no idea where they were or how to find them.

A man appeared at the exit. The face looked familiar. He stopped and fixed his stare on her. Through the jumble of bodies between them, she saw his hand go to his side, pulling his shirt out from his pants. He walked toward her.

She turned left and walked at a steady clip.

He mirrored her movements.

The luggage carousels divided them.

Every time she glanced over, the man stared back. There was no doubt why he was there. But why hadn't he acted yet?

She couldn't dwell on that. Thinking would only slow her down and reduce her reaction time.

An opening ten feet ahead provided her with an opportunity to escape. The man would have to circle around to reach the same hallway. Leaping over the railing into the baggage claim area would only draw the attention of the airport law enforcement.

She made her break, picking up her pace and using a store that opened up to the main lobby. From there, she turned right and hurried toward the other end of the room. She stopped and scanned the area, looking for the man. Figuring that he'd enter the lobby from the far end, she went back the way she came.

The gamble paid off. She returned to the baggage claim area and did not see the guy. And she didn't see Beck. So she headed toward the exit.

Stepping out onto the sidewalk, she saw a sky lit with artificial light. Traces of orange, red and pink colored the horizon. Exhaust and heat and humidity surrounded her, pressing down on her chest and causing her lungs to scream. Cars and taxis lined the curb, idling. Trunks popped open. People shook hands, hugged and kissed, saying their hellos and goodbyes.

She looked left and saw the man standing a hundred feet or so away. Her stare lingered a second too long. He felt it, presumably, and turned her way. Beyond the bubble of orange light, the sky was dark. But it didn't matter. It could have been noon where she stood. Recognition flashed on the guy's face, and he moved toward her.

Clarissa turned and weaved her way through the people coming and going. The level of activity astounded her, but she realized that most people lived busy lives Monday through Friday. The weekend came and they did whatever they could to wash away the taste left in their mouths after a week of soul crushing work.

Tires squealed next to her. She looked over as the window rolled down. A voice shouted her name. She kept moving. The car followed. The man shouted her name again. She looked over, but his face was hidden by the roof. She leaned forward.

"Get in," Beck shouted.

She turned toward him. He hit the brakes, then leaned over and opened the door. She swung it wide and jumped in.

"What's wrong?" he asked.

She looked back, pointed at the man twenty feet away and reaching for his sidearm. "Him! He's been following me."

Beck didn't wait for her to put on a seatbelt or close the door. He punched the accelerator. The tires took a few seconds to grip the asphalt. The car fishtailed and swerved toward the sidewalk. A couple of travelers jumped back. One extended his middle finger and shouted something. Secured by the seatbelt, Clarissa pulled her door shut as Beck corrected and raced toward the exit.

Past the confines of the airport, Beck said, "I can't believe they found us that quickly."

"How?" she asked.

"It had to be the phone. I made a call. They must've decided to watch anyone I know."

"Get rid of it."

"Already did. Tossed it in the trash after using it. But we should probably get rid of all of them."

She still didn't know if Beck and the man who chased her knew each other. Getting rid of the phone was eliminating the last lifeline she had if things went downhill. She tried to process the possible outcomes.

Most left her in a position where the phone would be useless. If she ended up alone and on the run, she could pick up a phone.

Beck rolled down her window. Warm air rushed in, overpowering the rental car's air conditioning. She pulled her phone from her pocket, took one last look at it, then tossed it onto the highway shoulder. In the side mirror she saw it bounce twice before disappearing into the dark.

He handed her two more and asked her to dispose of them. One at a time, she tossed them. She knew that if the phones were being tracked, they'd give away their initial position. Her concerns were settled when Beck exited I-395, then took Suitland Parkway to I-95. He took the northbound ramp and merged in with the thick Baltimore-bound traffic.

Thirty minutes passed. She wondered if Beck played the situation over in his head, or if he was using the time to clear his mind.

"Where are we headed?" she asked.

"Boston," he said.

She calculated the distance and time it would take to reach the city. They'd arrive around four or five in the morning.

"Why there?"

"A hunch."

"Guess that's better than anything I've got."

Beck glanced over and smiled.

For a moment she forgot about her concerns and put her trust in him. "If that's where you think we should go, I'm on board."

Alternating hands on the steering wheel, he said, "It's a solid hunch, Clarissa. Hogan left the country on vacation a few days ago."

"Really?"

"Convenient, right?"

"Very."

"Well, he's on his way back tonight. Paris to Boston. His flight is due to arrive around six in the morning. We'll be there to greet him."

"Did he take his family with him?"

"Yeah, but he left them behind. He's coming back because of the McCormick situation."

She nodded. "Do you think this puts him in the middle of it?"

"I think his reaction to seeing us will provide the answer to that question."

"Who gave you this information?"

"I can't say. If this got back to him in any way, it would cause problems you couldn't imagine." Beck paused for a beat. "But what I can tell you is he's solid. If we can't trust him, then we might as well turn ourselves in because we're as good as dead anyway."

She leaned her head back, rolled it toward Beck. "I'm sorry I doubted you."

"What?"

"Throughout this whole thing, Beck. I couldn't help but feel you were involved at times. I'm sorry. You were and are the only one who has my back. I'm with you until we get this thing figured out."

There was nothing else to talk about after that. Beck drove for three hours while Clarissa slept. Before she took over so he could catch a nap, they stopped at a 24-hour superstore and purchased two suitcases and two laptop backpacks to give the appearance of travelers. They also purchased a couple pay-as-you-go cell phones with the intention of using them to communicate only with each other unless an emergency arose.

As they approached Boston's Logan International, the first traces of sunlight hadn't yet reached the Boston Harbor. The edge of the water shimmered under city lights. The further her eyes scanned, the darker the water grew, turning black on the horizon.

She reached over and tapped Beck on the shoulder. He leaned forward, stretching his arms out, as the car burrowed into the tunnel, the last stretch of road before they reached their destination.

She glanced at the clock. It was two minutes after five a.m. In an hour's time, everything would change.

Chapter 47

The first few minutes would dictate whether Beck's source had sold them out. The man knew their destination. All he had to do was place a call and a team of local, state and federal law enforcement would be waiting to take them down.

They ditched the rental car in long-term parking, exiting the vehicle after a discussion on whether to retain their handguns. In the end, they decided to remain armed despite the problems it would pose if they were stopped. All an officer had to do was dislike the way they looked, or notice that they lingered without any intention of flying, and it'd be over. To minimize risk, they decided to enter through separate entrances, then remain close, but hide the fact that they arrived together.

Clarissa split off from Beck before they reached the sidewalk in front of the terminal. She went left. Beck went right. The lone officer out front seemed to ignore her as she wheeled her suitcase and pretended to talk on her cell phone.

She fought the urge to look back and locate Beck. They'd set the phones so that a single button-push would dial the other. If it rang and he didn't answer, then she knew everything was wrong, and she should leave.

Entering the building, she turned right. The majority of the self-check-in kiosks were empty. People lingered near windows and in line at the various airline counters. She kept moving forward until she spotted Beck. They made eye contact for a second, foregoing any other sign of acknowledgment.

Clarissa purchased a cup of coffee and a paperback. She tucked the book under her arm and carried the coffee over to a table near the arrival's gate. It didn't give her the best view, but that didn't matter. She only had to be nearby. Beck was going to watch for Hogan, using the excuse that his presence was required because of the threat. From where she was seated, she had visible contact with Beck. A hand signal would relay his initial thoughts to her.

They counted on Hogan being aware of what happened to Banner and Polanski. Either he'd been told, or he'd been involved with their killings.

She alternated looking at the paperback, the clock in front of her, and at Beck. She counted down the minutes to Hogan's arrival, wondering if his flight had been delayed.

Six came and passed. She looked in Beck's direction more frequently now, and shifted in her seat to face the man. When he placed both arms behind his back, she'd know that Beck had spotted Hogan.

At quarter after six, she saw the sign.

Clarissa rose, grabbed her bag, opened it and placed the book inside. She tossed her half-full coffee cup into the trashcan. A small crowd gathered in front of the arrival's gate. Not enough to shield her. Hogan might accept Beck being there. If he saw Clarissa, he'd know something was wrong and do what he could to alert the authorities. She had to move forward, though. She was the surprise element in the plan.

Lowering her head, she kept moving closer. Every few seconds she looked for a change in Beck's stance and hand placement. Both hands in front meant things were moving as planned, and he'd be heading her way. One hand behind his back meant Hogan balked. She'd then have to be ready for the man's next move.

Hogan emerged from the tunnel alone. He looked up and down the wide hallway. Clarissa held the phone to her head, blocking his view of her. Her hair hadn't been short the only time the two had met, but she didn't want to take any chances.

Beck swung both arms forward. He stepped away from the small group of people waiting in front of the gate. Hogan stopped. Beck let both hands drop. Clarissa waited to see where they went next.

Hogan said something. His eyes were narrowed. His posture suggested he didn't trust Beck being there. Was that because he feared Beck knew of his involvement? Everything to this point had been supposed by Clarissa and Beck. Despite Banner's damning statement, they lacked proof. They'd need for Hogan to be carrying evidence, physical or digital, or to confess. And alone, away from the airport, they could get him to.

Beck's hands moved forward again. The men approached each other. They shook hands. Clarissa spun as Beck extended his arm toward her. She kept her phone to the side of her head, blocking her face. After the men passed, she'd follow close behind. Outside, away from the building, she'd approach. Before Hogan could react to the situation, she'd have her gun planted in his lower back.

The glass she leaned against felt cold through her shirt and against her skin. She almost relished in the feeling after two days of heat and humidity and sweat. When she turned her head, she saw the reflections of those behind her. Beck and Hogan were close. She waited until she could no longer see them, then turned her head to the right. The men passed by. She fell in line behind them, remaining fifteen feet away until they stepped outside.

The first rays peeked over the parking structure. For the first time, it felt cool out. The humidity was low. Sweat still formed on her brow and around the spot where the pistol pressed against her lower back.

As they crossed the street, Clarissa quickened her pace. She reached behind her back, retrieved the pistol. She used the backpack to cover it. The garage was close. She'd abandon her luggage there.

Beck guided Hogan forward. The man asked him something, but Beck said nothing.

Clarissa was only a few feet away now.

The men stepped into the garage. Early morning light turned into orange haze. The air felt heavy, filled with exhaust. Headlights swung around in front of them as a car parked in an empty spot. Clarissa scanned the parking level. Aside from the car, there was no one else around.

She made her move.

Chapter 48

Clarissa rushed forward as high beams caused Beck and Hogan to turn their heads to the side. Hogan turned his far enough that he saw her approaching. His gaze shifted from her face to the pistol in her hands. He stopped, reached out for Beck. But Beck pulled away while reaching for his own weapon. His concern did not appear to be with Hogan, though. He was focused on something ahead of them.

The first shot that rang out sounded like a tin can slapping the street. The impact it had was far greater.

Hogan's body jerked, became rigid. His eyes were wide open, fixed on Clarissa. Before she realized what had happened, another shot was fired. Beck cried out in pain and dove to the side. Hogan fell where he stood, blood pooling around his head.

Clarissa spotted the shooter, although it was impossible to make him or her out in any detail because of the flood of white light coming from the headlights. She darted to her left as the third shot was fired. It hit the structure behind her, sending shards of concrete flying.

She dove in front of a vehicle. Behind her was a waist high wall. She could hop it as a last resort.

Loud cracks rang out and echoed throughout the garage. The bright light coming toward her disappeared. She peeked around the car's fender. Beck had shot out the headlights. She tried to locate him, but was unable to. She saw a man duck into the car and put it in reverse.

Following Beck's lead, Clarissa rose and fired at the dark sedan, shooting out the passenger side tires before the car disappeared behind other parked vehicles.

"Stay down," Beck called out.

She ignored him and began running toward the sound of his voice, while keeping an eye on the escaping vehicle. The sedan rounded the first corner. The driver would do one of three things, she figured. Escape, go for her, or go for Beck.

The driver eased the vehicle to a stop. The door opened. She saw the long barrel of the rifle poke into the air. Clarissa fired a shot, hitting the front windshield, but missing the man. He continued to rise. As his head emerged, Clarissa recognized him.

Sinclair.

"Get down," Beck called out.

Sinclair turned toward Beck and raised the rifle, using the doorframe to steady it. Beck fired, but missed high. Sinclair's shot followed. Clarissa couldn't tell if it hit Beck. The SIG drowned out all other noise.

Sinclair fell forward, hitting the door and collapsing to the ground.

Clarissa approached cautiously, looking for any sign of movement. She rounded the front of the vehicle with her pistol aimed at the ground. Any doubt that Sinclair had survived was erased at that moment.

"Is he dead?" Beck said from behind her.

She nodded without looking back. She didn't want him to see her crying. She pulled stale air in through her mouth and let it fill her lungs.

"I think I'm gonna need a doctor."

She turned around. Beck had been hit. Blood ran down his arm in streams. She looked for her backpack, thinking she could use the spare t-shirt as a tourniquet.

Blue and red lights bounced off the ceiling and walls. A couple blips of a siren followed. Several officers on foot came running toward them, guns drawn and shouting.

Clarissa tossed her pistol, then lowered herself to the ground, arms spread out wide. Beck got to his knees and held his hands out. Neither of them said anything. She knew Beck would get it cleared up as soon as he could.

As the officers pulled Clarissa to her feet, she caught one last glimpse of Sinclair. A single thought ran through her mind. Why? Why had he done this? No one benefited from it. Not even him. Or did he? She doubted she'd ever find out.

Chapter 49

The following Monday Clarissa waited on the steps leading up to the Capitol. The dome blocked the sunlight, but it didn't matter. It was a perfect early summer day. The temperature was in the seventies, and the humidity was nonexistent.

She and Beck were detained in Boston for less than a day. They'd brought both of them to the hospital. Him for the obvious gunshot wound. Her because she claimed she'd hit her head and needed to be treated for a concussion. The last thing she wanted was to be separated from Beck.

The cops declined to take her to the hospital. But after seeing Beck's credentials, and following the call he placed to the president, they deviated from their original plan.

While in the hospital, she found out that Beck's source had been President Rhodes. The things he knew, combined with what Beck told him, led the president to believe that Hogan was involved. But they couldn't send a team without being sure. He trusted that Beck could detain the man and bring him back, where they could question Hogan without anyone outside finding out.

It hadn't turned out that way. And up to this point, no one could tell them why.

They left Boston late that night by helicopter. Sunday morning she was debriefed and told that there would be no charges pressed against her, and they would not be performing any further investigation into her actions. Despite her waffling feelings, it turned out that having Beck around had been the best thing for her.

A man she'd never seen before, and expected to never see again, escorted her out of the Treasury Building after the meeting. Her footsteps rose loudly off the empty sidewalk, drowned out by the sound of an approaching vehicle. The car pulled up to the curb next to her. She glanced over and saw Beck leaning over the passenger seat. With a smile, he invited her to take a drive.

They took the longest route possible back to her apartment. They hardly spoke except for him mentioning that he had a meeting Monday morning, and he'd like to see her afterward. Clarissa was noncommittal toward him, but making plans to show up anyway.

She packed up her apartment Sunday afternoon. The task was easy. She didn't keep much on hand, considering she often had to leave for long stretches of time at a moment's notice. All the furnishings had come with the place. She only had her clothes and a few small effects to take care of. Her destination was still undecided. The layout of the departure board at the train station would help narrow down the choices, she supposed.

Sleep came easy that night, and she slept for almost ten hours, waking up around seven a.m. She showered, dressed, and put on minimal makeup in preparation for one last visit with Beck.

And so she waited on the steps of the Capitol, wondering why Beck had asked her to meet him there. He could have said thank you the day before. And he did. But he didn't leave it at that. There had to be something else. Something more. In a way, she hoped he'd ask to see her again. She'd beaten the odds and escaped from a job that would have swallowed her whole. She had survived an ordeal that could have put her in prison for the rest of her life, or reserved her a seat in the electric chair or gas chamber. Now, she no longer feared for her life.

And she saw Beck in a new light.

He had been with her through it all. It was hard to deny the connection she felt with him. But she wouldn't pursue it unless he brought it up.

An hour after arriving, she spotted him at the top of the steps. His right arm was in a sling, held tight to his torso. He smiled, waved to her, then jogged down the stairs.

She rose to meet him. "Still feeling okay?"

"The meds help with the pain, but I'm trying to wean myself off them."

She laughed. "It takes more than a couple days to become an addict."

He lifted an eyebrow. "You an expert?"

Rolling her eyes and wondering how much he knew about her past, Clarissa said, "Whatever." After a brief pause, she added, "Tell me why you wanted me to come down here."

"Walk with me?" He gestured toward the lawn.

He led her away from the Capitol, north to the Lower Senate Park. There were more people out than Clarissa had expected. They stuck to the sidewalk and benches having conversations with their headsets or someone physically present. None seemed to pay any attention to her and Beck.

Eventually, they found a bench away from others.

"There's a few things I wanted to discuss with you."

She nodded and said nothing.

"First, I found out how this all happened, and why. It turns out that both McCormick and Hogan were involved with a task force that is out to shut down all black ops. Doesn't matter who is running them, or who is sponsoring them." He paused and lowered his head. "Everything must cease if this plan goes through. Of course, it's not the kind of thing you're going to hear about on the news, but Sinclair, through his various channels, found out about it. And he knew who was behind it. He planned a counterattack to stop it. Now, this whole thing would have gone down one way or another, with or without your involvement. It was dumb luck on his part that Banner and Polanski brought him in on this thing with McCormick. He offered you up as a patsy if need be."

The betrayal struck her hard.

Beck continued. "Then he began the cleanup process, starting with Amy."

"Why Amy? And what about Adam?"

"Julie hadn't been lying when she told us she'd had him moved to a safe location. They are tracking down paternal grandparents, who he'll go live with in California. And, as for Amy, she had the unfortunate task of being assigned to watch over you."

Clarissa felt her cheeks redden and her eyes misted over. She still thought of Amy as an innocent woman. Someone whose only crime was residing in the building. The truth was more than that, though. She was about to ask Beck about the scope of Amy's job and involvement when two younger men dressed in navy blue suits approached. She held back, and when they passed, Beck continued.

"From there he turned on Julie and Banner. We suppose that they didn't know you and I were at Banner's house when they attacked."

"The man at the airport?"

"One of Sinclair's."

"How did he find us in Boston?"

"Sinclair was going to kill Hogan no matter what. He knew the flight plans. They believe Hogan told him, and that he expected Sinclair or one of his men to meet him and escort him back to D.C. Apparently, Sinclair had convinced Hogan that someone else was targeting high-ranking officials and he might be next. We think he blamed Jordan, but aren't quite sure. Anyway, Sinclair tracked Hogan through his phone. We just happened to be there at the same time."

"Jesus," she said. "How will they explain this?"

Beck shook his head. "Anything they say publicly is going to be general. They'll do their best to hide it. Sweep it under the rug. They have Sinclair's corpse, and he'll take the blame internally. Externally, if necessary. Though they'd prefer not to bring his name up for fear of someone uncovering all that Sinclair represented. And behind closed doors, McCormick is going to use this to convince others that black ops have to be stopped once and for all."

"McCormick?"

"Yeah, he's fine. They are letting the critical condition reports play out a couple days longer in case Sinclair had backup plans in place."

"What about Jordan?"

"If he goes down, McCormick goes down. That's not happening. So, he's likely going to stay on with the Service, but they'll move him to another role. He'll be on lock down, essentially."

Nodding, she asked, "What will the task force do?"

Beck shook his head. "Ironically, they'll perform the biggest black op ever, and terminate everyone they can find."

Her stomach tightened and her body tensed. She glanced around the park in an attempt to spot anyone watching them. "They'll come after me, Beck."

He reached out and placed his hand on her shoulder. "You're safe, Clarissa. All of your records have been erased. All of them. You aren't even mentioned in your father's records anymore. Effectively, you are a ghost. In a few days, we'll have a new identity established for you. And I'll be handling it, so you don't have to worry about anyone else knowing the new you."

The thought of not existing as Clarissa Abbot tore through her. In a way, she felt light, as though she could do anything she wanted now. But she also recalled the few remaining people who were close to her. They'd never find her, and she'd never be able to reveal herself to them if she wanted to remain off the radar for good. At this point, she had little choice. Accept the new identity, or be hunted down. No matter how far she ran, they'd catch up to her.

"I know this is hard." Beck pulled out a folder from his bag. "And I'm probably making it harder with this, at least now. But I hope the information in here helps ease your mind in some way."

"What's that?" she asked, tensing again.

"Inside are some files I thought you'd like to look at." He handed them to her.

"What are they?"

"Open it up and see."

"I don't like surprises, Beck. Tell me."

He inched over in his seat, glancing around. "The truth behind what happened to your parents."

She stared at the folder in her hands. It was close to an inch thick. For over a decade, she'd wanted the truth. Now that she held it in her hands, she wasn't sure she was ready to face it. At least, not seated on a park bench next to Beck. The time would come when she would open the folder and see the secrets that died with her mother and father. But not today.

"You're not going to look?" he asked.

"Not yet." She kept her gaze fixed on the folder.

"I think you'll feel somewhat vindicated when you do."

She placed her hands flat on the documents, lifted her head and turned toward him. His eyes wavered back and forth. She sensed he wanted to say something to her.

"Anything else?" she asked.

"What are your plans?" he asked.

Taking a deep breath, she shrugged. "Not sure yet. I'm leaving as soon as I can, though. I thought about returning to New York, but there's too many memories there. Too many people who know who I used to be. Too much trouble. And anywhere else I've lived is out. I mean, why go back to those places? New Orleans has always appealed to me. Might go there for a while. Then who knows where. Somewhere on the ocean, maybe? I know that I don't want to stay in one place for too long. Know what I mean?"

"Don't go."

Her breath caught in her throat. Her heart pounded against her chest. Her palms grew slick. She managed to say, "Why not?"

"To get this information, I had to give something up. Rather, I had to accept something I've turned down for quite some time now. But I can't go back to the White House, and I don't want to be stuck in a field office, so I agreed."

She had expected something else. Still processing his words and shaking her head, she said, "What are you talking about?"

"I've taken a special position. It's lots of travel, and it deals with major financial crimes around the world. Serious stuff. Bringing down major contributors to terrorist organizations, counterfeit, blood labor, and so on."

Feeling defeated, she rose and turned toward him. "That's great, Beck. But I don't see what it has to do with me staying."

"Part of what I negotiated with them was that I could pick my partner. Anyone, as long as they had experience as an operative." He looked away. "And you do."

"You're offering me a job?"

He nodded. The look on his face led her to believe there was more to it, though.

"I've just been through a nightmare, and I'm finally free, Beck. I think...I think I'm better off leaving. Send someone else to deliver the identity stuff."

She turned and walked away, leaving Beck behind on the bench. Plenty of times in her life there were times she leapt without looking. Made decisions that betrayed what she truly wanted.

And it always burned her.

She knew what she wanted now. It was more than a job. But if that's how it had to start, so be it. One question had to be answered first.

If she ran, would he follow?

Only then would she know she was meant to join him.

The ambient city noise drowned out the sounds of her own footsteps. She walked quickly, nearing the street. The sidewalk grew crowded. She turned north, resisting the urge to look back. To search for Beck. If she spotted him, she'd go to him. And it couldn't work that way.

She stopped at the intersection, waiting for the crosswalk light to turn. With every second that passed, she became surer that she would never see Beck again. She scanned the long line of cars traveling in both directions, looking for a break in traffic so she could take her chances dashing across the busy street. Anything to get away.

The gap never appeared.

The countdown on the westbound crosswalk light started at twenty. Twenty long seconds until the lights would change and she could continue on.

She waited, tapping her fingers against her thigh.

The light changed.

She took a step into the street.

"Clarissa, wait up."

She looked back, and through a mesh of bodies, saw Beck jogging toward her.

Sign up for L.T. Ryan's new release newsletter and be the first to find out when new Jack Noble novels are published (and usually at a discount for the first 48 hours). To sign up, simply fill out the form on the following page:

http://ltryan.com/newsletter/

As a thank you for signing up, you'll receive a complimentary copy of *The Recruit: A Jack Noble Short Story.*

If you enjoyed reading *Beyond Betrayal*, I would appreciate it if you would help others enjoy this book, too. How?

Lend it. This e-book is lending-enabled, so please, feel free to share it with a friend. All they need is an Amazon account and a Kindle, or Kindle reading app on their smart phone or computer.

Recommend it. Please help other readers find this book by recommending it to friends, readers' groups and discussion boards.

Review it. Please tell other readers why you liked this book by reviewing it at Amazon or Goodreads. Your opinion goes a long way in helping others decide if a book is for them. Also, a review doesn't have to be a big old report. Amazon requires 20 words to publish a review. If you do write a review, please send me an email at ltryan70@gmail.com so I can thank you with a personal email.

Like Jack. Join us on Facebook: https://www.facebook.com/JackNobleBooks

Other Books by L.T. Ryan

Jack Noble Series in Order

Noble Beginnings

A Deadly Distance

Noble Intentions Season One

Noble Intentions Season Two

Noble Intentions Season Three

Never Go Home

Noble Intentions Season Four - Coming 2014

Mitch Tanner Series

The Depth of Darkness

Untitled (Mitch Tanner 2) – Coming 2014

Untitled (Mitch Tanner 3) – Coming 2014

Affliction Z Series

Affliction Z: Patient Zero

Affliction Z: Abandoned Hope

Affliction Z: Book Three – Coming 2013

Receive email notification of new releases here:

http://ltryan.com/newsletter/

CPSIA information can be obtained
at www.ICGtesting.com
Printed in the USA
LVHW092304160220
647148LV00001B/271